THE POINT OF DEATH

THE POINT OF DEATH

Peter Tonkin

This first world edition published in Great Britain 2001 by
SEVERN HOUSE PUBLISHERS LTD of
9-15 High Street, Sutton, Surrey SM1 1DF.
This first world edition published in the USA 2002 by
SEVERN HOUSE PUBLISHERS INC of
595 Madison Avenue, New York, N.Y. 10022.

British Library Cataloguing in Publication Data

Tonkin, Peter
    The point of death. – (The master of defence)
    1. London (England) – History – 16th century – Fiction
    2. Detective and mystery stories
    I. Title
823. 9'14 [F]

ISBN 0-7278-5723-1

Typeset by Hewer Text Ltd.,
Edinburgh, Scotland.
Printed and bound in Great Britain by
MPG Books Ltd., Bodmin, Cornwall.

For Cham, Guy and Mark.
As always.

Those noblemen who could no longer rely on the safety of armour had to turn to the sword. They needed education in its use, and much of the available education they found unsatisfactory. Pressure from them produced a new race of Masters . . .

The History and Art of Personal Combat
Arthur Wise

CHAPTER ONE

The Master of Logic

Holland 1587

Tom Musgrave pounded out of the battlefield, running for his very life, wondering distantly: Am I likely to live through this? Or not? *Not* seemed to be most likely. Another shell exploded close behind him. Splinters and shot spattered the slick earth all around him. A wave of force gathered him up and hurled him forward.

Tom had easily topped the five-foot cross at the Market Gate of Carlisle Castle five years ago when he had first left home, and he stood two full cloth-yards tall today. There were those who called him 'Long Tom' these days, measuring him with speculative eyes. Now he measured his own length in the Flemish mud and skidded forward, all elbows and knees; then he jerked erect again, breathless, desperate and angered, at the heart of a sudden silence, looking away left for Talbot Law, his companion, to see whether he was still alive or not.

Talbot's strong, square figure was staggering erect too, at the far lip of the smoking crater that had so nearly claimed them both, looking at him and desperately waving him on.

Tom pounded forwards. The sudden cold striking into his brain told him he had lost his precious headgear in the blast but there was no going back for it now. On he ran, with desperate determination, up the slope towards the river road, his ears

1

ringing, able to hear nothing of the real world all around him, only the beating gallop of his own racing heart.

The crest of the rise revealed the river. It was sluggish, and of the same red-brown colour as the blood-soaked mud. It rolled roughly westward beneath a russet sky from one fortified bridgehead to the next. Between the tall English soldier and the dull water, at the foot of a cliff the height of a partisan pikestaff reaching down from his very toes, the road ran from Nijmagen on his right, away towards the distant coast. The embattled town stood threateningly close at hand, surrounded by sullen besieging armies and defended by grimly determined men.

Tom looked right and left again, his stomach growling with tension and hunger. The local roads were usually as well stuffed with soldiers as eggs are stuffed with meat, he thought. But, here, today, with the war advancing across the fields above it towards the shell-shattered outskirts of the town, this road was empty and still.

Except for the runaway horse.

Tom and Talbot Law had seen it both together at the same instant five minutes since, away in the far distance, galloping wildly out of the ruins of the Italian lines, past the rough window made by a shell crater in the bank side. Fleeing the dangers of the enemy-infested outskirts, it was following the river road, bound inevitably to come past here. Leaving the gathering battle, they had raced it, striking straight into the curve of its progress. And along this low track, here it came pounding now – Tom and Talbot's quarry; wild, terrified and screaming mad.

It was a big horse, bay beneath the mud and blood, square and solid, swift and very dangerous. Its eyes were rolling like Tom O' Bedlam's and its reins were flying free. Along behind it, one foot wedged in a strong stirrup, the beast dragged its rider. Tom spared not a glance for the battered corpse. His eyes were all for the animal. It meant the first square meal in a month to him and the camp for which he and Talbot were the foragers in chief. *Escalopes of equus*, he hazarded, continuing the Epicurean theme so close to the hearts of the starving, and turning to his hard-won Latin as he always did when exercising of his wit. Or *hotchpotch of hippos*. He was reaching for something even more adventurous, again in Greek – centaur pastries – when the mad banquet thundered up towards his boot-toes and he leaped.

Those rolling eyes saw sanely enough, like many a gibbering London beggar turning cutpurse behind an unwary back. The horse shied as Tom leaped, jerking its rein away from his grasping hand and meeting him with a square, muscular shoulder. Tom flew sideways and down like a fairground tumbler, the heaving flank grating past him as he fell, and the saddlebag slapping him in the face like a roaring boy set on a brawl. He anticipated yet more mud and the utter ruination of the last of his decent clothing, but things fell out differently. He landed not on the road at all, but upon the rider.

Tom found himself face to face with the corpse, looking down upon it like a lover. His long legs were caught up in the stirrup, his belly rested on the dead man's chest and his elbows held the shoulders down. Then Tom's added weight caused the horse to stumble. The stumble jerked the straps apart and the horse fell, shedding the saddle and the tangled men, even as Talbot Law, wily as a riever from Tom's own wild Borders, leaped down to wrap its head in his jerkin and bring it swiftly under control.

The four of them lay still for a moment, the two men living, the dead man and his horse. Then another black shell came hurling over the rise and slammed down into the mud nearby, sending up a pillar of earth and water too close for comfort. Half drowned and half deafened once again, they waited as the thunder of its echo rolled against the black walls of Nijmagen and under the shadowed arches of the great stone bridge it defended. Then, into the relative quiet afterwards, Talbot Law delivered a considered speech. 'Yon bastard culverin will be the death of us yet, Tom, unless we move. It's firing wild with a vengeance.'

'Like enough,' said Tom, preoccupied. 'But look here, old

Law . . .' He paused, glancing up and down the quiet road. 'There's something here needs a minute more of thought. Something of the greatest importance.'

Talbot shrugged and set to coaxing the horse to its feet. He and young Tom Musgrave were the strongest men in the English camp but not even they could carry a horse back to the lines. Once the horse was up, the boy was rapt, his eyes and fingers busy about the corpse in the mud. The solid west-countryman grinned with affection. Another explosion signalled the birth of a rolling barrage as all the guns at the Master-Gunner's command were fired off one by one. The horse jumped and whinnied, but remained quiet under Law's assured and gentle hand. 'We must hurry, Tom, that fusillade has been the signal to prepare attack each forenoon for a week.'

Tom looked up. 'You're right. Time for consideration is at an end. Listen, therefore, as I, the Master of Logic, explain my observations; for much of our future may well hang upon them. This new-made member of the Heavenly choir was singing an earthly song this dawn. That is obvious enough. But his song was an English catch. For, look. His shirt is Kentish wool and weave, and of the finest. His hose may be made of French cloth but they are of the English cut. His jerkin is Spanish leather, true, but it fits ill and has been foraged. It may well be a disguise, for he has come up through the enemy lines, has he not? All his weapons and armour are gone, but he rode well armed to be thus well preserved for our inspection, since the end, at least, of his ride was so rough.

'But these observations merely lead us on to another question, do they not? A pair of questions; a brace . . . Whither this young Englishman, coming through this battlefield? Whither went he and whence came he? He came out of the Italian lines, down by the river gate. I am certain of that. He rode wildly and bravely to his death – death by a bullet from a pistol or dag if the back of his head is anything to go by. Italian pistol, Dutch dag – either one might have done it, even though the Dutch are on the poor boy's side.'

4

'That Spanish jerkin would have fooled St Michael himself,' observed Law.

'True. And a fitting epitaph. But his good steed – a good English steed, from its tack, and the brand on its shoulder there, ran straight and true to the English lines. But why, old Law, but why?'

'This is good sport to hold two soldiers in a ditch at the onset of a battle, Tom,' growled Law, growing as restless as the horse and seeing no practical point to his friend's uncanny cleverness. 'Master of Logic or no, it'd go hard with us if the Sergeant at Arms's men found us here when they were out after deserters. Not even our Forager's Passes would save our necks for us then.'

'Maybe. But sometimes it is as well for a soldier to use his wits as his weapons. For, y'see, old Law, this was a man with a mission, and he was coming up to our lines from down there, below Nijmagen town, when he died. *Quod erat demonstrandum*, I believe.

'But we can move a little further, by exercise of a moment more of logic, if not of magic. Look, he wore gloves stout enough to have preserved his hands and what fingers are these, callused and black-nailed, singed and smelling of saltpetre? Are these the hands of a courtier to match the boy's fair face and fine apparel? Of a farmer? Of a soldier?'

'They're never the hands of a common soldier,' conceded Talbot Law, his low brow folding into a frown as he looked down at his own huge fists.

'No,' said Tom, quietly. 'They're an engineer's hands.'

'Ha!' laughed Talbot caught between wonder and revelation. How could he have missed such a simple truth? The sections of the army kept aloof from each other, but the engineers, with their mud and gunpowder stench, were well enough known to the rest.

Tom was pushing on, however, like a schoolmaster expounding on Logic. 'So what lies before us is a young engineer, sent from below Nijmagen up to our lines, in spite of the risks. Not a common hack-out-a-trench-and-set-taper-to-your-petard man

5

but a well-dressed youth, fair of face. An ensign, fit to ride to his death like a lusty lad for his commander and his God. A messenger.'

'You should try this at the Bartholomew Fair,' said Law. 'You'll prosper. Till you're taken for a witch.' He looked superstitiously around as though naming evil could summon it too.

'But a messenger supposes a message,' insisted Tom. His hands became busy at the young man's throat, pulling a pouch from beneath the fine Kentish wool of his shirt. 'And a message, in times such as these, carried at such a price, must speak of dreadful danger.' He opened the pouch to reveal a small square, folded and folded. With trembling fingers he unwrapped it and laid it open to the sullen morning. It was no mere piece of paper, but parchment of the highest quality. On its bottom right hand corner it carried a blood-red seal. Beside the seal, there was a ring. Tom looked neither at the seal nor the signet. His eyes were for the message alone:

aaaec. caaae.
cdabe. cdbee.

CHAPTER TWO

The Master of Cyphers

'If any man can read your code, this man can,' repeated Talbot. 'He's a Master of Cyphers if ever I saw one.'

''Tis an unusual thing to find an adept at codes in such a place,' countered Tom. He would fain have unfolded the secret message and studied it again but could not take the risk. He needed both hands to keep hold of his companion as he needed both thighs to stay astride the plunging horse's hips. Talbot Law, firmly in the roughly repaired saddle, thrashed their prospective dinner home across the battlefield, glad to be out of that ditch of a road where the ill-aimed culverins were set to blow them all to atomies.

'They've been common enough on any battlefield I've fought over,' growled Law. 'Spies swarm to wars like flies over corpses.'

'That's as may be. But none that I've heard of was tented with the pressed and mustered men.'

'He's not a spy. And he's not pressed. He's a gentleman volunteer like us, out to make his fortune.'

'He'll be lucky to see his coat money. Our brave captain may grow fat out of this but no one else in the band is likely to, unless we can come across some fine Dons or *Signors* to strip and ransom.'

'The Captain won't see much by all accounts. The Colonel and his lieutenants have it all to hand and we can go starve or

7

hang for them. They'll pay the dead before they pay us, though the six-month payment is long due, and not a muster master seen since the autumn gales set in behind us. The Italians are said to be protected by the devil with their fencing magic and their Ferarra blades. And the only Dons I've shook hands with so far are *tercio* men and likely to yield little more than cold steel, living or dead.'

The English lines were all astir with men donning their battle gear and preparing to fight hand to hand once the artillery had settled matters from a distance. The women and boys of the camp bid farewell to lovers and husbands, fathers and masters. The men who found themselves here alone, saw to each others' harnesses, looked to their own arms, practised their passes of defence, stood thoughtfully; prayed. The Captain's men, under the Sergeant at Arms, were roughly organising the band into the groups that would form the main attack.

The horse plunged into the camp like a band of Spaniards, scattering mud, men and confusion, until Talbot saw his woman. 'Bess,' he bellowed. 'Hold this jade 'gainst my return. Tom and I have business afoot.' No sooner had the solid woman grabbed the reins than Tom and Talbot were sprinting through the encampment. As he ran, Talbot held a series of short bellowed conversations, mostly question and answer. Tom ran at his shoulder, the letters of the code clear before his eyes – as though he held the paper up still. His mind wrestled with their meaning and, more terribly, with their implications. But he got to voice neither until after Talbot had found his quarry.

Talbot Law's Master of Cyphers was a slim man of middle height with a high forehead and fiercely intelligent eyes. Like Law, who hailed from Winchester, he spoke with a west-country burr, much at odds with Tom's flat northern tones. Even as Talbot was trying to explain their mission, the stranger led them into the tent he shared with some half-dozen others. This was deserted at the moment, private and light enough to see in now that the overcast morning was struggling towards the noon. 'Show me,' he ordered quietly, and gestured towards a table top already strewn with closely written papers. Tom took out the parchment and gave it to Talbot's man. Slowly, creaking a little as he moved in his battle gear, he sat. Tom watched narrow-eyed as the weight of the man's intelligence focussed down on the piece of parchment. There was silence within the tent that stood in sharp contrast to the commotion without.

'How is it you have come by a knowledge of codes?' Tom asked without thought.

'As with all other knowledge. A Master imparted it. A Cambridge man at that.'

'He is not with you?'

'He is not. He has other heights to storm.'

Tom looked down at the stranger as he sat, lost in thought. There was little wonder that Talbot should know the man and Tom should not. It was one of the unacknowledged facts of their relationship. Talbot knew everyone in the camp. Tom knew Talbot. And Bess, a little.

'These are no words, I think,' said the Master of Cyphers.

'Not Latin, nor Greek, nor any I have seen,' agreed Tom. Something in the stranger's tone making the obvious, over-simple observation seem wise and full of import.

The Master glanced up from the cypher. The edges of his eyes crinkled slightly, as though in the slightest of smiles, meeting Tom's open gaze. 'Words do not come naturally five letters at a time,' he explained. 'Poetry can be worked into pentameters, with five beats in a line, but that is measure. And measure, though it lies down with oratory and poetry, is not one with them. Rather it sings with music and dances with harmony. And, as the tree-trunk of oratory is the word and the root of it is the letter, so the body of harmony is mathematics and the limbs of it are numbers. This is what Aristotle and Signor Della Porta believed. And so do I.'

'And I,' said Tom, by no means overawed by such august company. He had never heard of Della Porta nor read his book on codes, *De Furtivis Literarum Notis*, but he had lived with

Aristotle, Caesar, Cato and all the rest since his first day at school. 'But what numbers are concealed within letters?'

'Roman numbers,' said Talbot before either of the others could speak. 'Needs no great scholar or spy down from Cambridge to tell us that!'

Tom's eyes met the stranger's once more and a shiver of shared excitement flashed between them, mixed with no little shared amusement. 'Dare they?' mused the stranger.

' 'Twould be simple enough,' said Tom.

'And effective . . .'

The two were sitting side by side poring over the parchment, wasting a good deal of precious paper and ink with their calculations when the Captain's men burst in.

'War's advancing,' the Sergeant at Arms, their leader, bellowed. 'The Captain's in the field and the General himself's a-horse. To your posts now or your necks'll answer for it.'

Talbot swept the men outside, one arm over the leader's shoulder and the other showing his Forager's Pass. A few moments later he came back alone. 'We've little enough leisure,' he warned. 'They'll be back soon and they'll have a noose with them next time. The Captain likes shirkers less than Spaniards.'

'And the General likes his men less than their money,' growled Tom.

'A poor enough fancy,' laughed his partner. 'Sharpen your wits on that.' He pushed across a neatly written set of Roman numerals:

iii – xxiii – xliv – xlv.

'A simple matter thus far,' he said as Tom pored over his workings. ' "A" equates with "i" or one, "b" with "v" or five, "c" with "x" or ten and "d" with "l" or fifty. "E", I believe marks the periods that define the numbers. The final "e" ends the message.'

'Three, twenty-three, forty-four and forty-five. What numbers are these?' wondered Tom, his mind ranging over infinities of possibility. The wise eyes alongside were also lost, for the numbers could refer to anything. Just the books alone beggared computation. Did they refer to lines in Virgil? Thoughts of Demosthenes? Histories of Plutarch? Speeches of Tully? Satires of Juvenal? Battles of Caesar? Adventures in Homer? Dicta of Socrates? Laws of Justinian? Theorums of Pythagoras? Tragedies by Sophocles or Euripides? Comedies of Aristophanes or Plautus . . .

'I hear numbers like that every Sabbath,' observed Talbot.

Again, Tom's eyes met the Master's. 'Were I to send a message from one captain of one faith to another, through the massed ranks of heresy, I could choose no better,' said Tom, careful to avoid the word *papist*, even here. 'But it would be safest with Tyndale . . .' He tensed to move.

The other was up before him, crossing to the doorway of the tent. 'Come,' he said quietly. ' 'Tis early for the chaplain to be gone. He'll be at prayer, not ministration. The misericords come later.'

The sight of three hale, hearty, well-armed men running through the camp at this stage of the battle turned a few heads. But then enquiring eyes recognised Talbot Law at least and returned to their business again. Behind and above the slushy, rough-tented midden of the pressed men's infantry lines stood the high, dry, gaudy and well-guarded marquees of the masters at arms, the captains, the colonels and the General. No mere mustered men here, but the sons of noble houses whose names were known at Court and whose families were titled for the towns, shires and counties which they owned. Only their squires and equerries remained now, little older than the boys down the hill and no wiser; a little better dressed, perhaps; a little better educated. The guards were from the Sergeant at Arms' men, even so, and they knew Talbot Law, as the Sergeant did. In a moment, old Law had wheedled Tom and the Master past them and into the Chaplain's tent.

The Chaplain was on his knees and there before him, on the lid of a travelling chest, lay open a copy of Tyndale's new Bible, translated from the original Greek and Latin scarcely sixty years before. So different in form and numbering from the Vulgate used in Rome.

'The third book must be Luke's Gospel,' said the Chaplain, turning to it as they explained their mission to him and held the Master's decypherment of the dead man's message under his bulging eyes. He was an elderly man of holy reputation; too honest, ancient and scholarly to be in the common run of camp-follower priests. Some said he had been the General's tutor as well as his chaplain and followed him now for love. 'And if we read the forty-fourth and forty-fifth verses of chapter twenty-three, we find, "And it was about the sixth hour and there was darkness over all the earth until about the ninth hour. And the sun was darkened and the veil of the temple was rent in the midst."' He looked at the three men blankly, his mouth working while his brain most patently was not. 'It tells of the death of the Lord himself,' he said. 'But what can that mean here and now to us or to our General?'

'It gives times of day and warns of darkness,' mused the Master of Cyphers. 'But there's little enough there. Perhaps we were wrong after all. And yet . . .'

'I've often wondered about that,' said Talbot, apparently more interested in the meaning of the text than any message it might conceal. 'If the Good Lord was taken before Pilate and scourged, then the people were asked whether to release Barabbas or no, all before Our Lord was led through the city up to Golgotha, how could it only be six in the morning? How could it only be the sixth hour?'

'Because the Jews counted their hours from the dawn of the day,' said the priest. 'Not from the midst of the night as do we.'

'So their first hour was our sixth . . .' said Talbot, with simple wonder.

'And the sixth hour will be midday!' snapped Tom. He turned to the others at once. 'Coming at such speed, with such moment – and in such fashion – from the engineers' lines to ours, and, like enough, from their captain to our General, it can only be a warning to stay our regular assault at noon. For at noon today, the world will go dark and the veil in the temple will be torn . . . Chaplain, how goes the clock?'

The poor priest shook his head, his face still vacant with shock. 'What should a priest do with a clock?' asked Talbot's friend coolly, leading the way back to the doorway. 'The General and the Colonel. Such men as these need to count the hours carefully . . .'

'Aye,' agreed Tom, stepping out into the light and glancing up at the overcast, hoping for sight of the sun. 'They'll count their minutes as carefully as they count their men.' He sniffed and shook his head. The clouds were too thick. It seemed halfway to night already. 'But I know which they'd be readier to lose. Law, how will we get into the General's tent?'

'This way,' answered Law and the three of them were off again.

CHAPTER THREE

The Made Men

I t was not until they were close beside the bright walls of the General's own palatial abode that Tom slowed. 'But wait. We do not need the clock. Whatever the hour, however near to noon, it is the General himself we need, for only he can hold the army back.'

The others paused beside him and turned, only to swing back again at once, called away from the prospect of the distant war by the immediate imperative of a scream. It was the scream of a woman and it came from within the tent itself. The gaudy portal stood a little way ahead and Tom reached it first, even as the terrible sound was repeated. There was a guard on duty, but he had swung round at the sound and was too busy looking inwards to see the three men coming up behind him – let alone to stop them. They simply charged him down and tore into the silken confines within.

The atrium of the tent was split into several chambers, floored with carpets, walled with cloth of gold and well stocked with servants who, like the guard, stood gaping. A third scream guided Tom like Theseus through the scented maze and he first tore into the inner sanctum and skidded to a halt. There, on a curtained bed at least as weighty as one of the ill-aimed culverins, stood a woman. Stark, panting, a golden hind at bay. She was scarcely more than a girl – perhaps sixteen. All her clothing was the riot of her tumbling hair, golden as the wires in the walls; all her defence was a dagger – scarcely more than a bare bodkin – and the power of her screams. The hair gave some pretence of decency to the pale, pink-tipped swell of her breasts, scratched and reddened though they were. But nothing could hide the cloud of golden brightness at her loins – nor the black bruises of abuse and the ruby-red streaks across her thigh.

Ranged against her stood a burly youth, little better dressed than she, and all at a point to push his rapine home, dagger or no dagger. He swung round with a snarl as the three men burst in. His hot gaze swept over them and pegged them all alike. 'Out, you whoreson peasants!' he spat.

'What, Prince Tarquin?' raged back Tom at once. 'And leave you to your ravishment? Sir, not I!'

His refusal enraged the boy beyond control. Naked as he was, he threw himself to one side and snatched up a sword belt. Hurling himself between his screaming victim and her would-be rescuers, he tore the sword from its scabbard and launched himself into the attack. Tom's own weapon whispered into the air, a good yard of razor steel, borne with honour by his father's grandfather at Bosworth Field itself. The blade began as broad as both his thumbs pushed together with a blood-runnel separating the sharpened edges. It ended with a flat, rounded point, but remained at its sharpest along the edge. It had a strong basket guard over the handle above the crosspiece, and a pommel half the size of a fist. The better part of a hundred years old, it was still a potent man-killer, and Tom had been well trained in its use. He stood open, square on to the charging boy, whose own advance was proceeded by a more fleshly blade before his steel one.

The boy struck first, and high. Tom saw the stroke coming and turned it away, edge to edge, using the instant of respite to catch a rag of the bed-curtain and wrap it, like the tail of a cloak, around his forearm. The boy had received some training and recovered swiftly, striking in at Tom again, high and from the right.

Given leisure, Tom would have taken time and exercised the both of them a little, especially as he was well armoured and facing a naked foe. But there was no time here – and now a girl to see to even before the secret message could be delivered. With contemptuous ease, therefore, remembering what his father had taught him of the method of the great English Sword-Master Silver, he turned the boy's blade with his cloth-wrapped fore-arm, stepped into the circle of the boy's reach and punched him in the face with the basket guard over his fist. There was a sound like an apprentice's foot striking the bladder of a foot-ball. As the boy reeled back towards the bed, spitting blood, Tom's left gauntlet closed on the wavering blade of his sword, at once disarming him and, for an instant, holding him upright. Tom's sword rose again and struck down like a club, driving the pommel with jarring force, down into the centre of the boy's forehead. There was a sharp report of steel on bone, as crisp as a shot from a pistol or a dag, and the boy's eyes rolled up. He slumped back on to the carpeted flooring, no longer so fierce; scarcely alive indeed. And, wrestling almost as closely with death, the naked girl collapsed on to the ground beside him.

Into the silence that followed there came the most unexpected sound – the tinkling clamour of a travelling clock, striking the half-hour.

'I must away,' spat Tom.

Talbot Law swung a little wildly, torn between the work here and the urgency he shared with Tom.

'I must find Bess and take the horse. Wait for her here,' said Tom, sliding his sword back into its sheath as he spoke. 'Bess must look to the girl. And the Master at Arms or the General must look to Sir Rapine the ravisher here. Only you, old Law, can hold the square till then.'

Talbot Law turned, almost desperately, to his friend. 'Will,' he said, 'could you . . .' the sweep of his gaze encompassed the tent and all the measureless evil done and pending therein.

The Master of Cyphers smiled. 'I'll go with Tom, old Law,' he said gently.

And so all their fates were sealed.

The horse's hooves struck sparks from the cobbles of Nijmagen town ten minutes later, but the bay was all but done and her gallop, which had slowed to a canter, staggered to a spavined walk now. Will slid off the broken jade's hips and ran along at its shoulder while Tom buried his heels yet again in the shuddering heave of its sides. The wreckage of the town's shattered outskirts rose around them, falling away from the almost mediaeval thrust of the fort-walled bridgehead. Here the English army was beginning to gather, standing beside their good Dutch allies, under the eyes of their leaders, William, Prince of Orange, and Robert Dudley, Earl of Leicester. Tom knew well enough where the generals would be. He would find them on a little eminence that gave a clear view of the great bastion of the portcullis of the castle that cut the road off from the bridge. Against these stone foundations the armies had been hurled every noon for a month like a relentless, steely tide. Up atop that ridge they would be sitting, at the far end of this very road, five minutes away, no more, behind wall after wall of guards. More than once of late the more daring of the defenders – the Italian bloods rather than the Spanish professional *tercio* men – had come around the back here, in true 'Hole land' fashion, hoping to stab the generals from behind.

From here on up, indeed, wild riding should give way to wary walking. This was where the horse's original owner had died. This was where the Italians were, with their half-magic swords from Ferarra. This was where the hard, quick-shooting Hollanders were, with their pistols and their wheel-lock dags, banned in England on pain of death since the days of Henry VIII.

Tom slid off the bay's back and dropped the reins. 'This is not a *carne vale*,' he warned the animal, 'unless this is my Shrove Tuesday.' Then, like his black-clad companion, all dull except for his breastplate and his sword-blade, he slid into the shadows under the ruins of the walls. He repeated the witticism to himself: this is not *goodbye to meat*, unless he ended up being *shriven* himself. And by God's grace it was indeed a Tuesday! As witticisms went, it was worthwhile, he thought, savouring its repetition to Talbot Law, should they ever meet again. Meet or *meat* again . . .

Tom's lip was still curling in a satisfied little smile when he ran into the Italians. They stepped out of a hollowed house, coming through the doorframe as though it still had walls around it. Tom ran headlong into them and, as he was drawn, it was they who were taken by surprise. A backhand flick sent his high-held blade between the top of gorget and the armoured down-swell of chinstrap, straight across the pallid vulnerability of a throat. The first Italian span away spraying blood even as Tom swung to face the next, sensing his dark companion falling in at his shoulder to face the third and last.

Echoing the English style which had despatched the rapist in the earl's tent a scant quarter-hour before, the two men stood square on to their opponents, the blades of their short swords held high, ready for the inward cut, the step forward, the punch and the pummelling. As this was war, both men also slid a long dagger out from its sheath across their buttocks and waited to go at it, hammer and tongs.

Ignoring their choking, drowning ex-companion, the Italians fell into an altogether different stance, however. It was a stance that Tom had never seen before, though he had heard it whispered of. Side-on, the Italians looked at their English opponents over their right shoulders. Before them they held, not the weighty, double-edged English short swords left over from the Wars of the Roses like Tom's, but brand-new, Ferarra-made, long, slim, needle-sharp rapiers.

Tom, confident of his strength and experience, swung into the attack first, only to find his first strike flicked away by a swift blade and an iron wrist. The return stroke struck at him like a snake, so fast he never saw it coming and luck alone set the point slithering off the boat-belly roundness of his breast-plate a hair's breadth from his own throat. He tore his left breast swinging in the dagger thrust, but the Italian had danced back immediately on missing his stroke. Feeling as clumsy as an ox, Tom stepped forward, falling into the familiar stance that had served himself so well all his life. That would serve him through to its fast-approaching end, by the look of things.

It was hard to say whether it was the sword or the way his

opponent used it that unnerved Tom more. A flurry of movement and a hiss on his left warned him that his companion was
in little better case than he was himself. In the face of the deadly
rapier, Will had begun a careful, skilful retreat, clearly looking
for some other help or advantage. Will was wise, thought Tom.
Attack had not worked; perhaps careful defence might reveal
something of use. He too stepped back, waiting, all too well
aware that time was ticking by with relentless pace.

Tom waited less than a second, and that fearsome blade was
hissing for his throat again, as the Italian threw himself forward, all his weight and strength behind the point. For all his
experience and agility, Tom was far too slow to stop it; instead
he turned it with a club-swing of his own blade, and the point
hissed past his throat – but through his very ear lobe. In came
the dagger again, swift enough to screech across the Italian's
back-plate before the burning kiss of the rapier was gone,
retreating along a line so true, that Tom's ear lobe didn't even
tear.

'I will put a pearl in that, when I go to Court,' said Tom, in
his flat but fluent Latin, all bravado to the end.

The Italian laughed, a light, mocking sound. Behind the
vizard of his chased silver helmet, his face looked young and
fresh; scarce bearded. The eyes narrowed and Tom jerked into
action again. He was quicker this time, warned by that flicker of
olive eyelids, but the boy's wrist was every bit as unyielding as
his blade and this time his target was clear. Tom's right earlobe
was spitted like a chicken ready for the fire. No sooner was the
fiery ice of the kiss there than it was gone again, and the
endgame of the duel was upon them.

'Now,' said the Italian youth, in liquid Latin fit to grace the
lips of Tully himself, 'you can wear a pair of ruby drops, down
to the courts of H—' He exploded forward on the aspirate of
the word and Tom turned his face helplessly aside, truly
expecting that terrible, unmatchable, unstoppable point to
pierce his eyeball and send him straight to the courts of Hades
indeed.

But, unaccountably, the Latin youth threw himself into

Tom's arms instead, their breastplates chiming together like cymbals.

Tom was thrown backward by the weight and power of the assault and came near to losing his feet. The Italian's helmet slammed into his face, rattled his teeth and all but flattened his nose. In a pure reflex, he wrapped his arms about his assailant, his mind still far away from thoughts of wrestling. His senses, in truth, were questing for the tiny, deadly wound that must, somewhere about his skewered body, be draining his life away.

But then the Italian's knees gave and the forward push of his power became the backward drag of his weight. Tom fell forward on to his knees with his erstwhile foe lying beneath him, like the body behind the horse which had started all this. The boy's lips moved but nothing issued from them except a choking froth of blood.

Moved by some motivation sprung secretly from the heart of Jesu himself, Tom snapped open the dying man's chinstrap and slid his helm away. How young he was. The curls on his forehead were dark only with sweat and the fluff on his chin might have caused a peach to blush. And yet this stripling had been set to finish him, here and now.

'Am I dying?' asked the boy, thickly, through the blood.

'Yes,' answered Tom, though he still had no idea why.

'Shrive me. Hear my confession.'

Tom looked up, away from the desperate pleading in those tar-dark eyes. A Dutch soldier stepped out into the street, a smoking dag in his hand. The wheel-lock pistol was old enough to have been banned in England fifty years since, but they were happy enough to employ it here. The soldier with the dag gave a brief, fierce grin. Tom was torn. The Hollander had saved him, not a doubt of that, and yet he was vexed that he had killed the boy at all. It was that thought, coupled with his simple goodness, that held the young Englishman here. Time was running away too swiftly and all the weight of the message, the fate of the army and the reputation of the General, stood in the scale against hearing the confession of a dying boy and sending him safe to Heaven.

'I can shrive you,' he told the boy in his barbarous Latin, as gently as he could. 'Tell me your sins, little brother, and I will shrive your soul.'

A hand descended on Tom's shoulder and he looked up. 'I will attend to him,' said the Master of Cyphers. 'You have other business in hand.'

Tom looked across the road to where the last Italian lay, still as death.

'How—?'

'I was taught by a Master. Tarleton, the Master Clown. He's a Master of Defence to boot. Even so, had the boy not glanced away at the sound of the shot that killed your man here . . .' He shrugged in silent eloquence. 'Still. It was the will of God. But you have your message to deliver. And time is short.'

Tom looked up, scarcely able to speak, torn between horror and revelation. 'Ask him . . . Will, ask . . .'

'I know. I shall ask, on my word. Now go. And Godspeed!'

Tom staggered to his feet and broke into a run once more. Only thews as young and hale as his could have kept moving after such a morning as this had been; long after even the horse had given up. But he was at the final furlong now and he was young and strong and desperate.

Sensing something of the urgency and the desperation of his young English ally, the Dutch soldier fell in behind him and paced him up the ruined road, reloading his ornate, triangular wheel-lock pistol as he ran.

Tom realised there was a second section to the Italian patrol when a ball slammed into his breastplate and ricocheted off across the street, leaving a numb track on his upper sword arm. The force of the bullet stopped him in his tracks and the Dutchman slammed into his left shoulder. 'Look for the smoke,' advised the Hollander tersely.

Shocked and breathless, Tom nevertheless had the wit to heed him and he saw at once a cloudy grey column rising from behind a ruined wall ten yards ahead. With the clap of his companion's hand on his arm, he threw himself into a run again, turning aside towards the tell-tale smoke. Within two seconds, he was vaulting over the low cairn of rubble, left hand as a pivot, right hand high and armed.

His opponent was a matchlock musketeer, no young dilettante reliant on his Ferrara blade and his swordsmanship, but a hardened professional, trained by the Spanish *tercio* men. As Tom leaped into the ruined house, the Italian looked up, partway through the reloading of his weapon. Without a pause, he hurled the smoking snake of his burning match straight into the young Englishman's face and used the momentary pause this won to catch up his weapon by the barrel. The musket's shoulder-piece was heavy and sharp on the underside so that the whole thing made an effective club – and a rudimentary axe. Up swung the heavy bludgeon, even as Tom cast the burning, saltpetre-coated musket-match aside and ran on in. But the sparks of blazing twine had blinded his eyes just as the shattered bricks and fallen tiles proved dangerously slippery under his feet and he fell forward. The dangerous edge of the long gun swung like a headsman's blade through the air that his head had just occupied. Forward he reached, in that long thrust that the young Italian swordsman had used to skewer his burning ear-lobes. The tip of his great-grandfather's sword jarred into the musketeer's groin and the short blade came near to tearing loose from his hand as he fell. There came a flat report, which echoed like the slamming of a door. It was a sound he knew now – the Dutchman has finished the business with his dag.

No sooner was he down than he was up again, blinking his streaming eyes clear – but the musketeer was gone. In his place there stood a soldier with a pistol, cocked and ready. Tom slowed, slithering. The pistol came up, but it was aimed well wide of him. He threw a glance sideways and saw his companion there, dag still smoking. The Dutchman was the target of the Italian pistoleer and for the moment, he was helpless. '*Morti!*' he called in Latin. 'Die!' The Italian began to turn, swinging the hollow barrel of his pistol round until it gaped at Tom like Hell's Mouth.

Tom's boots scrabbled for purchase on the slippery rubble

beneath them and, by the best of good fortune, found it. Just as the Italian swung round to face him, pistol levelled and steady, Tom found sure enough footing to lunge. Up went the point of his great-grandfather's sword that had killed many a usurping Tudor soldier in the blood bath of Bosworth Field. Down came the match of the pistol's match-lock into the powder-filled priming pan. Into the very mouth of the barrel plunged the sword-point, as thick as a thumb, running up the barrel just as the powder caught. Into the very throat of the thing went the steely weight of the good old sword, just at the moment that the charge exploded behind the tight-wedged ball.

The power of Tom's thrust threw the Italian soldier's pistol up into his face just at the moment of discharge. The twisting blade snapped off, the tip of it shattered for a hand's length by the destruction of the gun. The barrel exploded, soft iron unable to accommodate so many contrary forces. The blast blew off the Italian's face and hand as it hurled him backwards, a hollow-skulled corpse, into the rubble. Tom pulled his shattered, smoking sword back and found it a short sword indeed, while his hand and his arm were numb to the shoulder. He dragged himself erect and looked around. Two more dead enemies. The Hollander smiling, and waving his heartfelt thanks. Each of them owed the other a life now. They would surely be the closest of friends – or the bitterest of enemies. But there was no leisure to weigh the balance at this moment, with still a way to go before the English lines would be reached, with the last of the time running out.

As he came up among the outer guards, Tom tore the signet from its hiding place within the wrist-piece of his gauntlet. The first guard that saw it called his sergeant and the sergeant called the Captain himself. Within moments, Tom and his silent Dutch companion were being hurried through the lines towards the General himself. After having been thwarted so many times, it was strange to be pushed forward so easily – and so far. He was before the Earl of Leicester within less than five minutes – a wonder, had he been able to count so short a time.

'You are late,' snapped Lord Robert. 'Give me your message

at once.' His hand reached down imperiously, thumb and fingers at play like rapiers duelling.

Tom handed over the parchment at once. 'My lord,' he said. 'I am not the messenger. I found him dead upon the road and have brought his message to you in his place.'

Leicester's eyes, only a breath less powerful than those of the Queen herself, regarded him over the top of the parchment.

'And how did you fathom what this was – and calculate where to bring it?' he asked, turning away to share the contents of the message with a tall, hawk-eyed man at his side.

'By . . . By . . . By exercise of logic, your grace,' said Tom, having no expression other than this to describe what he and the Master of Cyphers had achieved.

'Through logic, then, you are a made man,' said the Earl, turning back after an instant of fierce, whispered conversation. 'You and any that have helped you. For you have saved my army this day.'

'Though, from the look of you I guess there was as much of bravery as logic,' added the other, his fierce eyes resting on Tom, as sharp as the Italian's steel, his voice easy and carrying, used to interrupting earls and captains general.

Lord Robert gave a tight smile. 'You're in the right of it, Master Poley,' he said. Then he turned. 'Captain, call the retreat,' he ordered. 'Call it at once, man, for Captain Ive tells me by this that at noon the walls of the citadel come down – and they will land upon the heads of any who still stand beneath them, be they friend or foe. Quick, man, for there is no time left and yet much to do!'

Ten minutes later, as the English army took to their heels under the jeering insults of the Italian and Spanish defenders, an earthquake shock of buried thunder rolled all along the south-facing wall. As though stone could become sea, the whole outer keep curved over and broke like a tumbling wave. The shock of it cascading on to the vacant mud below made the whole of the battlefield heave as though great breakers were speeding across it to set the tents of the English army dancing like the sails of a fleet at sea. And to make one or two of the English soldiers unsteady on their feet as they turned like the tide out of apparent retreat into a full, full-throated charge.

Four men stood amid the rubble that had been the walls of Nijmagen at sunset that evening. They were weary after a day of battle but cheery and laden with spoils. Each of them was also richer by a thousand pounds and, on the promise of Lord Robert himself, free to follow his own desires.

'What of the girl and her ravisher?' Tom had liberty to enquire at last. But all he got from Talbot was a thin-lipped scowl and a shrug by way of reply. When he asked what the others' plans were, however, Talbot was the first to speak.

'I will stay with the army,' decided Talbot. 'At the end of this campaign, Bess and I will settle back in London, or home in Winchester. Look for us at the sign of the Boar's Head, the Bishop or the Anchor. A tapster's life for me, that I may each night regale my customers with the story of this day!'

The Dutchman's name was Ugo Stell. He was a silent sort, but during a day of fierce street-fighting, he and Tom had discovered an ability to read each others' thoughts that came unsettlingly close to witchcraft. They were a deadly team indeed, with the broadsword and wheel-lock pistol. 'I go with the boy,' he said, in thick English, pointing with his chin at Tom.

'Well I cannot say where I will go,' said Tom.

'South,' said the Master of Cyphers. 'The Italian left the men who saved his soul at the last all his armour and his sword, his horse, his pack-horse and his saddle-bags – well stocked by all I could discover. And most of all, young Tom, he left you your heart's desire.' Like an actor he rode the moment, until, just the very instant before even Tom himself could ask what was his heart's desire, he said, 'Ridolfo Capo Ferro, of Siena.'

'What?' demanded Talbot Law. 'Who?'

'Tom knows. It's the name of the man who taught the Italian boy to use a sword. Ridolfo Capo Ferro of Siena. The Master of all Masters of the Science of Defence.'

'So,' said Tom to Ugo. 'We go south.' But then he turned back to the other. 'And what shall you do?'

Again that smile which just curled the lips below the dark moustache and folded the skin at the corners of those wise eyes into the finest of wrinkles. 'Home to England. I have a wife and family at home in the country. I have a profession in the city and, with my thousand pounds and my booty, a fine chance to become a sharer in the finest enterprise that any man could dream of.'

It was only later, after the farewells, under the wide sunset at the end of another long ride, in the first camp on the way south that Tom pulled off his gauntlet to see a little piece of paper come fluttering out into the firelight. Wearily, he picked it up and looked at it. It was the sheet that had belonged to Will, the Master of Cyphers. On one side it was covered with a series of calculations proving with mathematical precision that 'aaabe' could be the same as 'iiiv.' With a grunt of satisfied amusement he began to fold it, ready to put it away. Then he noticed that there was writing on the other side as well. In a neat, clear, firm hand, it said:

THE FIRST PART OF THE CONTENTION OF THE TWO FAMOUS HOUSES OF YORK AND LANCASTER

by

WILLIAM SHAKESPEARE

CHAPTER FOUR

Three Deaths

I

September 1588

Robert Dudley, Earl of Leicester, was tired. He had been utterly tired when he set out for Buckstones to try and repair some of the exhaustion of arranging the celebrations at Tilbury to mark the defeat of the Spanish Armada. He was still tired now; tired and lonely. Almost, in fact, alone. His retinue was small – certainly for the most powerful man in the country, the power behind Queen Elizabeth's throne. He was old, too – fifty-five now. The tall vigour of the 'Sweet Robin' that Elizabeth the girl had fallen so deeply in love with was stooped and white-haired portliness now. The year that had passed since the siege at Nijmagen had treated him badly. It was as though the slipping away of power and popularity had broadened his belly and hunched his shoulders and badger-striped his beard.

But he was beginning to marshal his resources. Once he had finished taking the waters at Buckstones, he was sure, he would be back in the saddle and back in power. Then let those puppies Essex, Southampton, Cotehel and their circle look to their laurels. Then let the strutting popinjays Drake and Raleigh dancing around Lord Howard of Effingham try to stand so tall.

He'd be back in the Netherlands again, wielding power like the almost-King he had become.

For a moment he dreamed of the walls of Nijmagen and the bright-eyed, excited young man with the message who had allowed him to snatch one final jewel-bright victory out of the dark jaws of defeat.

Then, coming back to the more painful, less glorious and much less clear-cut present, he looked down at the papers he was working on. Most of them were reports to the Council urging that Essex and his faction and Raleigh and his 'School of Night' needed closer watching than ever now that the Earl was approaching his majority and the bluff West Country sailor, Elizabeth's 'Shepherd of the Ocean', was shining so brightly at Court.

There was a gentle tap at his chamber door. He looked up and called, 'Enter.'

A servant entered with a tray that bore a package and a tall goblet made of green Venetian glass full of the thick claret wine he liked to sip in the evenings. Robert Dudley accommodatingly moved the papers he was working on to one side, making room on his table for the tray.

The package was from the Queen. He recognised the wrapping and the seal. He had written to her a couple of days ago and she had answered by sending him medicine. He tore open the package with a smile. It contained a little vial of liquid. From any other source he would have tested it or disposed of it, but the Queen was always so careful herself – all her food and drink was tasted by at least three separate people before it even approached her table, let alone her lips. He broke the seal and threw the medicine back, following its oily foulness down his throat with a good draught of the wine.

He knew at once he had been poisoned. The concoction hit his belly with a wrenching twinge like an assassin's knife – which, he wryly thought, it probably was. He tried to get up but his legs had already betrayed him. The twisting agony in his stomach intensified, but oddly, the clarity of his mind remained.

Two ideas occurred to him at exactly the same moment. That

he should call for aid before his voice betrayed him also. And that his beloved queen had sent him this poison.

He sucked in a shuddering breath, but as he tensed his stomach to release that great bellow, it betrayed him also, sending up a great wash of burning, agonising vomit. He made some quiet choking sounds as he sat stricken, watching the contents of his belly dissolving the letters he had been writing. Then he toppled sideways off the chair and slumped on to the floor. The whole of his body was in open revolt. He couldn't even blink his eyes and his vision clouded with tears. This angered the clarity of his dying mind. That he should be thought to have cried at the last. Unless, of course, they thought he was crying of a broken heart, poisoned by the queen he had loved.

They thought nothing of the sort. His doctors reported to Her Majesty that the Earl of Leicester had died of a seizure resulting from his long consumptive illness to the belly. The Queen locked herself in her room with grief and did not come out until Sir Francis Walsingham, Secretary to the Council, gave orders that the door be broken in.

II

April 1590

Sir Francis Walsingham, Secretary to the Council and the Queen's closest and most trusted advisor now that Leicester was dead, sat in his office at White Hall Palace. He looked into the eager face of the young man opposite. 'The package is from Tom, you say.'

'It is, Sir Francis. Tom sent it up from Scadbury with me and asked that I place it in your hands. It is a sovereign remedy, he says, against the affliction from which you suffer, sir.'

Walsingham looked into those eager, burning eyes. He was not particularly pleased that Tom should have been discussing the great infection of his waters, cod and testicle stones which was currently making his life so hard to bear. But, as the leader of the Queen's first and most effective secret service, he knew the power of that new, and Heaven-sanctioned source of information, pillow talk. And this was after all one of his own men, a Cambridge man like Robert Poley, the leader of his spies. One of his adopted son's closest friends. 'Very well,' he said. 'I will take it. My thanks to you for your trouble.'

As good as his word, he took the noxious potion the instant the young man had left, washing it down with a draught of water. He knew as soon as he had swallowed it that it was death. His stomach clenched and he fought to vomit as he felt the liquid coursing through his veins. He heaved himself out of his chair, hoping to make it to the door and summon aid. His legs betrayed him and were joined in their treachery by everything else below his waist. A waterfall of urine cascaded out of him. Thin yellow bile exploded from his mouth and nose. He choked and gasped, his body twisting in seizure then stilling. But his mind remained clear. As his secretary burst in, crying aloud with shock and horror. As help was summoned. As he was lifted on to a pallet, carried out to a carriage which bore him home to his austere establishment in St Mary's Papey, the house he occupied hard by Bevis Marks beside the London city wall.

Sir Francis's mind remained trapped in his useless body, wide awake and helpless while Robert Poley, his master intelligencer, came in and looked through his papers. Where would Poley go, now that he no longer had Sir Francis's protection? The old man wondered. To Essex, so hungry for power? To the quiet Robert Cecil who would make such good use of those papers? To his own impatient son Tom down at Scadbury? They would all give a man like Poley much employment.

Poley was replaced by another with free access to St Mary's Papey – Thomas Phellippes, Sir Francis's cypher and code expert and sometime right-hand man. Phellippes, as ever, came in with the brutal Richard Baines – the man they used if a throat needed cutting or an arm or two breaking. They found that his papers were all gone and looked coldly down on him. Then they left. Like Poley, they would be heading for the Court and new employment, under some other lord's livery.

Of course Sir Francis's son, Tom, was summoned up from his great house at Scadbury. But the old man was dead by the time Tom arrived. And that was perhaps as well; for had it not been Tom who sent the poison up in the hands of his vital young friend?

They told the Queen the man she called her 'Moor' had died of a seizure. And they never found his papers, which named every spy and suspect from the Queen's side to the kennel, in all the broad land and as far afield as Reims and Rome itself.

III

April 1594

Ferdinando Stanley, Lord Strange, Earl of Derby, sat in his private room in Lathom House, reading a letter which had been sent to him by two of his men. Lord Strange's Men they called themselves, and wore his livery badges, enjoying his patronage. But he had not expected that they should write to him in this fashion. This was the sort of information that should go to the Council or to Mr Secretary Cecil, if it were true. *If it were true.*

Had it come from another source, he might have consigned it to the fire that burned just beyond the irons at his feet. But he knew the writing – it was Will Shakespeare's sure enough. And the information seemed to have come from the new man, Julius Morton. And he had impressed Ferdinando as a man with wit and contacts. And, of course, the information was to do with Essex and the crew he had gathered around him. Yes, even if Morton's suspicions were ill founded, they would make useful ammunition to one of the Walter Raleigh, 'School of the Night', faction. Useful bargaining counters to a man already in trouble with the Council and the Court for being used as a Catholic figurehead now that Phellippes and Poley's exposure of the Babbington Plot had rid the country of a nest of conspirators and their Queen of Scots as well.

But Morton and anyone else who shared this information had better take care, thought Lord Strange darkly. For such accusations could be almost unimaginably dangerous. Especially if there was even the tiniest tincture of truth about them.

A servant tapped at the door. 'Enter,' called Lord Strange.

It was a bowl of strawberries, from his own estate, grown under glass against a south-facing wall in the new Italian fashion. The first of the season. As he read on, Lord Strange began to eat them, his mind so consumed by the content of the letter that he did not notice their unusually tart flavour.

The first hint he got that he had been poisoned was when his stomach suddenly spasmed. A great wave of yellow bile washed, scalding, up his throat and out over Will Shakespeare's careful writing. The paper, horribly weighted, slopped down into his lap, and Lord Strange's clear, trapped mind, watched with distant horror as the writing and then the paper itself began to dissolve.

When they found him, some hours later, the well-spattered fire irons had begun to dissolve as well.

CHAPTER FIVE

The Deadly Blade

London, June 1594

Tom Musgrave stood at the curtain behind the stage-left entrance on to the thrust of the Rose Theatre's stage, marvelling at the manner in which Will Kempe, the greatest clown of the age, could turn an audience from thunders of laughter to whispers of fear.

'I bite my thumb, sir . . .' called the suddenly dangerous clown, in the words Will Shakespeare had chosen from the bagfull of Italian insults Tom had brought back with him from his years at school in Siena. The fencing master knew what the next sounds must be – the serpentine hisses of rapiers as Kempe and his companions on the stage drew their long, dangerous, stillstrange swords against their Montague and Capulet enemies. So the first-ever performance of the new play of *Romeo and Juliet* got fully under way.

Tom was not so certain of what the audience's reaction would be to the wild rapier play. After all the rehearsals at both acting and fencing in the new Italian style with the new Italian weapons, this was the first time the deadly foreign sword-style had been seen on the stage, outside private performances. Rapier play was still whispered as a black art here, like lock-picking, gun-smithing and witchcraft.

Tom swung back, his mouth dry and his throat tight with the tension they were all feeling. The theatres had just reopened after two years of the Plague – this was their one chance to repair their fortunes – a chance made infinitely more important by the recent death of their patron Ferdinando Stanley, Lord Strange. The last few golden angels from his bounty would keep them going until his affairs were wound up and the actors truly became masterless men, vagrants, beggars.

In the shadows by the tiring house, he could see Assistant Sword-Master Ugo Stell, going through Tybalt's deadly *passado* with his lead-coated blade, as Will Shakespeare himself rehearsed his tragic, unexpected death as Mercutio.

During the last few busy weeks, the new star of Lord Strange's Men, Julius Morton, had learned Mercutio's part – but he was nowhere to be found this afternoon, so Will Shakespeare himself was planning to double as Escalus the Prince of Verona and his witty, half-mad, ill-fated nephew Mercutio.

But halfway through the action, Mercutio was doomed to die, centre-stage, first victim of the black art of rapier play. Under Ugo's watchful eye, therefore, the lethal Italian pass went home again, thrusting the yard-long skewer of the rapier apparently through the playwright's breast. Will, seemingly slaughtered, clutched at the little bag of red vinegar beneath his shirt – but not hard enough to burst it into life's-blood yet.

Abruptly, a wave of sound broke in over the fencing master, causing him to spin on his heel and reach for his weapon. His eyes raked the Rose Theatre's backstage area as though it had been a Holland battlefield or a Siena stews. The bookkeeper, doubling as prompt, was gesturing wildly, shouting silently through the bear-baiting bellow of the crowd. There was something seriously amiss.

Two of the company, costumed as the Lords Montague and Capulet, hurled themselves out on to the stage and the others pushed nearer, with Tom at the vanguard and Ugo by his side. Round the edge of the curtain, Tom could see pandemonium on the stage, and the simple unbelieving awe of the audience beyond. A full battle was in progress, swords dazzling and spitting, blade against blade, pikes and partisans waving. This was a far greater riot than any they'd rehearsed. The short hairs on Tom's neck pricked.

In through the far curtain, the late Julius Morton came sliding in a flurry of rushes, bursting back from the stage itself. He was breathless and his face was pale. 'They are all at war out there,' he snapped, his voice carrying through an ebb in the bellowing. 'Two or three braggarts on the stage stools have snatched out their weapons and joined in our civil strife. Tom, Will, we must bring this to conclusion soon or there will be more than vinegar shed.'

Will Shakespeare brushed past Tom's shoulder. He had changed into his costume and was drawing himself up to represent the Prince of Verona. The fencing master swung in behind him. He used the last freedom before the heaving press of bodies to slither out his blade, all too well aware that his alone of all the company was not blunted with a coating of dull lead.

The afternoon was sultry and overcast, an imminent threat of thunder making the whole high heaven reflect their little turmoil here. The seven sides of the Rose's galleries rose up against the roiling clouds, threatening the thrust of the stage and the milling men upon it. Even after his increasingly close association with Will and all the rest, Tom found it disorientating to be under so many eyes. In the hectic months since his return, he had given exhibition bouts in plenty of the new Italian style taught him by Capo Ferro – but never before a house as large or as thrilling as this one. And never on a stage as full of fighting men.

All among the actors, adding deadly reality to their carefully rehearsed pretence, a dozen rich gallants who had paid extra to sit up on the stage itself, had joined in the apparent riot. Bodies hurled this way and that, blades whipped in fans of light and lightning thrusts. Tom's eyes narrowed, trying to discriminate the deadly silver flash of the unguarded point from the dullness of the leaden ones. Pikestaffs, partisans, staves were flourished. There was no room for grand movements – and had he not been drawn already, he would have been helpless. In a press like this it was easy enough to see how Kit Marlowe must have died little more than a year since, fighting to get out his long blade in the little back room of Mistress Bull's house at Deptford while Ingram Frizer's dagger went in through his eye.

Will Shakespeare strode forward, filling his princely robes and role, preparing to claim the stage and Tom went with him, close behind. All around was a babel of sound, no word clear amid the grunts and gasps.

No word clear save one, suddenly: '*Mercutio!*'

Hearing the name, Will Shakespeare, caught between one role and the next, swung back. Tom felt a jarring push and a sliding tug at his arm. Will froze, then stepped back and turned away once more. The press of bodies around Tom eased immediately as the citizens of Verona with their pikestaffs seemed to reclaim the peace. Will strode to the front of the stage and raised his hands. 'Rebellious subjects, enemies to peace,' he bellowed in the prince's voice.

And order was restored.

Tom met Julius Morton in the stultifying gloom immediately backstage the instant after his exit. The new man had on Mercutio's gaudy jerkin now, and was ready to accompany Dick Burbage who was playing Romeo onstage in a few moments' time. Will followed Tom off and strode over to the tiring room to pull off the prince's robes. No sooner had he begun to do so than he called, his voice low but urgent, 'Tom!'

Tom hurried across to his friend and found him standing with the royal cloth of gold on his left shoulder and his hand upon his ribs. 'I've been hit,' he said. Tom went forward at once and pulled Will's shirt up. Across the outer curve of his ribs, a little below his left breast, stood a ragged welt, sluggishly weeping blood.

'This was a close matter,' said Tom grimly. 'You are lucky the blade did not strike true or things would have gone badly for you, Will.'

'And from the look of things, I have you to thank for turning the point,' said the actor, gesturing. Tom looked down and remembered the sudden numb tugging through his flesh. The outer swell of his left arm was in like case a finger's breadth above the elbow; his sleeve bright with blood.

'I had not thought yours a dangerous profession,' said Tom. 'Until now.'

'There have been those that found it so,' said Will.

'Kit Marlowe, from your tales of him,' said Tom.

'But it was not this, among all his other interests, which got him killed.'

'And I doubt this thrust was much to do with acting either. Or with playmaking, unless your Puritan critics have armed themselves with something mightier than pen or pamphlet. Are you still a Master of Cyphers, Will?'

'Of letters only, these days.' There was less easy affability than Tom was used to hearing in Will's voice as he replied.

'And no fathers or husbands jealous of wives or daughters seduced away?'

'None of recent note.' The voice was icy now. A stranger's voice.

'Then it is accident and nothing more, Will,' concluded Tom. 'But from the look of these scratches I would say that we should look about ourselves. For out there on the stage there is a blade the equal of mine. From Ferrara or Toledo it has come to London and to Bankside and the Rose. Such blades are drawn to drink heart's blood, Will. You, who have written such a play as this must know that better than most. Look about you and pray that heart's blood may not be yours or mine.'

The two men's eyes met, each pair, friendly enough on the surface but guarded in their depths. Had either man been able to see into the future even a little way, a word or two might have been spoken now and a wilderness of sorrow saved. But both were blind to the future and so they guarded their tongues an instant longer.

A roar of laughter called them back to the business on the

stage where Kempe once again reigned supreme. Had either been ready to say more, the chance was gone, for all the company was suddenly a-bustle with preparations for the Capulets' ill-starred banquet.

CHAPTER SIX

The Murder of Mercutio

T he murder of Mercutio was the turning point of the drama's action. Its manner was so much a part of the grim message of the play that the relentless approach of this first public execution of the lethal rapier *passado* began to gain an unbearable weight and moment. Tom, who had used the teachings of Maestro Capo Ferro to devise the deadly duel, felt a keenness of suspense he thought he had left on the battlefields of his youth. Will Shakespeare, who had seen the dangers of the new weaponry and written it all down in his play, was hardly heartier. Both had lost a deal of blood, however, and would later blame the lowering of their spirits on that fact. Ugo Stell and Dick Burbage, who had practised for hours, were hang-dog in the tiring house and only Dick's genius as an actor made him seem to shine with happiness onstage when he acted the love-struck Romeo. All the rehearsals, the warnings and the care, seemed, of a sudden, so petty in the face of the danger. Among the cunningly contrived stage deaths of past actors – even to the excesses of Kit Marlowe's Tamburlaine and Barabbas – the calculated, casual realism of this one was new and shocking to them all.

Because of this, as the lines that brought the dreadful moment closer were spoken, so those who had limited occupation on stage began to gather hard behind the entrance curtains, looking warily out at the relentlessly unfolding drama on the

Rose's stage. Something of the impending gloom communi-
cated itself even to the audience, for as the sultry, thunderous
afternoon wore on, not even Kempe in the Nurse's costume
could keep their laughter loud. Not even Burbage could lighten
their unease. Not even the great Ned Alleyn, dressed as the holy
Friar Lawrence, could raise their drooping spirits. In fact the
only man there seemingly unaware of the gathering gloom was
Mercutio himself – or Julius Morton, who was playing him as a
pale shadow of the dead mercurial genius Kit Marlowe, whose
character had informed the part, ghost-like, in the first place.

Morton was full of frenetic spark and sport. It was his
fantastic duels of wit with Romeo, his ribald sallies at the
Nurse, which raised the loudest guffaws. His flights of fantasy
held the whole theatre entranced, and had both the bookkeeper, Tom Pope, and Will himself scrabbling among the
prompt books to discover whether he spoke the true lines as
written or not.

At last there were only Morton and the boy playing Benvolio
on the straw-strewn boards, between the rows of fashionable
gentlemen who had paid their extra sixpence for a stool in the
public eye up on the stage itself. Morton was sometimes speaking Mercutio's lines and sometimes extemporising, talking of
the heat, the Capulets, the dangers of mad blood and swordplay. Will was seated by the bookkeeper. As Tom gave up his
examination of the seated gallants and his quest to identify
which of them might possess the deadly sword, he glanced
across the cavernous backstage and caught the playwright's
eye. Will had a tight smile – a flash of teeth, thought Tom, like
the grin of an angry dog.

Sly, who played the sneering Capulet swordsman Tybalt, the
King of Cats with such a lethal scratch, thrust past Tom with an
arrogant rudeness that would have earned a challenge anywhere else, and swaggered out on to the stage, already deep in
character. His movement left the curtain caught back and
round it, Tom could see more clearly right across the stage.
Once again the solid thrust of wood was filling with brightly
costumed men – for Tybalt did not arrive alone. Face to face in

the centre of a gathering crowd, Sly and Morton confronted each other as Tybalt and Mercutio, their characters in the play. Tom could see well beyond them now, to the wide-eyed gaping of the groundlings who could once again scent deadly violence in the heavy wind. Over by Will and the prompt, Dick Burbage pushed through the stage-right curtain and out on to the boards. A gasp went round the galleries as Tybalt's wrathful, rolling eye fell upon Romeo, the object of his deadly rage. Insult and counter-insult flew. Tybalt advanced. But Romeo began to fall back; refusing to fight; refusing to say why, and accepting jibe after deadly jibe meekly. Until Mercutio himself, enraged beyond control by his friend's abject grovelling cowardice, ripped out his rapier and threw himself into the attack.

The duel exploded at once. No mere street-brawl this, but an exhibition bout, as carefully choreographed as any galliard danced at the Queen's bright Court across the river. The glittering clash of the swords ran counterpoint to the snarling of the duellists, and, running fleet-foot, through the sharp steel heart of it, Romeo himself desperately trying to beat the blades down with his very hands. The company onstage fell back into a horseshoe of bodies, its end open wide to the audience, giving the three men room to move. No sooner did they do so than the sixpenny gallants were up off their stools again, suddenly the only people in the packed house unable to see the action. Real, fashionable finery pushed between the lordly cast-offs that the actors wore. Tension simmered, after the explosion into violence of the earlier battle scenes. The self-important gentlemen jostled increasingly roughly for a better view. The actors, sticking grimly to their marks with the deadly dazzle of rapier blades scant inches from their noses, pushed back. The three wild characters with their two clashing, shimmering foils whirled around the barrier of their companions' broad breasts.

Until, abruptly, the tableau centre stage was frozen. Romeo held Mercutio back, his arms wrapped like hoops around his friend. Tybalt stood with his blade thrust beneath Romeo's arm, its tip apparently buried in Mercutio's very heart. Every entranced eye in the theatre, front of house and backstage alike,

41

had seen the vicious, lethal thrust beneath Romeo's innocent arm, and understood that Mercutio was dead.

'Mercutio will fall now,' said Will, suddenly at Tom's shoulder. 'His life and his lines are done. As are Morton's extempore additions to my good play.'

But the mordant playmaker was wrong. Mercutio did not fall. Instead, Morton's left arm swung wide, jerkily, puppet-like, into the face of the nearest actor. Morton wrenched himself out of Burbage's grasp with a guttural kind of scream and staggered sideways drunkenly. Off the chests of the stunned actors he bounced, like a bear at the baiting, trapped within the pit wall. 'I am hurt!' he shouted, with such force, shock and horror that the actors and the audience alike gasped. Burbage glanced back into the darkness backstage behind the curtains and went after the suddenly mad Morton.

'A plague on both your houses,' Morton was yelling into the faces of the stunned actors too slow to move out of his way. 'I am sped!' He was tugging at the edges of his doublet as he raved. Burbage caught up with him. 'Courage, man,' he ad-libbed half-heartedly. 'The hurt cannot be much . . .'

Morton's doublet was wide now. The lawn of his shirt shone white. No stain of vinegar, even, marked it. Will was still wearing the little bag of fake blood himself. 'It's not as deep as a well,' snarled Morton, suddenly overwhelmed with helpless rage. 'Nor so wide as a church door. But 'tis enough. 'Twill serve!' He opened his hand and smeared red across his fellow-actor's face. 'A rat! A cat to scratch a man to death. Help me into the house or I shall faint!'

Morton hurled himself on to Burbage with such force that they nearly fell. But then they staggered sideways as the stunned company fell back out of their way. Even the braggarts began to slink towards their stools, overcome by the terrible power of the moment. 'A plague on both your houses,' screamed Morton as Burbage ran him, stumbling, off the stage into the darkness of the tiring house. 'They have made worms' meat of me!'

Backstage, Burbage handed the tottering weight of Morton to Tom and Will. As they hurried the sagging actor back away from the stage curtain, the playmaker spat questions and threats at the actor who had extemporised such a lengthy death-speech for himself, but Morton disdained to answer him. None too gently, Tom and Will released the man and turned with a final threat, rushing to get to their places for the next fierce duel – between Tybalt and Romeo himself.

It was at the end of this, when Tybalt too lay bleeding dark red vinegar on to the rushes that dressed the bare boards of the stage and Will, in the person of Escalus the Prince, was hearing from Benvolio the detail of the murderous brawls, that Ugo Stell came up to Tom, with the tall figure of Ned Alleyn, still dressed in the friar's robes beside him.

'Tom,' said Ugo quietly. 'It's Julius Morton.'

'Tell him he'd better make haste away. If Will catches him in this mood, he really will make worms' meat of him.'

'Too late,' said Ned Alleyn, his voice deep and dark with worry.

'He's worms' meat already,' said Ugo, grimly matter-of-fact.

'He's dead?' Tom suddenly thought of the simple weight of the man he and Will had hauled backstage. There was a certain weight that was special to death. He had felt it often enough in the past. How could he have missed it or mistaken it now? 'Dead?' he demanded again.

'Dead as mutton,' confirmed Ned Alleyn. 'Though how and why are mysteries far beyond my understanding. What are we going to do?'

CHAPTER SEVEN

Worms' Meat

'**B**ring him in here, swiftly!' commanded Tom.
'Shall I send for the physician?' asked Ned Alleyn,
uncharacteristically hesitant in the face of the shocking event.

'Not yet,' said Tom as the three of them swung the sagging
weight of Julius Morton's body through the doorway and into
the tiring house. Here the crabbed little wardrobe keeper swept
a jumble of bright cloth off the long tiring table an instant
before the corpse crashed down on to the boards, the dull
thump of its landing masked by a wave of applause.

'The doctor would warn the constables or the Bishop's
Bailiff. Thank God the Queen's not at Westminster, the width
of the river away, or it would be Household men investigating
things to boot. Sir William Danby and his crew, like as not; just
as it was for Marlowe last year. And in the meantime, where
shall we be, awaiting Her Majesty's pleasure? Not on the
boards of the Rose, my friend! Especially not with Lord Strange
dead and gone and no one to plead our case at Court.'

'We'd be waiting in the Limbo at Newgate Prison, like as
not,' said a newcomer disgustedly. At the sound of his voice
they all fell back respectfully, except Tom who was busy with
the body. 'Or in the Marshalsea,' continued the newcomer,
Philip Henslowe, owner and proprietor of the theatre, the
company, the wood yards by the river and the baiting pits
nearby. 'The Marshalsea where we can pass a merry afternoon

with Master Topcliffe and his red-hot irons as our business goes to rack and ruin.'

Henslowe had little sense of humour, so it was only Tom who cracked a grim guffaw at the unwitting wit of the final phrase, for it was literally true. Topcliffe, the Archbishop's Pursuivant and the Queen's Rackmaster, would rack them and ruin them all if they fell into his clutches.

A roar of laughter swept strangely into the suffocating room, recalling the grim occupants to the relentless progress of the play outside in the real world. 'God's life,' swore Alleyn, 'my cue!' and he was gone with a swish of his friar's robes.

'On with it, all of you,' ordered Tom. 'I will see to this!' And, glad to pass the terrible weights of action, decision and responsibility to the fencing master, even Henslowe slunk away. Tom glanced around the dim, sultry, suddenly deserted little room with its mean window half shuttered. On an impulse, he crossed to this and threw the shutters wide, letting a shaft of sudden sunlight into the room. As he did so, he looked down across the old garden towards Bankside and there, on the corner of Rose Alley, where it ran north through Dead Man's Place to the river, stood a gallant looking up. For a moment more the man stood, still amid the bustle, staring back at the Rose as though expecting some matter of great moment to happen any instant now. Something about the man struck Tom. The darkness of his olive skin, perhaps, the glistening of his oiled black curls, the glint of ruby at his ear – a pair to the ruby in Tom's own lobes. As their eyes seemed to meet across the better part of one hundred yards, it was as though a flash of recognition passed between them. Then the man was gone into the crowd towards Bankend and the wherries at St Mary Overie Stairs, leaving nothing but an impression of tobacco doublet slashed with red, black cloak and long, long sword swinging against a broad right thigh.

Another burst of applause drowned Tom's purposeful tread as he crossed back towards the table with its silent burden. As he stood beside the still form, his eyes narrowed, focussing his thoughts as his mind whirred into action. What was it about poor Julius Morton that bespoke death so clearly? The still, staring, soulless eyes, perhaps. The utter pallor of his face. The stillness of his parted lips and chest, which lay like warm marble beneath Tom's first gentle touch. The stillness at the cooling column of his throat. But more. Even with the absence of blood upon that fine, linen shirt – so excellent a match for his white cheeks now – there was the languor of his limbs. The weight of them. The almost studied carelessness with which his left hand was disposed across the broad boards, its fingers half curled in some final, dying gesture. The hand that had swung wide at the crucial moment, striking one actor and smearing another with bright blood. It was the hand . . .

Tom took a step or two up the table and leaned over to look more closely at the hand. Gently, he folded out the loose grasp of the fingers as though opening the petals of a rose. There, in the centre of the palm, was a tiny pool of blood. Tom remembered the smear that the dying man had left on the shocked Dick Burbage. Frowning, Tom reached into the breast of his jerkin for the Italian lace kerchief he always kept there. Three deft dabs revealed a wound – scarcely more than a knife cut – as though the man had stabbed himself while sharpening a quill for a pen.

Tom's broad forehead folded in a deepening frown as he turned the dead hand over. There, on the back, a pin-prick, scarcely enough to release a ruby drop from the fat vein running along the back of it. Tom tugged at the red-gold point of his beard and thought. Only a poisoned blade could bring death from a wound as small as this – but no poison Tom had heard of would work as swiftly as this one must have done. And Tom knew a great deal about poisons, one way and another. He had learned a good deal more than the science of defence with Maestro Capo Ferro at Siena. He made a mental note to keep a watch on Dick Burbage's face. If there was poison in the blood Morton had wiped upon it then the skin would blister and fester. And Death would enlarge his kingdom by one more actor's soul.

Deep in thought now, far removed from the howls of sorrow

46

on the stage, Tom folded the wounded hand across the still
chest, then he cast it aside again, in the grip of growing
revelation. Short of breath suddenly, he tore Morton's shirt-
front wide. The man was dark, his chest matted with hair, but a
moment's careful search revealed, just below his left nipple,
where the oily curls were thickest – and most heavily tenanted
with fleas – another cut. A cut such as a slightly larger pen-
knife, big brother to that which might have cut his hand, might
have made.

Shouts of warning and outrage from the audience. A flickering disturbance to the thick light. A distant rumble of thunder
and the first stealthy whisper of rain in the old rose garden
outside. Tom heaved the dead man up on to his side. As he
moved the corpse, there came a sluggish slopping, as of a quart
or so of liquid on the move in the hollow of a barrel. Tom pulled
the fine, creased linen out of the dead man's belt above the
dagger he wore across his buttocks. Half-balancing the fallen
column of the man, holding him still with one hand as he pulled
the voluminous linen up to the lightly furred shoulders, Tom
stripped Morton's back bare. And there, on the inner curve of
his ribs, running in through the inner edge of his shoulder blade
almost into the ridged range of his spine, was a wound the
width of a little finger. A tiny mouth with a coral gape and a
dead black throat, reaching straight into the barrel of his chest.
And, as though the weight of Tom's understanding had some
magic property, a stream of dark heart's blood burst out of it.
The black stream caused Tom to leap back – though its stain
would hardly have discoloured his black breeches or boots. He
used the movement to spin himself into physical action. A
glance out of the window raked across the innocent bustle
moving to and from the Bankside. Then he was out into the
backstage area, even as Julius Morton, apparently merely
asleep, rolled languidly back on to his back upon the table
and began to examine the ceiling with bright but heavy-lidded
eyes. The dripping sounds grew louder. Moved out of the
garden and into the Rose.

The wardrobe keeper was there, still clutching his precious

cloth. 'You'll have some cleaning-up to do,' spat Tom in an undertone as he sprinted for the stage. He knew already he would be too late but he had to make assurance double sure. His long sword spat out of its scabbard, echoing warlike sounds from the stage itself. His shoulder hit the pillar by the stage curtain hard and, breathing a swift prayer of thanks that Master Griggs the carpenter had built Master Henslowe's theatre so stoutly, he used the rapier blade to ease back the heavy brocade. Across the stage, Dick Burbage danced in the final, desperate duel of the play and the County Paris was preparing to die. They were alone onstage except for the sixpenny gallants, so it was easy enough for Tom to see that one of the stools, which had all been full until Julius Morton's murder, stood starkly empty now. One of the courtly blades who had joined unbidden in the sword fights and the riots was gone.

Then, so was the chance for further speculation. All of the actors came milling up around him, ready to go onstage again to complete the final, vital section of their play. All of their futures depended upon it. And the play could go on of course, for Mercutio, after all, was dead.

Tom caught hold of Will's princely sleeve and pulled him aside. 'It was murder,' he said, his voice low. 'He has been run through from behind. It was a master's stroke. Only the finest of blades could have done it. Only the blade that came so close to us, I think. And the man that wielded it has gone.'

'But how could it have been done, Tom? On the stage of the Rose under the eyes of half of London and no one the wiser?'

'Not only *How?*, Will, but *Why?* This was a deep plot, carefully laid. And a tangled web behind it, like as not.'

'But what are we to do, Tom?'

Tom opened his mouth to answer. To answer that he did not know. But Will was gone on to the stage and the voice of the Prince rang out across the Rose.

Abruptly Ugo Stell was there, with the bookkeeper in tow. 'Tell Tom what you told me,' ordered the Dutchman quietly. Pope held up the prompt book. It was covered in scrawled additions – mostly to Julius Morton's speeches. 'I noted what Mercutio said at the end, Master Tom,' he said breathlessly. 'The speech about plagues and houses and making worms' meat of the man. For Master Will had written nothing like it in his original book. There's nothing like that in the original at all.'

'But you have it written down?'

'Every word, truly, sir. But what's the significance?'

'I have a suspicion,' answered Tom, glaring out on to the stage where Will was delivering the Prince of Verona's doom on Romeo, all unaware of the doom awaiting him back here, 'that there may be a message hidden within it. A message from a murdered man who dared not make his dying message clear. There is work for a Master of Cyphers here.'

'And for a Master of Logic,' added Ugo.

'And for a Master of Defence, I shouldn't wonder,' concluded Tom, grimly. And all too soon he was to learn just how true those last words were.

CHAPTER EIGHT

A Death Re-played

Later that afternoon the whole company except for Julius Morton was again assembled on the Rose's stage. The whole company of actors, that was. The Bookkeeper was at work in Master Henslowe's office copying out with laborious accuracy every word the dying Morton had spoken, marking the difference between those which followed Master Shakespeare's original and those that he had extemporised for himself.

As the wet boards and sodden rushes out on the stage itself steamed lazily under the gathering weight of the next thunderstorm, it seemed to more than one mind there that Julius was as fully among them as any of the others, passing spectrally from one ghostly wisp to the next. And in fact he was figured there in person as Will paced out his last moments, rolling in Dick Burbage's arms across the brawny chests of all the others. The badly shaken Sly, still half convinced that he must have struck the fatal blow after all, worked carefully and precisely as Tom, narrow-eyed, watched the whole performance, with Ugo by his side.

The actors were all at their points. Inevitably, after so much rehearsal of such a dangerous piece of action destined to be repeated over and over, every man there knew to within a whisker where every part of his body must be placed. The only difference, apart from the absence of the little tragedy's principal actor, was the equally crucial absence of the sword-wielding sixpenny gallants. But the actors were beginning to build up a clear picture of who among the courtly audience was where, when they left their stools.

'Now,' called Burbage and Sly together.

'Hold,' commanded Tom. The action froze. Will was standing in a slight crouch, trapped against the rock-steady chest of Hemminge, held by the encircling arm of Dick Burbage. Sly, caught in the act of bouncing off Condell's solid front, balanced the length of his leaded rapier precisely, ready to thrust under Dick's arm, apparently into the depths of Will's unprotected breast. 'Look about you,' commanded Tom. 'Stir your memories. Who else was close by at this very moment? Where were they facing? What were they doing? What did they look like?'

Of course a babel of answers arose at once, for there had been eight gallants up from their stools in the midst of the action and all of the horseshoe of actors had seen at least one of them. Tom held up his hand for peace, then he put a simple order on the matter by starting with the outer ends of the half-circle, and establishing through the testimony of at least two actors apiece what each of those eight men had been doing at the vital moment. The outer two – one on each side – had simply been pushing against the wall of actors apparently seeking a clearer view. Those next upstage behind them, at that very moment, had been caught between what was being enacted by the actors and what was going on among the other four of the unruly audience behind them on the stage. Here, between the steady backs of Hemminge and Condell and the curtains over the exits, there were four braggarts at swordplay. Whether two against two or three against one it was hard to say for the mêlée had been brief and none too well observed. Both Hemminge and Condell were agreed, however, in placing one dark, fragrant, black-clad gallant the closest behind them.

'I felt his shoulders against my shoulders, jostling me

roughly,' said Hemminge. 'He was hard at work, and I have, I calculate, a round dozen bruises on my ribs, courtesy of his elbows as he fought.'

'The air around me was all a-hiss with foreign tongue and spitting blades – and a-hum with fragrant garlic,' added Condell.

'So, he fought with his back to you against at least one other upstage. But he turned, when?'

'Turned?' asked Hemminge.

'Look around you, man. You see how Morton stood at your front and this gallant stood at your back. To run his blade beneath your own arm and through Morton to his very hand, he must have turned and thrust.'

'No,' said both Hemminge and Condell in a kind of chorus. 'He never turned, Tom.'

'They're in the right of it, Tom,' added Sly. 'I was watching my timing and my thrust but I swear I'd have noticed any man turning in that crowd behind Master Hemminge there.'

'The boy's right,' called the gruff voice of the Gatherer across the pit. 'I was up here on the upper three-penny gallery and I saw well enough. None of your roaring boys turned. And at the end of the swordplay they sheathed and sat like lambs, no harm done. There were upwards of twelve hundred souls in the house this afternoon and not an eye saw aught amiss for all they told me on their way out at the end. Not an eye dry, Master Will; but not an eye saw one jot or tittle amiss, on my life.'

The fact that the Gatherer was talking to Will abruptly awoke Tom to the fact that his friend had been standing frozen for a considerable time. 'Will, are you strong enough to stay there for a while longer?'

'For a while, Tom. Why? What have you in mind?'

But Tom was paying the motionless playwright scant attention. 'Ugo. Get me one of the leaded blades and stain it with soot from a taper. Bring it to me where the black-clad gallant stood. Then bring another for yourself. Leaded or not – it is your choice; we will try a pass or two in enactment of this strange bout.'

While Ugo ran to do his bidding, Tom positioned himself where the black-clad swordsman had stood. Much to poor Sly's disquiet as it chanced – for Tom's own clothing was a work-manlike shadow of the gallant's courtly fashion. As he waited for his associate to return with the swords, Tom jostled his way into perfect position.

'Ha,' gasped Hemminge. 'Your elbows strike the very bruises, Tom. You are a very image of the man.'

'I hope not,' said Will dryly. 'Another such as Tom would be one blade too many.'

Something in the ironic quip made Tom frown even as his lip curled in acknowledgement of a palpable hit. Then Ugo was there. 'Here.' He tossed the tallow-marked blade to Tom and fell into the first position as taught him by Maestro Capo Ferro. The blades clashed as Tom fended off his friend easily, the greater part of his mind occupied with feeling what exactly lay behind him; not before him. His back and elbows were surprisingly sensitive. It was easy, he soon discovered, to sense where the solid trunks of Hemminge and Condell stood and to plumb the vacancy between them. A glance over his shoulder revealed the white cloud of Will's billowing lawn shirt. Then it was the act of only a moment to perform the secret variant on the deadly *Punto Reverso* that Capo Ferro had taught him. The foil's handle twisted in his hand almost as though it had life of its own. The soot-stained blade slammed up into his right arm-pit, its point sticking out behind his back. Safe in the knowledge that it was well and safely leaded, he pulled his right hand sharply in towards his own breast and was rewarded by a sharp cry from behind. He stepped forward, swinging the sword out to defend himself once more. But Ugo's blade was at his heart.

Now it was Tom's turn to freeze. 'Too slow, Tom,' said Ugo, heavily.

'Aye, and a mite wild to boot. I am hurt, sir, but not killed.' Will's voice echoed Ugo's, but the dry irony was gone. The playwright seemed genuinely shaken. Even though the black line from the sooty blade ran along his ribs almost exactly over the welt he had received earlier on that deadly day, he nevertheless saw as clearly as the rest of them that Tom had unmasked the dark heart of the murder.

But Tom was not satisfied. The blade had gone awry. Unless the duellist opposed to the murderer were a confederate willing to hold the killing stroke as Ugo had done, then that moment of defencelessness would have spelt death for the murderer in any case. He stood, racking his brains for the one vital element he had overlooked – the one thing that would turn this rough botch into a mirror simulacrum of the lethal act.

As he stood – and the rest stood, still frozen at his command – the rain started again. A stealthy pattering like the footfalls of a prowling cat hunting rats among the rushes. The association of sounds made Tom think of the tiring house with its blood-dripping occupant and the way the pattering of blood had made the most recent downpour seem to come into the room from the rose garden when he had first discovered the cause of Morton's death. And, in a flash, even as the others, groaning, turned to find shelter from the gathering storm, Tom thought of the window, the rose garden and the black-clad gallant standing at the corner of Dead Man's Alley looking back. The gallant standing with a rapier hanging across the solid breadth of his right thigh.

'Hold,' bellowed Tom, freezing them all once again. Freezing them all as though they had been struck with the same icy touch as Tom's own heart had been. For only two sorts of swordsmen wore their foils like that – left-handers and ambidexters.

Tom was actually shaking as he swapped the leaded rapier to his own left hand and slid his long Ferrara blade out into the right. Ugo stood before him, white to the lips – the only man there to see as clearly as Tom the horrible danger of what he was proposing. At Tom's curt nod, the Hollander fell to again. Both he and Tom knew that Ugo could have had a companion at his side almost as well-tutored as he was, and Tom would have held them both in play. But what Tom was doing now he had never essayed outside the main salon of Maestro Capo Ferro's school in Siena, for an ability such as this was dangerously close to witchcraft and was even more likely than his uncanny ability with logic and deduction to get him hanged as a witch.

'Hey,' called Tom, thrusting forward with his right hand as he reversed the point in his left. The motion was so swift that not even the increasingly intrigued actors realised what was going on. Tom straightened, keeping Ugo easily in play. Behind him, Will cried out with shock and surprise, lurching forward into Dick Burbage's arms. The pair of them lurched against Sly and Condell and – but for the slap – the re-enactment was terrifyingly perfect. And, when they looked, in the muggy dryness of the tiring house a few minutes later, the black mark on Will's shirt was on the very point that the blade had run through Julius Morton's linen with so much more deadly effect.

Inevitably, it was Will who pressed him hardest to reveal exactly what he had done to reproduce the method of the murder so perfectly. But Tom remained reticent. Of all the men there, only Ugo, he believed – and hoped – understood exactly what he had done. The ability to fight with both hands at once – using two rapiers instead of one, or rapier and dagger – was one of Capo Ferro's most closely guarded secrets. Up until now, Tom had remained quietly confident that he was the only man in England who could perform the mystery at such an elevated level. Now, as the conversation around him began to gather, taking a course which it was all too easy to predict, Tom was increasingly, uneasily, aware that they were going to ask him to go out in search of this man. To find him, to find out what he was doing and to find out why he had done it to Julius Morton.

The murderous stranger was, perhaps, the one man in England who could kill Tom in fair combat – and he was, therefore, the man Tom should be most eager to avoid. And yet, as the afternoon wore on and the thunder gathered over the thatched roof of the Rose, bringing with it the sort of weather best suited to the kind of deliberations going on within, he felt a boundless excitement gathering in his breast.

'We want no authorities brought in on this,' emphasised Master Henslowe again. 'For two years and more we have been at starvation's door and now that the Plague has relented, I'll be damned before I let Fortune play us foul. Or any more foul, given the evil turn the whore gave us in the death of Lord Strange. City, Court and Bishop's Bailiff, all would close us down. And you all heard Master Doorkeeper – it was a big house and not a dry eye. As long as the play runs, our fortunes are on the mend and it will run for ten days more at the least – two houses a day after this, before we approach My Lord Chamberlain to seek preferment to the Queen.'

'We will need to approach my Lord Strange's executors in any case,' said Ned Alleyn. 'We work under his protection still, in theory. If we also work outside the law, those looking after his affairs will need to be alerted, if not warned.'

'A dangerous move, surely?' suggested Master Hemminge, the steady churchwarden. 'Like as not, they'll warn Sir William Danby himself and close us anyway. It is the lawful thing to do.'

'Perhaps,' said Henslowe a little shortly, unused to the frank discussion the Burbages allowed in their company – preferring to limit discussion to that between himself and his son-in-law and leading man Ned Alleyn.

'On the other hand,' added Will, 'a coded warning in the right ear might allow continued protection of our poor enterprise here should anything go wrong in the near future.'

'And a good deal could go wrong,' continued Tom. When he paused to order his thoughts, even Master Henslowe sat silently, not a little awed by what the Master of Logic had achieved in the case so far. 'For a start, we have Julius Morton. We have him but we cannot keep him long. What shall we do with him? Dump him in the Fleet River and let him wash away with the rest of the sewerage? Smuggle him over the river and leave him near his lodgings, another corpse in the nearest dark alley?'

'There are dark alleys enough up in Holborn, I suppose, well without London Wall, but we cannot risk it. He cannot go anywhere he might be found,' said Henslowe at once. 'All the world knows he played with us today. If he is found dead tonight then the Bishop's Bailiff will be at our door tomorrow. Though in God's truth he lived convenient enough to the Fleet River, nearer there than Southampton House.'

'That's your neck of the woods, Will,' said Dick Burbage. 'My Lord of Southampton's your patron. Perhaps he was funding Morton too.'

'I never saw him at Southampton House nor down in the country,' said Will dismissively. 'Half the bright young men in London live along High Holborn, for it's close to the Inns of Court for preferment and the mercury baths for the pox.'

'Danby, or Rackmaster Topcliffe, or the Bishop's Bailiff,' said Ned Alleyn, bringing them back to the matter in hand. 'Depending on whose jurisdiction the guts are washed up in.'

'Then we must put him where he will never be found – or hide him until our investigation is complete,' said Tom.

'And our run is finished and our future's secure,' added Burbage and Henslowe together.

'Where is the nearest graveyard?' asked Will.

'Behind St Mary Overie Church hard by the bridge,' answered Henslowe who knew the South Bank well – particularly as he owned so much of it.

'There are new-made graves there, I'll be bound,' said Will. 'We could add to their number tonight.'

'There's a risk,' warned Hemminge, the churchwarden. 'If you played such a trick at my church at St Mary Aldermanbury, the sexton would be on your heels fast enough. And the authorities would be called in by the week's end.'

'Then,' said Tom grimly, 'we'd best stow him where the recording's not so nice. Where's the nearest plague pit?'

Again it was Henslowe who answered most readily – too readily, for he did not immediately see where the question was leading. 'There's a new pit out beyond the Paris Garden, round towards Lambeth Palace,' he said. 'It's but poorly closed off. I fear the authorities are expecting to reopen it soon enough.'

'Is it well guarded?' wondered Tom.

'A couple of boys and a dog o' Sundays.' Henslowe shrugged dismissively. 'Who'd be mad enough to break in there?'

'Who indeed?' asked Tom, glancing across at Will and Ugo.

CHAPTER NINE

Bull Pit and Plague Pit

The company broke up just before ten. Those careful of their pennies wanted to be free to cross the Bridge before the City Gates closed; those like Hemminge and Condell more careful of their souls and reputations, wanted to be free of the Bankside before all Hell was let loose. But in truth there was little to keep them. All the plans they could make were laid and wanted nothing but action. From tomorrow they would be putting on a second performance between five and seven – giving patrons an unrivalled opportunity to spend the early afternoon at Master Henslowe's baiting pits, the early evening in his playhouse and the night in his taverns and brothels close-by.

As full darkness came and Bow Bells echoed distantly, chiming their nightly ten o'clock peal, Tom, Ugo and Will followed Henslowe himself out into Rose Alley. Between them, Tom and Ugo pulled the small cart favoured by the Wardrobe Master, piled with old rags of long-faded finery. Its ancient wheels creaked and its axle shuddered as they pulled it out into the street which was little more than a path worn in the grass and a little bridge over a stream. As though its venerable frame found the weight of these piled scraps of tawdry far heavier than usual, it continued to complain. A link boy waited to guide the busy entrepreneur to whichever of his adventures he wished to visit next. 'Bull Pit,' he ordered gruffly. The four of them slopped through the muddy pathways with the puddle of golden light appearing to brighten and dim in opposition to the light around them, which varied in turn, according to the vagaries of the moon behind the last of the fleeing stormclouds. The axle of the ancient cart squeaked and howled as the notion took it. Maid Lane wound between the half-open fields behind the Bankside tenements and the great places of entertainment. To the south of the Lane lay the Winchester Park, running up to Winchester Palace itself, London domicile of the Bishop who owned most of the land between here and Lambeth and whose Law ran south of the Thames. Almost before the last echo of Bow Bells died, their ears were assaulted by the howling of the dogs Henslowe kept kennelled in the gardens behind both the Bear Pit and the Bull Pit. Right into Bear Gardens they turned then left through a little cut to the Bull Pit itself.

The Gatherer guarded the door still, though the last bull of the day had long-since gone screaming down to death. He let the four of them into the great wooden-walled space, not so very different in design from the Rose. But whereas the walls of the theatre were decorated with gilding and paint, here they were spattered with blood and offal. There the air reeked of groundlings and – occasionally – Master Henslowe's beloved gunpowder effects. Here it stank of odour and death. And not a little lust.

Round the walled 'O' of the pit itself, with its central pole and scratched, splintered walls they scurried, pulling the Wardrobe Master's protesting cart into what would have been the tiring room if this had been a theatre. This room was, literally, a shambles. Four bulls hung from a great gantry, ready to be wherried across the river first thing in the morning to be butchered and sold at the City Shambles hard behind St Paul's where Cheapside met Paternoster Row. The bulls' faces were largely gone, their throats, chests, legs, bellies and privities ripped to pieces. And, beside them, stood a cart more than twice the size of that between Tom and Ugo. This cart was strong, new, well maintained, its axle well greased and solid. It needed to be strong, for it was piled high with dead dogs. From every crack and fissure along its high-boarded sides ran rivulets of thick, dark blood to gather on the axle and grease the wheels before it gathered thickly on the ground.

Henslowe gestured and the Gatherer left them alone. Tom heaved the Wardrobe Master's finery aside to reveal Julius Morton, blue and stiffening by now, his face a bloodless, waxen mask with wide eyes and an all but lipless gape. Henslowe himself caught the corpse's heels as Tom took the shoulders and together they swung him on to the dog cart. Then, careful to avoid the gathering blood, Tom hurled over a length of rope and several solid iron carpenter's instruments to lie on the dead man's chest. Will and Ugo put their clothing at greater risk by pulling dead dogs from beneath him to pile up atop him, until the corpse – and the pile of tools it carried – was completely hidden. 'You know what to do,' said Master Henslowe. 'Then, Master Shakespeare, I would most warmly commend you to your bed. You'll be doubling as Mercutio tomorrow and twice a day after that until we can train up another man. Here . . .' He reached into the bag the Gatherer had left and pulled out a handful of pennies. 'Take a wherry from Stangate Stairs or Horseferry hard by the palace.'

'Stangate Stairs to Fresh Wharf,' said Will as they pushed the heavy but silent cart out into the moonstruck night. 'Please God it is slack water or we'll never shoot the Bridge.'

'It's still a fair walk from up to your lodgings at St Helen's,' added Tom. 'You'd best walk light and careful, Will. Either that or bed down at the Boar's Head. Henslowe gave you enough for a bawd, let alone a boat.'

Will fell silent at that and Tom smiled. The Boar's Head Tavern was part of Henslowe's empire. The women who worked there were a cut above the rest, except for the girls at the Elephant, which Tom himself preferred. Will had a good deal to think about. As had they all.

Speed and logic dictated that they should be wheeling their doubly grim burden along Bankside and into Upper Ground – thence along the South Bank to Lambeth Palace, whither they were ultimately bound. Although the Scavenger had an agreement with Henslowe – a mutually rewarding one – for the disposal of dead dogs and occasional offal, every now and then a larger assignment of canine meat would be sent directly to Lambeth Palace to be fed to the Archbishop of Canterbury's pack of hounds. Should anyone demand an explanation tonight, this was the one they were prepared to give.

But of course their real objective was the old plague pit which lay in the King's Field, hard by the Scavenger's own Laystall or rubbish pile. The moonlight led them along Maid Lane to Gravel Lane and there they turned south, running down below the bawdy brightness of the Paris Garden towards Sunmer Street. No sooner had they turned south than Tom began to suspect they were being followed.

Will seemed to have no such worries, however. If he had done so he would have stayed quiet, straining like Tom to catch any suspect rustle, whisper or footfall in the moonshadows at their heels. Instead, he fell into a low, muttered conversation about what the meeting of the Rose's company had agreed before they broke up into the gathering night. As soon as Morton was hidden well away – hidden it was now agreed in some place whence he might be retrieved should circumstances so dictate – Tom was to take up his next and most personal responsibility. He was to search out the deadly ambidexter swordsman. Not too hard a task, in all truth; for the man was like to be unique and he would inevitably flash through Tom's orbit, or that of his acquaintance, like a meteor through the night. But discovering the murderer's identity would get them little further unless they could put him in the hands of the law and get the truth of the matter racked out of him. But they would have to be careful how they did this, of course. 'We're as like to end up on Rackmaster Topcliffe's bed as the murderer is,' puffed Will, throwing his weight against the increasingly unwieldy cart. 'So we must present a complete picture to the Crowner's Quest. Like Robert Poley did at poor Kit Marlowe's death last year.'

'The nearest way to do that is to go through his rooms before the authorities can, I agree,' said Tom. 'Which end of Holborn did he live? Not up by Southampton House—'

'No,' said Will coldly. Will had spent much of the last few years on the fringes of the Earl of Southampton's circle, and had been his servant for the last eighteen months, dedicating some of his greatest poetry to his master and – some said – sharing his bed from time to time as Marlowe had sometime shared Tom Walsingham's. Will had left the young earl's household mere weeks since to rejoin the Burbages – and the recently formed Rose Company. There were whispers that Southampton, like the Earl of Leicester seven years ago, had given him a thousand pounds. But sign of such riches was there none.

'Morton's rooms are at the east end, past the Inns, near Turnagain Lane,' said Will now, breaking Tom's chain of thought.

'Close on Alsatia,' said Tom. 'A man of many parts, then, if he is privy to that thieves' den as well as the inns and the theatres. But not Southampton House, you say?'

'Not while I have been there.'

'Better known, perhaps, at Essex House, then. The two are close enough.'

'In all but distance,' admitted Will.

'I must across to Westminster in the morning at any rate,' continued Tom, quietly, ears a-strain for that near-silent foot-fall close behind, mind focused on what Will was letting slip about the relationships between the great Earls of Southampton and Essex to whom he had been so close, and the murky world of thievery and murder which clung to their cloak-tails like mud. 'I'm happy enough to talk to my Lord Strange's secretary. Even though Lord Strange is dead we still may have some call on his name and his purse. My name is on the list of the Rose's company and they know I can speak for Masters Henslowe, Burbage and the rest of you. But I am also known at Court as Master of Defence. More and more of them are making their pilgrimage out to my long room at Blackfriars. Lords of all stripe and seniority among them. Their Graces of Essex and Southampton soon enough, I daresay. And to be frank, my name is not unknown in certain corridors. The Musgraves are captains of the Bewcastle Waste. My Uncle Tom reports direct to My Lord Chamberlain and the Council.'

'Hist . . .' spat Ugo. 'We are followed.'

Tom nodded and the three of them fell silent again. They were coming close to the edge of the King's Field now. Beyond that stretched Lambeth Marsh, a sodden desert crossed by paths a little dryer than the mire. The King's Field was higher, a slight eminence around which the Thames wound between the twin cities of London and Westminster on the north bank and the separate conurbations of Bankside and Lambeth on the south. As the three men and the dog-filled cart slowed to turn upwards along a pale path towards the Scavenger's dust heaps and the plague pits nearby, three men stepped out of the shadows, blocking their way. They held clubs and long, hook-topped poles.

'Whaddayou want here, cully?' said the largest, the leader.

Tom stepped forward, hand on sword-hilt, casual but ready enough. 'We're about Master Henslowe's business.'

'Oh aye? What business be that?'

'To carry these carrion dogs down to the Archbishop's palace at Lambeth.'

'They're Scavenger's meat, them dogs. Scavenger's like to want them, Master Henslowe's business or no.'

'The Scavenger'll have to take them then,' said Tom easily, and his sword whipped out into the moonlight like quicksilver.

'*Hold!*' cried a great voice, even as the three ruffians took their first steps into battle. A light flared. Four large men stood under a flaring torch across the north-running reach of the road. The Watch did not patrol south of the river – nor in some areas north of it, Alsatia among them. Or rather the City Watch did not. These men were something else entirely. These were the Bailiff's men. As the Bishop of Winchester owned the South bank up to Lambeth Palace Walls, the officers employed by his Bailiff had jurisdiction to take down felons and lock them in his prison at the Clink. Under the aegis of the Bailiff, these men were the law south of the river. Tom, Will and Ugo knew it. The

Scavenger's men knew it. 'If those dogs be bound to my Lord Archbishop,' said the leader of the watchmen, 'then it is Master Henslowe's business and the Archbishop's business. It is no business for the Scavenger or his men. Go trawl your hooks through some other midden, club some of these triple-damned wildcats.'

Thus was the law laid down.

Had they been concerned about any guards – or indeed any noise – the cats laid their fears speedily to rest. The Scavenger's dust heap was alive with them, hunting the rats that also infested the place, quarrelling, courting, screaming at the moon. Tom essayed some dry exercise of his wit to cover some understandable nervousness as they unloaded Julius Morton and fell to with the crowbars and jemmies from his chest. On the third repetition he gave up, his words drowned by the cacophony of the cats – even though they were several hundred yards away on the dust heaps while the three men broke open the unguarded mouth of the King's Field Plague Pit.

Under the skirts of the departing cloud cover, the winds were light and flighty, flirting from one way, then another, to ruffle hair and stroke cheeks like the coolest fingers of the hottest bawd. But they brought with them more sensations than delicate touch. They brought with them a range of odours which would have turned the stomach of the most hardened practitioner of physicke. From the river – though it was the cleanest part of London – came the stenches of mud, effluent, putrefaction and fish – living, recently deceased, long dead, rotten and near mummified. From the dust heaps came the stench of rotting food, clothing, excrement, overlain with a burning dose of wildcat scent, excrement and urine. But this was as nothing compared to the stench which came with the opening of the first rough board across the black maw of the plague pit. Mercifully, the moon was too low to penetrate far into the hollow where the dead lay. Carefully numbered in their hundreds in each of the boroughs and parishes where they had died, carefully entered into the records by the clerks, alerted by the Searchers whose job it was to search through the bodies, looking for information, valuables and probable cause of death. But away from the parish registers, the records simply stopped. No one knew how many unnumbered hundreds or thousands of corpses mouldered down here. And none of the three living men up here was going down for a closer look. Awed, they stood and stared into the black Hell's mouth they had opened. Little brightnesses winked back at them – white, red, green. Little scuttlings and scurryings told them of things alive down there – rats at the very least. Wild cats too, for the area was overrun with them. God alone knew what else. And God was welcome to the knowledge, thought the three of them all alike.

'To business,' ordered Tom after a moment. They looped a noose around Julius Morton's body and pulled it tight beneath his arms, then they lowered him into the pit. As soon as the weight of the body came off the rope, Tom reached over to loop it round the lowest beam and tie it into place. If the time came, it would be an easy enough matter to pull him up again. Then it was but a matter of minutes before the covering was back in place, exactly as they had found it, and not even the most careful watch-keeper would have been any the wiser.

It was as well they were quick about their work, for the wind, as fickle as the bawd it pretended to be, was carrying the reek of the carrion dogs up to the army of wildcats on the Scavenger's heaps, and the dangerous creatures were sidling down to explore already.

The three of them turned away with great relief to finish their mission – they really did, after all, have to deliver Master Henslowe's dog meat to the Archbishop's Master of Hounds. Over the crest of the hill, the rough track they had been following led swiftly and easily down to the brightness of the Archbishop's lower garden gate hard by his kennels. The cart ran easily and began to rumble almost merrily, speeding downwards towards the light. So that none of the three adventurers knew of the seething black sea of wildcats which spread like liquid tar over the wooden mouth of the Plague Pit, then paused there to lick up the cold dogs' blood.

So that the black-clad man who had followed them from the Rose, overheard much of their conversation and overseen most of their work, had to kick the screeching creatures viciously out of the way before he could kneel and check in detail exactly what they had been doing here.

CHAPTER TEN

The Mistress of the Game

Will's wherry dropped Tom at Goat Stairs, having swung north to drop the sleepy Ugo at Blackfriars. Then, as it was slack tide at midnight, it turned to run eastward ready to shoot the bridge and drop the weary playwright at Fresh Wharf. Tom, unlike his two companions, felt full of restless energy still. He tossed a two-penny groat into the boatman's hand and turned to run up the bustle on the stairs into the seething cauldron of Bankside.

The atmosphere, the excitement, gripped him at once. Since the closing of the City Gates, the whole area had changed its character. The cooling air was full of a heady mix of lust and danger. All sense of control and order, loosely in place during the day, was gone now. There was a feeling that the only rules were what a man made up for himself – and this, in Elizabeth's strictly ordered society, was as powerful as the most potent drug. Like the City Watch, God's own ordinance did not seem to run here. And the rules the Bishop of Winchester's men enforced had little enough in common with the commandments his Worship preached o' Sundays. This was Greene's graveyard where the poor mad poet had run with a whore, sister to the King of Cutpurses, Cutting Ball, famously hanged at Tyburn five years back; who had scrawled off his poems, plays and pamphlets while being consumed by the pox. And if Kit Marlowe had lost his life downriver in Deptford, here was where he had caused the death warrant to be written. It was no wonder that Master Henslowe, who owned so much, slept safe in his bed, far, far away from here; or that Hemminge and Condell crossed the river at nightfall to escape the dark temptations; it was no wonder the straitlaced Ugo or the weary Will, with two shows on the morrow, should cross the river or run the bridge rather than coming here. For there was nothing forbidden on the Bankside, if a man had the means to pay.

Tom shouldered his way along the busy thoroughfare, past the fronts of tavern after tavern. There were no normal houses there – the stews separated merely by alleys that bore their names, leading back into gardens – walled for the most part – that were simply extensions of the business. He pushed past the Rose Tavern, past the Bear, the Hartshorn, Ad Leonem and the Horseshoe, all within fifty yards. Then he paused. The Elephant stood slightly back, its form squarer and taller than the rest, its famous grey sign dull in the pale moonlight. Beside it, on the far side of Oliphant Alley stood the Herte, its sign much clearer, the white deer catching the silver from the sky. Although it was a masculine hart on the sign, everyone knew that it was the fair soft female hinds within that the customers came to see. Hinds, jades, bawds, trugs, sluts, trollops, trulls or whores to the better class clients who thronged here. Morts, stales, doxies, punks or bitches to the cant of local thieves. Winchester geese, named for the Bishop who owned the place. Mistresses of the game. And the games were without number or limit.

As Tom, careful of his purse, pushed across to the wide-flung portal of the Elephant, a vagary of conversation came through the hectic babble to his ear. 'Nah there's a mort in this stew thinks herself a proper coney-catcher. Foreign doxy. Italian. Thinks she's the queen of cozeners. But there's me for one as'd be happy to play her at her own game.'

The moment he heard this, Tom was shouldering towards the source of it – that dark alley between the two taverns. His ears were pricked for more of the thieves' cant, flowing apparently unremarked through the noise and bustle all around. There was a gang of professional card-sharps close by planning to rob the game he was planning to join by the sound of things. His eyes narrowed.

'Morts in these places is all trulls. And trulls is none too clever, leastways up in Islington they ain't. We can turn her from a bitch to a bird in less time it takes to tell. Shall I be setter? I can do the Kentish gab.' His accent deepened, became that of a well-to-do businessman.

'Aye. We need no verser for she's at play. Jack, you be the barnacle, and I'll be the setter and Sam, you be the purchase, for you have the pale young courtier's look about you. Now walk gentle and cut benely. We're country cousins tonight.'

Out of the shadowy mouth of the alley three sturdy ruffians, looking indeed like well-to-do yokels up from Kent with the first of the season's apples and cider, wandered into the place. Looking less conspicuous and much less out of place, Tom followed them in.

The Elephant was heaving. In effect, like most of the taverns here, it was a private house with a licence to serve drink and allow gaming. The room Tom entered now was a good, big parlour, lit with candles and flambards. At a dozen or so tables sat a range of employees and customers. The whores for hire walked about, some of them doubling as waitresses, their white belly-cheats or aprons announcing that they were for hire. Most of the tables were laden with drink – a range of types from cider through ale to various wines, all in a range of vessels – pewter, leather, thick green glass. At the back of the parlour roared an open fire and the potman's wife tended a cauldron as assiduously as he tended the barrels. The tables nearest the fire were laden with platters and spoons – of pewter, wood and horn. These were shared by anyone hungry enough to be partaking of the pottage also for sale. At the table nearest the fire sat three young girls with their tops open and their soft white breasts on display. Opposite them, eyes bulging, sat the real country cousins, parting with groat after groat as the girls ate and ate. These were not whores – the country cousins would get no ease from them – but they pulled in almost as much money. Tom's lip twisted in a half smile. The smell of the pottage wafted past his nose, but the odours of earlier in the night had killed his appetite. And he had other games afoot. He pushed on through.

Behind the main parlour there were other, smaller rooms, leading past the busy staircase to the equally busy garden, from where he could hear the lazy, lascivious playing of a lute. And a boy, singing a languid love song. In the first of the rooms sat the card-players. Tom eased himself round the door, eyes busy. The three coney-catchers, playing their parts too well, were still outside drooling over the merchandise. Tom could set himself up to take more of a hand in the game.

The table was dominated by the most beautiful woman he had seen on the Bankside. Broad shoulders supported alike a deep bosom of ivory-white and a long, slim neck. Her face was oval, her mouth wide and generous, her nose short, her wide eyes the colour of dark Sicilian olives. Her forehead was broad, high, unlined and capped with a gleaming wave of ebony hair. The arms reaching past the beautifully proportioned, perfectly presented cleavage were round and slightly dimpled. The hands were long, the fingers exceptionally so, capped with almond-shaped nails buffed to an opaline sheen.

Their eyes met. '*Signor?*' At the sound of her warm, deep voice, the two men at play opposite her turned, frowning. They were both young gentlemen and were dressed like courtiers. Tom could hold his own in this company as well as in any other. '*Signorina,*' he said easily. 'Gentlemen. Thomas Musgrave, Master of Defence.' His smile widened. They had heard of him. The lady's eyes flickered up and down, speakingly.

'Constanza d'Agostino,' she said, her voice deep, vibrant. He bowed. Their eyes met as he straightened; something hot passed between them.

He sat. A glance across the table-top told him all he needed to know about the game and the stakes. He reached into his purse as the cards fell in front of him and scattered a handful of gold across the plain deal boards. There was little conversation, for Triomphe was a demanding game, and all the players were desperate to win. As he held hand after hand, Tom secretly checked the edges of the cards for folds or marks. He studied their backs as well as their faces. He glanced furtively around the room looking for mirrors, glasses, reflective surfaces. The audience – mostly watching the lady rather than the play – was restless, passing trade. There were no barnacles amongst them, spying cards and sending signals. So no one at the table was coney-catching or cheating yet. None of the other players was a setter, in charge of a cheating game; none of them was a purchase set to walk away with the ill-gotten gains. The pile of gold in front of the beautiful Italian was there because she was a better player than the other two, and Tom was able to hold his own as he waited for the three from Oliphant Alley outside.

'The King of Cups takes it,' he said at last, and reached across for the little pot of gold. As he did so, the atmosphere in the room changed and without looking up he knew who had arrived at last.

'D'ye play, Mistress?' demanded the setter. Tom looked round like the other two, as jealous as they to be sharing the intimate interest of the bella donna. In the light he looked more presentable. A solid merchant – as well-dressed as Henslowe, though with none of the quiet élan which bespoke Tom to be a gentleman. This was the setter, though, getting ready to rob the game. 'Paul Carter. Merchant of Chiddingstone, up from Kent with a load of apples – best on the Cheap tomorrow. Now, what's our game?'

'Triomphe,' supplied Sigorina Constanza as the big man settled himself at the table.

'Ha. I'm a Mumchance man myself,' admitted Master Carter, getting out his gold, but he fell to easily enough. A moment or two later a pale, almost courtly young man joined them. He introduced himself as Samuel something and mumbled into the fluff of his beard so that Sam was all they heard of him. Tom glanced at the two courtiers but they didn't recognise the newcomer. This would be the purchase, then, thought Tom and began to look around for Jack the barnacle.

As he looked, so the lady's luck began to change in earnest.

The pile of gold that had adorned the boards beneath the shadow of her bosom began to drift with relentless inevitability towards the pale young gentleman called Sam. Master Carter made a great play of sharing everyone else's growing frustration, but his hearty acceptance of his bad luck kept the atmosphere light and the game going.

At last Tom saw the barnacle. Jack had positioned himself with practised care in a corner out of the lady's sight but where his sharp eyes could see her hand reflected in a pewter mirror, and the cards that Tom and the two courtiers held into the bargain. His signals to Master Carter were subtle but clear enough.

Tom's eyes sought out la bella Constanza's and they shared a speaking look. The high ivory forehead folded into the slightest of frowns, the olive eyes vanished beneath black velvet curtains of lashes. The next hand seemed to stretch out almost endlessly. At first it looked as though the knave of swords would take the trick, but the knave of money turned up miraculously – then the queen of cups. The pile of coins in the middle of the table became a kind of Scylla or whirlpool, gulping in every piece of gold there. Tom glanced up and down, keeping an eye on the increasingly pallid barnacle reflected in the pewter mirror. His gestures were becoming wilder and more obvious now and good Master Carter was frowning with a combination of confusion and irritation. Tom left his hand face down on the table, offering one last card to be exchanged. He felt the faintest stirring of a toe-point against his instep from the fair dealer opposite and his card arrived face down atop his hand.

'*Benedicite*,' crowed Sam the purchase. 'I have it all.' Such was the tension that he glanced across at Paul Carter with a relieved grin.

'Best show us your cards then, sirrah,' suggested the merchant from Chiddingstone.

Master Sam laid his hand for all to see. He had all the royal cups running down from the queen past knave to the six. He reached across to pull the pile of gold into his shaking hands. Tom glanced up. The barnacle was gone. The coney was caught. Everyone at the table was in ruins, every scrap of gilt and white money there on the smooth, cool boards.

'I think not, Master Sam,' he said quietly. Lazily he reached across and used the top card from the pile in front of him to flip the others over. Every club lay revealed, in order from the ace to the eight. 'Or shall I call you Master Purchase, to go with Master Setter here?'

Both the coney-catchers sprang erect, each of them reaching into the folds of their clothing for a weapon, but Tom's rapier was lying across the table before their rummaging was anywhere near done. 'Go,' he said. 'Collect your Barnacle Jack, and vanish or your next resting place will be in the Clink. 'Tis only ten doors up.' He raised his voice suddenly, his northern drawl lost in courtly imperiousness. 'Tapster, call the Watch.' His voice dropped a little. 'We'll see how the Bishop's Bailiff likes coney-catchers down from Damnation Alley.'

By the time he had finished this little speech, Tom was talking to vacancy. Indeed the two young courtiers had vanished as well, leaving only Tom and the beautiful card-player, face to face across the table.

'Another hand, *Signorina*?' asked Tom, gathering up the winning hand and pushing it back towards her.

Their eyes met over the pile of silver and gold.

'You have won all, *Signor*. I have nothing left to play for but my honour.'

'All of the trash against that one jewel, then,' he said. 'At any hazard you will.'

'Well,' she temporised, 'like the failed cheat Master Paul from Chiddingstone . . .'

'Who is likely to be waiting outside in Oliphant Alley with his friends and their filchmen, ready to beat my brains out before I can get to my sword . . .'

'I like the sudden death of Mumchance . . .'

She put the cards in a pile. 'Queen,' she said quietly, 'of denaro.' And split the pack to reveal a deuce.

Tom smiled and reached across. 'Knave of swords,' he said and split in his turn, holding the card for her to see without looking at it himself. Her eyes went from his face to his card and she smiled. 'Swords it is,' she said. 'Though which is the Master and which is the Knave, alas I cannot tell.'

Constanza had a room up in the private section of the Elephant up near the eaves. It was spacious enough to accommodate a sizeable bed and an eager pair of lovers, with a window opening at its end to show a gleaming view north across the quicksilver river from the Bridge to the Bridewell. As they looked across at it, they pulled leaves from the pots of basil Constanza kept on her windowsill here and chewed them to freshen their breath in the Italian fashion.

The city was mostly dark, but it glittered beneath the waning moon as though silversmiths had been at work alongside the thatchers and the tilers on the roofs. Since he had brought Constanza back from Siena last year, Tom had seen her housed in his own rooms and then in a wider range of accommodation – for she was not such a woman as could ever stay faithful to just one man. Nor was she a woman content to live off a man's earnings when she had abilities that would make her independent of any man, no matter how hotly she burned for him from time to time.

But Tom was here on business more important than cards or carnality. As he often did, without second thoughts, he came to her for gossip. As they stood at their favourite end of her room, chewing on their salad of fragrant herbs, gazing across the city the thieves' cant called Romeville, centre of the world, he pulled loose the laces of her clothing leisurely, caressing her under layer after layer. And they talked.

'Bella,' he began, using her love-name as he untied the knots at the back of her bodice, easing her warm ivory shoulders free, 'have you heard of any strangers in town of late?'

The tone of the question warned her that he meant the sort of strangers she might hear about. 'Gambling men? Or Mediterranean men?' she asked, her voice trembling a little now.

He pushed the wings of her bodice wide and fell to loosening the catches holding her fashionable skirts under the decorated swell of her farthingale. Her own hands were unloosening the farthingale's fastenings, shaking with desire as they did so.

'Mediterranean men,' he said, easing her out of her skirts and leaving her in her warm, damp, fragrant shift. 'I seek a Master with skills the equal of my own. And, I think, an ambidexter.'

She caught her breath; but that could have been revelation, superstition or reaction to his fingers running up the velvet column of her thigh to settle like birds nesting in the shadow bush up there.

'None from Italy of recent note,' she breathed as his fingers fluttered and settled, playing and pecking like restless chicks. 'Nor France. I have heard of no Greeks, nor Ottomans, nor any new merchants from Jerusalem, from Alexandria, from Aleppo . . .'

Tom suddenly realised that she was drawing out the list in order to continue the sensation of his caresses at the tops of her thighs. He substituted a lover's pinch for his more gentle ministrations.

The ravishment of her delicate flesh drew a quiet squeal from her, compound of a tincture of agony and a tun of acquiescence. 'There is a Spaniard lately arrived,' she admitted, twisting free and falling back on to the bed as Tom rose to strip off his black garments.

'A Spaniard? Hell's teeth. What could a Spaniard do here? Now?'

'Word is that he is seen at Essex House. A Don fresh from Cadiz, reporting to my Lord of Essex on matters in the Queen's business. Friend to the Don that's there already, Don Perez. Essex you know has quite a Spanish court there. Your man will be one of them, I am certain.'

That was almost information enough. Almost, but not quite. For Tom lived in a new world now, where information was not merely a pastime or an investment – where it could be a cutting edge and a coffin. Or, rather, a noose in the maw of a plague pit.

Tom pulled off his shirt and, being but little of the Puritan attitude these days, he slid the smock up Constanza's shuddering length and cast it aside before he began to practise his most powerful assaults in the battles of love – techniques, like those at cards, among other, darker, things, that he had learned at Siena, though not in the school of Maestro Capo Ferro. Almost coldly he worked on her body, bringing her burning voluptuousness soaring nearer and nearer to climax. At the crest of the wave, he paused, lingering out her desires. 'How do you come to know these things?' he asked her.

Her eyelids flickered. Her eyes seemed to engulf him, grown huge and dark, as though she had drizzled belladonna in them, as Italian lovers are sometimes said to do. 'I hear it by the way,' she breathed. 'I hear everything that happens in the south. My ears are like seashells. They carry a whisper of their home in their depth, be they never so far away.'

CHAPTER ELEVEN

The Master of the North

A little before noon next day Tom stepped out of the wherry on to the lowest of the Whitehall Stairs and tossed a groat downwards before turning to run on up. He had been back to his rooms in Blackfriars already to change and was wearing his finest. Black cloth of the Italian cut, Spanish kid boots. Boat-bellied doublet in the fashion of Spanish armour, dagged with slashes puffed with tobacco silk, and black galligaskins of the latest style, loose across his thigh but laced tight at the knee behind the high tops of his beloved boots. His short black cloak was laced with silver and left the hilt of his rapier convenient to his kid-gloved hands. He was out of the very point of fashion only in that he disdained a hat. Even so, he could have passed for any sort of a courtier, up to a man possessed of a title, and would have walked into the Presence Chamber without too much difficulty.

Except that the Court was not here at Whitehall. It was at Nonesuch, and likely to move again soon. For the Court was where the Queen was. Her own law ran 'under the verge' within thirteen miles of her person in any direction. The power of the throne resided where she did and she could sign state papers at Whitehall, Westminster, Nonesuch, Richmond or Hampton Court. She had even done so from ships she had been visiting: 'from *Due Repulse*, where this day I have been, Elizabeth R'.

The governance of the country in summer followed her from palace to palace.

Or, most of it did. For messages – messengers – came from all over the kingdom, all over the continent; sometimes even from remoter parts of the world, nowadays. And the palaces at Whitehall and Westminster retained small secretarial staffs to meet such men and redirect them to where the Queen was at the present time, and to oversee any other little routine matters that did not require Her Majesty's direct personal involvement.

And one such secretarial guide was Walter Collingwood, Secretary to a committee of the Court of Star Chamber, who had added to his other duties that of winding up the last details of the estate of the late Ferdinando Stanley, Earl of Derby, patron of the Burbages' Company, Lord Strange. Lord Strange had died less than two months since and the last of his bequest to his players was keeping the Burbage half of the Rose Company afloat while they sought another patron. But they could only do that if *Romeo and Juliet* was a great enough success to attract the attention of the distant Court away down in Surrey.

There was a guard at the top of the steps. 'State your business,' he challenged.

Tom was well enough prepared for this. 'I come to see the Secretary Collingwood,' he said. 'I have come from the Rose. The theatre.'

The guard paused for an instant, then he turned and poked his head into a small guard chamber. 'Take this man to Secretary Collingwood,' he said; and a guide appeared like a spirit summoned to take Tom in hand.

Tom knew something about palaces. Around the Campo in Siena there were fourteen of them not counting the Palazzo Publico. And he had travelled widely in his studies – and in respite from his studies. He had seen most of the major palaces in Italy – the Duomo, the Doge's Palace, the palaces at Rome. Further afield, he had visited Versailles and the Louvre in Paris. He had been to the Alhambra. Whitehall Palace was bigger than any of them. There were twenty-three acres of it, from Whitehall Stairs at Thames'side in the east to the Royal hunting grounds of the Green Park, which ran away westward almost endlessly; from Westminster Abbey in the south to Charing Cross. Like the Louvre, it had public roadways running through it spanned by great gates which doubled as bridges leading from one section to another. Tom had stood on the greatest of these thoroughfares, King Street, to see the Queen on Sundays. He had joined the jostle on Accession Day during his first November back, to see the tilting and the splendour.

But the maze of rabbit-warren passages he walked through now went far beyond any part of the palace he had ever imagined, let alone visited. At last his guide turned into a small, dark antechamber and motioned Tom to wait as he went through into the next room. Standing in the shadowy cell, Tom looked through the next door into a larger, brighter chamber with wide windows looking over the river. Like an actor, he rehearsed in his head what he wanted to say to Secretary Collingwood, for the murder of a man among the players he had supported could damage the reputation of even a deceased patron – and rouse the ire of the rest of the Stanleys, one of the most powerful families – dynasties – in the country.

Tom's years of travel and study abroad had hardened him in many ways. The quick-thinking, decisive, deadly man standing in Secretary Collingwood's antechamber was as far removed from the callow youth of the Flanders battlefield as the Ferrara blade at his side was removed from his great-grandfather's short sword. But even so, there was a stench of such naked power in these corridors that even the new Tom, the deadly blade and icy detective, could not help but rehearse his coded warning again.

'Come through.'

Tom moved, sweeping in through the half-open door, pausing to deliver a careful bow, straightening swiftly to look the Secretary in the face, drawing in his breath as he did so.

But he was not allowed to deliver his well-rehearsed message yet.

'You are late,' snapped Collingwood. 'You have kept matters waiting for a day too long. Have you any idea what it can cost them to be away from Her Majesty's side so long? Come through, man.' The folded, wizened, grey-bearded man twirled even as Tom's mouth opened. In a twinkling he had crossed the room, a-buzz with energy and urgency.

'Sir Walter, you mistake me.' Tom was not a man to allow misapprehensions such as this to go unchallenged. But Collingwood had crossed to a hanging and, sweeping a curtain of cloth-of-gold aside, he was opening another door secreted behind it. 'Sir Walter.' But Sir Walter was gone through and Tom had no choice other than to follow.

He found himself in another passage, ill-lit and twisting. Collingwood was dressed like any clerk in a long, dark gown and Tom cast all thoughts of further conversation aside as he hurried forward, fighting to keep the old man in sight.

As he half ran through the maze of passages on the Secretary's hurrying heels, however, Tom was unable to stop some part of his mind whirling away in wild speculation. He had been mistaken for someone else, that was clear. Someone from the Rose. Now, there were in Southwark alone the Rose and the Little Rose – two taverns side by side. God alone knew how many taverns were named for the Red Rose of York, the White Rose of Lancaster, and the red and white Tudor rose of peace. And yet had he not told the keeper of the water gate 'Rose Theatre'? He was certain that he had. Allowing that, then, he had to assume that there was someone working at the Rose who was also working for Collingwood and whoever Collingwood was taking him to see. Someone who was due to have been here a day since. Someone who had failed to keep his tryst.

It was most likely to be Morton for two reasons. Firstly because he obviously could not keep even the most urgent appointment now – and was alone among the Rose Company in being unable to do so. Secondly, Tom knew the Company men like brothers – except for Morton. Had any of the others – except, perhaps, the Wardrobe Master or the Gatherer – been in contact with men such as this, Tom would have known it.

Except, he admitted grudgingly, switching to his next train of thought, except for Master Henslowe himself. Morton it was, then.

But who was Morton like to be visiting at Whitehall? Someone who had come down from Nonesuch, from the Queen's very side, to talk to him. And what in God's name was going on, that the murder of a nameless actor was suddenly leading Tom into the company of such as stood by Her Majesty's own side?

But then the time for speculation was abruptly at an end. Secretary Collingwood opened a door and the pair of them tumbled into another chamber. No waiting room or antechamber this, but a Presence Chamber fit for the Queen herself. There were two men seated in the gracious apartment: one at a table in the centre of the room and another, away over in the shadows in the corner, his face hidden.

'Here's your man, my lord,' said Collingwood, from the depths of a bow. Tom stooped too, for a swift glance around the table had told him all too much.

Tom had never seen Secretary Collingwood before and would never until now have known him in a crowd. They lived in an age where the faces even of the most powerful were known to but a few. Portraits were painted for state rooms in powerful family houses, not for public gaze. Pictures of the famous were rare and only recently appearing in pamphlets. Her Majesty's countenance was familiar as it had once looked, in profile, from coin and seal. Other than that, common men like Tom would only recognise those they had seen at important occasions in attendance to the Queen, whose offices, arms or liveries they knew. In this pictureless society, it was possible for a full-sized portrait of Henry VIII painted on a wall in the cellars here to make old courtiers shake with fear ten years after his death when they saw it.

But Tom knew the face of the man at the head of the table well enough. He had seen Henry Carey, nephew to Anne Boleyn and cousin of the Queen, when he had been the Master of Berwick, Warden of the East Marches and Lord of the

North. He had seen him as Lord Hunsdon processing out of Somerset house to Church on Sundays. He had seen him as Lord Chamberlain riding beside the Master of the Horse, the Earl of Essex, when Her Majesty rode forth in state. He had kept careful eye upon him, too; for this was the man to whom his uncle Tom Musgrave reported, by messenger twice a month, as though his life depended upon it, the state of the Borders from Gretna to Berwick, from Newcastle to Home Castle.

'I am not the man you stay for, Lord Henry,' said Tom at once. 'But I bring you news of him.' Tom had been raised on tales of what this man had done in the Borders and he knew that the time for codes and secret messages was long past. As well try to shally with the Lord of the North as with Her Majesty herself. The truth might save them. Anything else was like to bury them, Rose and all. Six hundred men had been hanged in aftermath of the last raid he had quelled. Six hundred more than the dead already choking Hell Beck. It was the better part of twenty-five years since, but Tom had been there, a child, to see and learn.

He straightened now, to look into that long, thoughtful face with its almost semicircular black eyebrows with their slightly protuberant, dark-brown, intelligent and fiercely independent eyes. The high cheekbones and broad jaw supporting a full, white-silver beard. 'I am Thomas Musgrave, Lord Henry, of Bewcastle in your own West March and nephew to the Lord of Bewcastle himself. It chances that I can tell you of Julius Morton, and, perhaps, serve you.'

There was silence. Tom stood, tall and proud, waiting for his fate to come to him. He looked into the Lord Chamberlain's eyes and the Queen's own eyes looked back at him with the most uncanny family resemblance.

Then the figure in the corner spoke. His voice was a familiar, cold drawl; one that had lain in Tom's memory and rung in his dreams since he stood on that hilltop by Nijmagen with his message seven years ago. 'Here's a strange thing,' said the familiar voice. 'This is the second time to my certain knowledge that our young Master of Logic has stood before the Queen's right-hand man armed with far more knowledge than a mortal has a right to know.' The stranger in the shadows stood, and stepped out into the light. Once again Tom found himself confronted by the lean face, icy eyes and cool, unnerving intelligence of this man who interrupted dukes without a second thought.

'Tell the Lord Chamberlain what you know – what you think you know,' the stranger ordered. 'And bear in mind that evasion and equivocation are like to make you close acquainted with the Tower and with Rackmaster Topcliffe.'

Had Tom been unnerved by the stranger's threat, his disquiet would not have lasted long, for Lord Henry Carey leaned forward suddenly. 'I know this man,' he said quietly. 'I know his uncle and his family. They have been of service to me. And that is more than you have been of late, Master Poley; more than Topcliffe has ever been. So think on that.'

But Tom hardly heard. He launched into what he had learned and deduced, fighting to pull everything so far into enough of a pattern to impress the Council. 'Julius Morton might have been your man and working about your business, Lord Henry, but he was using the Rose as a mask or vizzard to cover the truth. And he had somehow contrived to move beyond the bounds of your protection, for he has been murdered, not a day since, at the Rose itself. I believe he saw his death coming and hoped to avoid it on the Rose's stage – perhaps escape it there a while. But it was waiting for him there and there it took him in spite of all. He was murdered by a secret blow from a rapier blade of the finest quality, wielded by a great Master. He died, but not at once. Dying, he spoke in cyphers, I believe, giving a message to someone in the audience, passing a plague on two houses and talking of worms' meat and I know not what else. But I have a note of every word he spoke and a Master of Cyphers to translate them. I have examined the body and seen that Morton was run through the chest from back to front so that the wound is widest near the spine, narrower near the left pap and narrowest of all where it pricked his hand. I have acted the murder over and believe it could only be performed by an ambidexter; and I find that there is such a man, a Master of Spain, currently given entertainment at Essex House. I have hidden the body where none are likely to disturb it and I have hurried hither to tell my Lord Strange's executor of the situation and seek his advice, for we are still Lord Strange's Men and careful of his honour and reputation.'

'God's my life,' gasped Lord Henry, half awed, half amused. 'I would I had some such as you to be careful of my reputation. Is there anything he has missed?' He turned to the stranger, Poley.

'How would summoning the law harm Lord Strange's reputation?' he asked now. 'The reputation of a murdered man can stand a deal of shaking ere it fall.'

Murdered? thought Tom. Now no one had yet seen fit to mention that fact to him. And yet someone in the Rose Company should have known – should have said – something.

'Perhaps it would not, sir,' he persisted as his mind span, weighing alternatives. 'We sought only time and wise council. Perhaps we have done wrong. Certainly, had Her Majesty been at Westminster, or here, we would have called for justice under the verge, safe in the knowledge that Sir William Danby—' He stopped then, for the association of the names made the scales fall from his eyes, like Saul on the road to Damascus, and he wasn't at all sure that he liked what he could see. The shock of it was enough to make him set aside all thoughts of Lord Strange being murdered. His mind was simply knocked on to a new line of thinking entirely.

'Go on,' prompted Lord Henry. 'What would you have done next had we not called you here in error?'

'Reported to Sir Walter, warned him of the situation.'

'Say he had felt Lord Strange's name to rest safe with you; what then?' Lord Henry's interest appeared genuine, almost academic. As though Tom's willingness to work outside the law and the social system made him some kind of rare specimen. Some kind of new tobacco to be savoured thoughtfully, in a long pipe.

'Searched Morton's room, my lord. It seems to me that

having hid the body puts us out of step with the law, even the Bishop's law in Bankside. So I would want to arm myself with the greatest store of knowledge I could gain before I went beating on the Bailiff's door.'

Lord Henry shook his head in wonder. He looked across at both Poley and Collingwood. 'It is almost as though the hand of God is in this,' he said with genuine wonder. 'We have lost our man and at once found a better man to replace him. And beyond the room, what then?'

'Find out the identity of the Spanish assassin if I could. Start to search for the contact Morton was trying to give his message to. Find out what exactly Morton's employment was whose wages were half a fathom of cold steel in his heart.'

Lord Henry threw himself back in his chair. 'A Master of Logic indeed. I doubt that even Pythagoras turned spy could have expounded a deadly theorem as clear as this. But it leaves us at a crossroad, does it not, with only two ways left to follow.'

'Should Master Musgrave wait without?' suggested Collingwood.

'No. You brought him in – and I see you are still a little pale from the shock. But you were moved by God's own hand I doubt not. And the Master of Logic here can see our paths before us as clearly as we – and if he could not, he would doubtless be listening at the keyhole.

'Master Musgrave. Either we must employ you or bury you. That is all there is of the matter. I have told Master Poley here that I know you and your family. I have regard to your uncle, the Lord of Bewcastle, even though he has taken the title for himself with none of our giving. I know your father, I believe, and your brother the blacksmith. I would prefer to employ you. But such is the moment of what we are about here, that if there is a shadow of a doubt, a shadow of a shade, then I will order you dead without a second thought.'

'And I will wield the blade,' said Poley.

'As you did with Kit Marlowe last year. I doubt it not,' said Tom, looking Poley straight in the eye. 'The content of Sir

William Danby's Crowner's Quest has been the gossip of Bankside this half-year and more.'

'Then you know it was Ingram Frizer who held the knife, not I.'

'Master Poley, I care not who the puppet was. I know who pulled the strings.'

'Now, if I really thought you did know that,' said Robert Poley quietly, 'then your life would be over for certain.'

The two men measured each other with calculating eyes. Then Poley turned. 'He is a master indeed, my lord. To throw such a weapon away untested would be a mortal sin. Will you work for me, Master of Logic?'

'Doing what?'

'Performing the actions you have described. The search, the contact, the identification. But this time you will not be alone – you will be using my men, my contacts, my information, to speed you on your way. And, may I remind you of the alternative.' His hand vanished into his clothing. Tom's hand slammed on to his sword-hilt. Poley's reappeared as though by magic, armed with a double-barrelled dag.

'If the springs on the wheel lock have been wound since I came in, they'll likely misfire now,' said Tom. 'Two steps and I'll have you skewered.

'Care to risk it?' asked Poley, quietly. 'Do, or die.'

CHAPTER TWELVE

The Man Who Murdered Marlowe

T he wrath of Lord Henry was terrible to see. It was
identical to the wrath of his cousin the Queen and echoed
in many ways that of his maternal Uncle King Henry, whose
rages were infamous. His anger now would have crushed most
men – would have annihilated Walter Collingwood had it been
so aimed. It was just enough to stop Tom and Poley killing each
other. For the time being. And to ally them in the same cause, in
the Council's business and under Lord Henry's command. For
the moment.

The pair of them took a wherry from Whitehall Stairs to
Blackfriars Steps. As the little boat swept eastward with the
current so they settled back into conference – but at Poley's
frown towards the wherryman's large ears, they talked of
generalities as though they were friends. Their first destination
was Tom's fencing school where he would change his clothes
into something more serviceable and less conspicuous. There
they would make further plans, for their next task would have
to be to search Morton's rooms.

'Do you fence, Master Poley?' asked the social Tom as the
wherry slid under Bridewell and into the stinking outflow of the
Fleet River.

'Not in the Italian style,' answered Poley shortly.

'But you carry a rapier, and a good one by the looks of it.'

'The best money can buy. The handle is from Ferrara like

your own, but the blade is German. One of the new blades from Solingen.'

'I have heard of these blades but I must admit that I have never seen one. Perhaps you will permit me to inspect it at my school.'

'Perhaps. In time. On better acquaintance, if it comes.'

Out they leaped at Blackfriars Steps and swaggered side by side up into Water Lane. 'Even so,' continued Tom, 'It is God's own pity to carry such a weapon and not to use it well.'

'I prefer to rely on other defences, as you know.'

Tom's school was in a long building backing on to the Wall with its front in Blackfriars hard by Ludgate – the path and the prison – a mere step or two from the bustling heart of the city, St Paul's. It was situated above a haberdashery and was carefully sited there. The haberdasher, Master Robert Aske, kept fashionable, quiet, fragrant premises, bright with buttons, tapes, ribbons, sequins, lengths of lace, cloth of gold, shoe-buckles, feathers, Spanish pins and needles and thread to attach them with, all at the very point of the pinnacle of fashion. He and Tom had a simple agreement which worked to their mutual advantage – Tom's rent was low but it was rare indeed for one of his fashionable pupils not to supplement his wardrobe on the way in or out of school. And Tom's simple advantage was that this successful retail was one of the few businesses in London that did not generate the most noxious of odours. Had his school stood above a spicer's or a baker's, it would have served, perhaps, for the smells wafting upwards would not have been offensive. But above a tanner's, a dyer's, a butcher's, a pie-man's, a cheese merchant's, a blacksmith's, it would scarcely have been possible to breathe.

Ugo met them at the top of the stairs. He was standing in the little reception area outside the fencing room with a handful of the sticks Tom used to train the absolute beginners in the basics. 'Who's this?' he asked. 'A new client? You'll have trouble fitting him in today. Your hours are busy between this and sunset.'

'No,' said Tom forthrightly. 'He's a spy.'

'God's . . .' spat Poley, pulling out his dag once again and levelling it at Tom.

Tom paid no attention. Walking forward unhurriedly, he opened a door into a long, bright room further illuminated by his most expensive possession – even including his Ferrara blades. Poley froze in little short of wonder, looking into the largest, longest mirror he had ever seen. 'You haven't reset the springs on that dag,' said Tom conversationally. 'It'll be all but useless by now, Master Poley. Ugo's a gunsmith. Do you want him to take a look at it? From the sound of things we'll be going through Alsatia between darkfall and the Bellman. You'll likely need it then.'

Poley pulled the triggers, both of them. Ugo knocked the dag up with the sticks he was carrying so that, had it fired, it would have peppered the ceiling. But nothing of the sort happened. The pistol fell from Poley's grasp and Ugo caught it.

Tom turned and his sword was in his hand, the point of it exactly on the bridge of Poley's long, slightly hooked nose. 'Almost everyone I know in London,' said Tom quietly, 'would like you to feel what Kit Marlowe felt during the last few seconds of his life, Master Poley. It is time for you to make up your mind to it. Work with me as equal, not puppet master, with plain dealing and honesty, and I will serve your ends to the top of my bent. And those of Lord Hunsdon too. But if you are looking to work with shifting, equivocating or double dealing, then tell me now and you can talk things over with Marlowe himself. His spirit is not so far above us but yours could overtake him, I doubt not.'

'Ha!' laughed Poley, without moving his face a whisker. 'You taunt me with words from Shakespeare's new play.'

Tom stood back and lowered his point, eyeing Poley with new respect. 'Fix his pistol, Ugo,' he said. Ugo vanished. 'You were there?' Tom continued in almost the same breath. 'There has only been one performance. How else could you know the line? You must have been there.'

'I have spoken with one that was.'

'Morton's contact?'

90

'Alas, no. Someone who was watching Morton's contact.'

'But also someone who was watching the play – and closely if they gave you a flavour of the lines. Too closely, perhaps, if he and you have lost sight of Morton's man.'

'As you say. But, in the spirit of forthright dealing, I must tell you that the recipient of Morton's message was no man.'

'A boy?'

Poley shook his head.

Tom frowned. In this new world of spy-craft he felt he was learning the rules swiftly and well. They were not so very different from the rules in his other worlds of fencing and acting – nothing was quite what it seemed and all was feign and feint. Even so, it required that he stretch his view of the way the world worked to accept a female spy. But then he thought of Constanza, her cards and her contacts and he realised – he already knew one. His mind seemed to explode then, teeming with questions for Poley, but before he could utter even the first of them, Ugo came back. 'It needs new springs,' he said, handing the dag to Lord Hunsdon's spy. 'But I fixed it for the time being. The first student's due on the stroke of noon, Tom,' he warned, and behind his words all the bells from St Dunstan's to St Paul's struck the hour, and time for further conference was at an end.

Six hours later, Tom was aflame. Never the type of Master to stand against the wall calling time, distance and proportion, rapping out his minim rests, he worked with his students toe to toe and blade against blade. Twelve half-hour lessons had left his muscles hot and supple and his heart singing as it thundered. And, if the truth be known, his blood-lust just within bounds.

With a white linen cloth draped round his neck above his black collar, he walked through to the back rooms where Ugo had placed a ewer of washing water and a jug of drinking water purchased from the water carrier at the corner of Paul's Churchyard. A swift wash and Tom was through into the smallest room in the house. Here, lit by a narrow garret supplemented by a pair of carefully protected lamps, was Ugo's workshop. Here lay a range of paraphernalia that would be likely to get him arrested if the authorities knew of it. Particularly as he was Dutch and the influx of foreigners from the Low Countries had been the cause of riots in the streets and a great deal of disquiet in the corridors of power of late.

Ugo looked up from his work. 'You play fast and loose with your own life, Tom, but have a care to mine.'

'I will, Ugo. But think on. This Poley has a direct line to Court. He works for the Lord Chamberlain and the good Lord alone knows who else. And he lives in a world I was born to live in. He walks paths I was made to tread. I feel as Will must have felt first seeing his play up on a stage.'

'Poley is deadly dangerous. The hand that can raise us up could cast us down as easy.'

'True. And you are more at risk than I am at the moment. But he is at risk himself. Think who he is. I have but to name him on the Bankside and cry clubs and his brains will be in the kennel quicker than it takes to tell. He knows this. I will have a care, however. I know you are at risk. But always remember, we owe a debt to Julius Morton. Like Kit Marlowe, whatever else he was he was one of us, and Master Henslowe, Will and the rest are looking to us to unmask the man who did the murder – and the hand behind the hand. Master Poley is about the same business. The hounds of Athens and the hounds of Troy would run together if they were hunting the same quarry. So we may run with Master Poley for a while. And so he must be made privy to this place.'

'He guesses at it already. I fixed his dag.'

'I had to make sure he came back, Ugo. Things are not settled between us. He has not yet told me of the matter Morton was looking into for him – though I suspect it must have something to do with the murder of Lord Strange. Be that as it may, he might well decide to search Morton's rooms and vanish. There are places yet the Council's writ might not run. That would be very bad for us because we still stand outside the law holding the body of a murdered spy. There is much we have to learn before we are safe and all secure – and he knows much of it if he can be tempted into telling. His co-operation would make our task easier and quicker. But he knows we need him more than he needs us at the moment. So, give him a sniff at what you have in here and he will be back like a roaring boy after tobacco and we have him to hand like a haggard hawk.'

'Let us hope,' said Ugo dryly, 'that he has not studied his Machiavel as well as you did in Siena.'

Their conversation was terminated by the arrival of its subject. Poley's eyes grew round at the sight of Ugo's workshop with its piles of black powder, measured and unmeasured, its scales and mixing bowls. Its rows of moulds for making shot of varying weights. Its little furnace for melting lead and its little leaden ingots. Its assemblance of barrels in varying sizes and of varying lengths and compositions. Its array of handles carved in wood, strengthened with metals of all sorts. Its seemingly infinite variety of firing mechanisms from matchlocks through wheel locks to dog locks and snaphaunces. Tom watched the spy gaze around like a bumpkin at Court, thinking that Ugo was safe in this man's hands until he got possession of this cornucopia. A man who carried a Solingen blade but relied on an elderly wheel lock would never cast away such riches as this except at the final extremity. 'Ready to go?' Tom asked him quietly.

He had to repeat himself twice before he received any reply from Poley.

'Why have you not been in Morton's lodging already?' asked Tom as soon as the two of them stepped out into the evening. The sun was somewhere far beyond Green Park, all but its upper brightness hidden by London Wall. Around them, especially up against the great, grey, stone cliff of the defensive works, the houses reached up to three storeys and four, jutting out in overhangs that closed off all but the thinnest lines of sky. Not that either man was foolish enough to look up. At their feet the roads sloped into central gutters or kennels, choked with household waste and excrement as yet unclaimed by the City Scavenger. Tom disdained them and cleaned his boots in consequence, but he saw Poley wore fashionable slippers over his shoes to protect them from the filth whose odour assailed their noses like the stench of the plague. There were cats everywhere, most of them alive. Anyone who wished to remain upright was always careful of where he put his feet.

Turning through Ludgate, they got a flicker of setting sunlight from the west before their attention was claimed by inmates of Ludgate gaol begging through the bars. Tom handed down a penny or two without a second thought, but Poley lingered, bestowing his charity on the pinkest cheek and the fullest bosom. These were gentlefolk for the most part, fallen upon hard times and, uniquely in all the London jails, it contained women of passable looks who disdained whoring to eke out their penury. But, Poley no doubt calculated, the kindness of a gentleman to a gentlewoman in distress might garner a reward in time.

Then they were through Ludgate and into Alsatia, and their way craved wary walking of another kind. 'You said Holborn,' said Tom quietly, his eyes narrow as the Fleet Bridge approached.

'I was misinformed. He was roomed at a house in Hanging Sword Court.'

When they reached the place, Tom saw at once why Poley had not ventured here this afternoon. Hanging Sword Court was near enough the heart of Alsatia. The City Watch did not come south of Fleet Street nor west of the Bridewell out the length of Whitefriars; they did not dare. There wasn't even the Bishop's Law to run in these streets, nor a brutal bailiff to enforce it. The place was a-bustle with lean-faced, narrow-eyed men in russet and fustian; men with black teeth, sallow skins and sharp daggers. More than once Tom saw the gleam of a steel thumb – a new fashion among cutpurses. He was glad enough that he had left his own purse at home, safe on Ugo's bench in the space left by the gun he carried in its stead. Poley, he assumed, had brought his own. He hoped it was the one Ugo had fixed.

Before they could attract too much unwelcome attention, however, they turned into Hanging Sword Court. It was as over-built and as narrow as any of the streets nearby. A glance upward allowed Tom to calculate that it would be easy enough to jump from one top-storey window to that opposite. The place was shadowed, nearly dark, and the shadows seemed to have attained a kind of physical form with the power of the stench it contained. The kennel down the middle of the road did not run away – though it angled down to the river, parallel with the Fleet River a street or two eastward – but was stopped instead by the back wall of a house. The wall, as blank and grey as the City Wall itself at first glance, had a great stinking pile of rubbish piled against it; and here again the cats ran wild, hunting all the rats and mice tunnelling through the mess.

As they came up to the house, Poley began looking around. An intelligence far meaner than Tom's would swiftly have deduced the spy had left a guard of some kind to keep an eye on the place. But before any watcher appeared, another man hurried up to Poley. 'Well met, Master,' he puffed.

'In good time.' Poley stopped looking around, but not, Tom thought, because he had found what he was looking for. 'You have your picks?'

'If you have my price.'

'You'll be paid inside. Now make haste.'

The lock-pick led them up to a doorway in the wall that Tom had failed to notice, probably because it was so close to the enormous rubbish pile. The little man fell to work on the door's big, old-fashioned-looking lock and Tom turned to look back up the Court towards Fleet Street. The filthy little byway had been empty when he and Poley entered it but it was rapidly filling with people now. All of them men. None of them here by accident. And none of them, by the look of things, used to observing the laws about compulsory Church attendance o' Sundays.

'Poley. Tell your man to make haste.'

Poley turned at Tom's word and spat a curse. His hand disappeared into his clothing but Tom's fingers closed on his forearm. 'It's early days for that,' he said. 'Especially as you've only two shots.'

He walked forward. 'Give you good den, gentles,' he called easily as he moved. 'How can I serve you?' There were six of them, he calculated, now that proximity allowed him to see more clearly. Armed with an assortment of knives and clubs.

'Serve us, cully?' called one of them in reply. 'Why by rendering up your gold, your weapons and your duds. Or you'll likely render us up your very life and soul. And you won't be the first today.' He glanced meaningfully at the rubbish heap against the wall – but Tom knew better than to look over his shoulder.

Instead, one of Ugo's finest appeared in Tom's fist then. It was a snaphaunce pistol, but unlike Poley's double-barrel it was the last word in modern armoury. For it was a revolver. It boasted six chambers, all loaded and capped, which were primed in turn by the pulling-back of the cock-head. Tom snapped back the head and targeted the speaker. 'A little lead, perhaps, if you come any closer,' he warned.

'Charge.'

Tom shot the first man in the chest and cocked again in an instant. The second discharge sent a second man sprawling across the feet of his companions and broke the charge. Even so, it required a third shot to stop them. 'I make that one dead and two like to be crippled,' said Tom.

'And all of Alsatia roused,' snarled one of the survivors.

'Until they arrive, it's just we few,' said Tom. 'So who'd like to die next?'

'Tom,' called Poley. 'We're in.'

Tom walked backwards unerringly to the open door, with Ugo's pistol aimed straight for the leader's face. Only as he entered the doorway itself did Tom risk a glance to one side, mindful of what the dead man said earlier.

There, from the rubbish pile, the dead eyes of Poley's watcher stared up at him. Beneath the gape of his mouth, the gape of his cut throat was wider. Then the door slammed shut and Poley swung a great balk of wood down across it.

'Not even the whole of Alsatia could break through that now,' he said with satisfaction.

'True, but on the other hand there had better be another way out of here,' said Tom.

Out in Fleet Street the man in black who had been watching Tom since the incident of the Rose continued to observe the ebbing and flowing of the men of Alsatia as they carried out the dead and wounded and then began to gather in angry conversation, temporarily thwarted by the impenetrability of the battlements protecting Julius Morton's apartments. Then he began to work his way round, certain that there must be another way out of the house – down towards the river, perhaps. That would be the way they would have to come now. Out into Salisbury Court and then down past Bridewell, perhaps.

And as the black-clad watcher moved, made briefly conspicuous as he was going in the opposite direction to everyone else, Ugo Stell pocketed the second snaphaunce revolver and fell in behind the sinister stranger, watching him from the far side of the street.

CHAPTER THIRTEEN

The Bishop's Bailiff

Immediately behind the bolted door was a tiny chamber filled with almost Stygian darkness. Only the faintest grey glimmer showed where a stairwell reached upwards towards Morton's living quarters. Here the three of them paused to gain their breath. As they did so, Tom slipped the half-empty revolver back into his clothing. 'We'll never get out of here alive,' snarled the lock-pick. His words were emphasised by a tremendous *crash* against the door immediately behind them. With a strangled cry, the lock-pick pushed past Poley and began to run up the stairs. He had gone perhaps half a dozen steps before there came a sharp click and a short, vicious whirring sound. The lock-pick was blasted bodily back down the stairs and the sound of his skull hitting the inside of the door gave pause to the thunderous blows raining outside it. His heels drummed briefly against the lower boards, but that was no more than the passing of his spirit, thought Tom. No one was going to survive a crossbow bolt pinning their head to a door like that. And sure enough, the lock-pick's movements stopped almost immediately. Tom went down on his knees at once. It occurred to him that he might essay a quick prayer while he was down there, but this was not the primary objective of the action. It took him out of range of anything else unpleasant hidden upstairs. It also allowed him to progress up towards the light by gradual degrees, checking for more booby traps. But the broken ends of the trip wire attached to the trigger of the crossbow were all that defended the stairwell. Easing himself up over the top step into a surprisingly large and airy chamber, Tom asked, 'Is there likely to be anything else like that hidden up here, Master Poley?'

'I cannot begin to guess.'

'You knew him, surely. You can hazard . . .'

'I had no idea he was so . . .'

'Terrified? I understand. Best take care, then. And, while we have so much privacy from prying eyes and listening ears, now is the best time I think for you to tell me what you conceive to be afoot here.'

It was at this point in their conversation that the battering on the door below was resumed, and the speed of their actions began to gain increasing urgency.

'Tell me what you believe,' countered Poley defensively. 'I will add, subtract or correct as necessity dictates.' Tom picked himself up and Poley followed suit, continuing, 'To do anything else would be impossible. I have been an intelligencer for nigh on fifteen years. I have seen plots come and go, kings and queens, lords and ladies, soldiers and courtiers, ministers of state, aye and spies in plenty. It is as though we sit atop a pyramid of Egypt here. We seem to be on the littlest point – one murder and a little mystery; but away beneath us stretch great walls aslope into the very heart of the desert, hiding secrets without limit and murders without number. You tell me what you can see from your little pyramid point and I will shield you from the momentous depths on which we sit.'

'Like dwarfs on the shoulders of giants,' said Tom softly, remembering Aristotle's words culled from Socrates, read somewhere in his schooling. Something in the man's words touched him deeply. Truth, perhaps; or something sounding like it. 'Very well. You had set Morton to cull information on something of greatest moment to the Chamberlain and the Council. Were I a betting man, I would suppose that it was a part of the matter of Lord Strange's death, for Morton was

Strange's man and I learn now that my lord was murdered. You had furnished him with protection and with contacts. But the more he discovered, the less he disclosed to you and the more fearful he became. And things came to a crisis yesterday when he discovered something that he knew would kill him. He came here. He set his trap, so he expected trouble to follow him home at least. He contacted his woman and whoever else. You already suspected he was running out of your control and so you had him and his woman followed but you lost him to the Spanish assassin – who we must assume to be at least a part of what he feared. And you have lost her to you know not who or what. You are beset on every side. Your watcher here is dead – perhaps killed by the men of Alsatia. They were suspiciously swift to exercise their rights to life and death upon us. Logic dictates that the guts in the rubbish below is your watcher from the Rose, so if there is anything he has not told you about the play, the death or the missing woman you are too late to hear it now. And yet, beset though you may be, you cannot afford to lose control of this, whatever it is, for if it scares Lord Hunsdon, then it is like to terrify the rest of us and that can only mean the Queen's at risk, or someone very close to her. And you, the spider of intelligence, had all the threads within your grasp until a day or so ago. And now they are all slipping away faster than quicksilver.'

As Tom exercised his mastery of logic, the two men, mindful of the battering on the door below, had been searching carefully through the room. There was a tumbled, truckle bed along one wall. Its ill-piled coverings the only untidy things in a fastidious room. At the end of the bed stood a table and, upon this, neatly piled papers. Beyond that there stood a clothes press, its top shut. Above that a bowl and jug, both wanting water. Above the bed, covered for the most part in greased paper, windows looked out at windows a yard or so away. Tom knelt and pushed his rapier under the bed, hooking out a pair of slippers. Again with his blade, gingerly, he lifted the coverings but disturbed little more than a flea or two.

Poley was busy with the papers. 'Mostly copies of his lines.

What is this madness about Queen Mab? Is it a part of the new play?'

'It is. Anything else?' Tom crossed to Poley's side and began to glance through the papers too, swiftly sorting out the speeches from *Romeo and Juliet*, setting them apart to return to the Rose. 'Was he getting funds from your purse – or the Council's?' he asked.

'Something. Sometimes.'

'Then you weren't paying him enough. Look.' A series of letters to courtiers begging for preferment. 'If you want a man to focus on the matter in hand, then you remove his most pressing distractions,' he said. 'I should suggest that pinchpenny spycraft is next to worthless.'

'True, but only partly so. Spies have deep purses and many distractions. Do you think I could ever have paid Julius Morton enough money to stop him getting distracted?'

'Probably not. But he needed all his wits about him yesterday and look, he was begging the Earl of Southampton to grant him an audience. And Essex too, by God.'

'Let me see those.'

'Wait. There's one here sealed. It's heavy. Stiff.'

'Give it here to me. Give all of it—'

'No. Wait. When I was in Italy, I heard of a device . . .' Tom laid the letter down and stood back. He slid the point of his sword beneath the seal and twisted, as anyone might do wishing to open it. One section of the paper snapped back and a hail of little darts leaped out. Because both men were standing well back, the pins harmed neither of them, but had they been opening the thing in the normal way they would have been blinded at the very least. 'Spanish pins,' said Tom. 'Poisoned, like as not.' He went up to the letter and moved it gingerly. 'Safe now,' he said. 'God's teeth, there's writing in it.' He flipped the package over and glanced at the front. There was a name scrawled there. But like the rest of Morton's room, his writing was neat. Easy to read. 'It's for you,' said Tom and handed it to Poley.

'We'd best take all of these papers,' said the spymaster, his voice shaken and low. He snatched up a solid-looking leather document wallet and began to stuff the papers into it as swiftly as he could.

'As long as it's not too much to carry,' warned Tom. 'And as long as we can move it swiftly . . .'

The battering at the door had suddenly been succeeded by a sinister splintering sound.

Tom turned to the last of the items Morton had left in the room. He crouched and slid his sword under the lid of the clothes press, easing it up fractionally. He had placed himself carefully so that the last of the light shone over his shoulder into the widening crack. The moment he saw the silver thread which stretched tautly down from the lid into the black depths of the box he stopped, slid his sword out and stood.

Below stairs, the door crashed wide. 'Time to go,' he decided. He took a step back, holding his sword level with his shoulders across his chest. Then he turned and threw himself bodily at the window. He dived through the waxed paper and flew over the three-foot gap a couple of stories above the street to crash through the facing window into the house opposite. He rolled forward, careful of his sword, and rose to his feet. Shrugging the wreckage of the window frames from his shoulders, he pounded through a series of small, empty rooms with Poley close at his heels.

They had just reached the next outside window, overhanging the broad brown wash of the Fleet River itself, when the first of their pursuers reached the window of Morton's room. The pursuer had a clear view through the ruined walls and open doors at the pair of them and had he been carrying one of Ugo's guns he might have done some harm, for they were standing, momentarily irresolute, stopped dead by the stench arising from the putrid river below. But all he had was a club. And then his opportunity to do anything at all stopped, for one of his confederates threw open the lid of Morton's clothes press, and just had time to scream something mercifully unintelligible before the three pounds of gunpowder it contained blew up. The top of Morton's room – and the house at the end of

Hanging Sword Court – disappeared. A wall of sooty fire rolled outwards along the corridor opened by the fleeing intelligencers. Tom's uncharacteristic hesitation ended. The pair of them plunged through the window and into the Fleet River beneath a breath of flame worthy of Hell's mouth itself.

It was the dead horse that saved them. It was unusual to find a horse in the Fleet River. Under normal circumstances the poor creature would have been skinned and butchered like any sheep or cow in the nearest shambles. But for some reason it had escaped this fate and was floating leisurely down towards the Thames. Its belly was swollen with gases and its legs stuck out straight and stiff. It was just possible for two men floundering in the thick sewage of the river's flow to scramble up on to its flank and pull themselves free of the liquid ordure to the waist. And it allowed Master Robert Poley, intelligencer and spymaster to the Council, to pull the leather wallet full of Julius Morton's secret letters clear of the water and keep its contents safe.

The wherryman who worked at Blackfriars Steps recognised Tom, otherwise he would never have paused mid-stream, under the last light of the westering sun as it shone up the Thames over the little hill at Charing Cross. The wherryman was part way through a fare, but he stopped rowing and reached over to pull the pair of them into his pitching little ferryboat. Had he not performed this simple act of kindness, they would, likely as not, have been swept away under the bridge and away with the tide, like the horse.

The ferryman was halfway through taking a staid and solemn young clerk across to the Bankside and thither they went, Tom at least, amused to be the object of so much icy disdain as he sat stinking beside Poley in the bow. His position there allowed him to look back at the brightness of the fire blazing among the rooftops of Alsatia in behind the imposing edifices of Bridewell. 'They'd best be quick up there,' he said to his malodorous companion, 'or Morton's legacy is like to consume all of Alsatia and half the inns of court.'

As they landed at Falcon Stairs, the young clerk ran instantly upwards, eager to be away from them lest anyone he knew – or didn't know come to that – might associate him with their rancid stench. Watching him with wry amusement Tom spoke to Poley. 'The Elephant has a privy bathhouse. We can clean ourselves and talk in private there.'

'If we pay for private use and care nothing for the scandal,' said Poley stiffly.

Tom laughed again. 'The scandal is in the way we look and smell, not whether we be lovers of Sodom. And, come to think of it, your reputation should be safe enough if it survived an association with Marlowe. What did he say? "Who loves not boys and tobacco is a fool"?'

So, with many expressions of gratitude to the wherryman who departed to wash out his boat, the bedraggled secret agents mounted the Falcon Stairs and slopped out on to the Bankside. For once the bustle did not much affect them. As though they had signs warning that they carried Plague, they walked at the centre of a rough circle cleared for them by their stench. Poley stayed hangdog, trying to make himself invisible, avoiding as far as he could the light thrown downwards by the blazing flambards in front of every tavern and the last of the light in the clear sapphire sky. Tom swaggered, as far as he was able, and met every eye; noted every wrinkled nostril and superior sniff at scented kerchief and orange and clove pomander. He still carried his sword naked – for Heaven alone knew what filth might be in his scabbard – so that all in all, he came as close to a careless saunter as circumstances would allow.

Which, as it turned out, was a mistake.

They had only made it as far as the Little Rose when the three card-sharps from last night reappeared, armed with clubs and looking for revenge. The first Tom knew of it was when the fluid circle of men and women fighting to avoid approaching too close was replaced by a solid wall, three pairs of shoulders wide. He looked up and recognised at once the three frowning faces looking at him. 'Stay back, Poley,' he said quietly. Then, seeing the reflexive movement of his companion's hand, he added, 'Remember, wet guns don't work.'

Then the three thugs were upon him. They were all wielding long clubs and were clearly expert in their use. Tom's rapier kept them at bay at first as he pulled his long dagger out of his belt, but they were determined men, a practised team, all of whom had felt the whip's hot kiss as they clyed the jerk and cared nothing for a little pain.

They spread out, effectively blocking the Bankside, trapping Tom in the middle of the thoroughfare and holding Poley between Tom and the water. The intelligencer began to fall back and distracted Tom for an instant as he vanished. Tom frowned, doubting that he would see the whole of Morton's correspondence now. He'd be lucky to see Poley, come to that, once he let him out of his sight. Tom too began to fall back, trying to keep Poley in the corner of his vision. To no avail. When his fair weather friend was gone, Tom turned to give all his attention to his enemies.

And none too soon. The first club stroke came high from his left. He stabbed in under it, moving like lightning, and felt his point pierce a thigh before the blow sang past his shoulder. Immediately he sliced right as though the blade had an edge, tearing the point out of one column of flesh and stabbing upwards at a second as his knee kissed the Bankside earth and his dagger stabbed wide at the third assailant. Two clubs crashed together where his head had been and he threw himself upwards and forward, tearing the muscles of his chest to bring dagger and rapier together into the face of his central attacker. Too close to use the blade as Capo Ferro had taught him, he used the knuckle guard as his father had taught him, smashing his assailant's nose, turning his head and exposing his neck to the thirteen inches of razor dagger.

But just at that moment, the thug on his right swung his club in a powerful round-house blow. Tom ducked. The heavy wood thundered just above his head and swung over his opponent's head as well, taking as it did so, the upright blade of his sword.

Any other sword would have spun out of his grip, but this rapier had a handle that fitted right over his hand, like a glove. As well as the wire-bound haft, it had solid hooks, like triggers, for his thumb and forefinger. It was impossible to knock the sword out of his grip. The pommel jumped back into his face. The knuckle guard smashed into his opponent's nose again. Tom hissed as the shock of the blow shot like lightening up his right forearm. That shock turned the dagger, however, so that it sliced into shoulder rather than throat.

Tom threw himself forward and sideways to his left, using that instant of purchase of steel in flesh on which to hang his turn. The third bully had been quiet during the last part of the mêlée. He would be up to something now, Tom calculated fiercely, hoping some feeling would come back into his numb right hand while he worked with the dagger in his left. He was. Tom jerked his dagger free and leaned in under a downward blow, stabbing at a slight but solid midriff. The blade sank home into an old-fashioned codpiece at the same moment that the club landed square across his shoulders. The weight of the blow tore him down and his dagger tore at an angle across into the top of a thigh. Hot blood squirted into his face, adding to the overwhelming storm of sensations that would have incapacitated a lesser man. His right hand spasmed and burned. Pins and needles stabbed from right wrist to elbow. The weight of the club across his back drove the air out of him and all but shattered his spine between his shoulder blades. The roadway hit his knee again, jarring him to the hip. Once again he used the knee and the dagger as steady points against which to turn and he threw himself to the right even as the wounded man fell screaming back into the river. The way he did so all but twisted Tom's dagger out of his grip and snapped the blade near halfway down its length.

Tom's right arm was an agony, but it lost little of its cunning, driving the length of his rapier straight into the hip of the second attacker who had exposed himself over-confidently by raising his club with both hands. Half the blade slid through the muscles and tendons of the hip joint, the point flashing out into the light behind his buttock. The man screamed and froze. At that instant the central attacker, the big man who was not from Chiddingstone, brought down his club in turn. It hit the blade immediately in front of Tom's knuckle guard and snapped it at once – though at some considerable cost to his companion's hip. Tom fell now, on to his right knee as well. As though at prayer he tore his two hands together and thrust the two blades, broken as they were, into his opponent's groin. The action, desperate enough, was sufficient to make the man jump back and so the last blow of the battle, which would have killed Tom where he knelt as truly as the headsman's axe, missed the crown of his head where it had been aimed, and kissed the temple instead, whispering past his collarbone as he slumped forward into the mud and blood the very moment that Poley arrived with the Watch.

When he came round he was one huge ache, he was slumped in a chair, stinking out an office in the outer area of the Clink Prison. As he came to, he had no idea exactly where he was but he soon began to work things out when he saw the uniform of the man Poley was talking to. Behind the huddled pair of them was a grille beyond which he could see down into the arched cloisters of the prison with its sad company of tightly chained prisoners.

Their conversation stopped when Poley saw Tom's eyelids flicker, and the intelligencer crossed to his young associate. The other man rose and stood looking down through the grille into the dark, hellish circles of his private hell. 'Are you all right?' Poley asked.

'My body is afire,' croaked Tom, 'but I can feel nothing major amiss.'

'They're heating the water at the Elephant. There's an Italian woman there says bathing will ease your hurts and quell the stench.'

'Yes.'

Tom's eyes remained fixed on the second man. He wore the badges of the Bishop's Bailiff, and no one else in Southwark was likely to have an office the like of this. But there was something about him that disturbed Tom deeply. Something he could not quite put his finger on.

Until the Bishop's Bailiff turned, and his face came into the light.

'Hello, young Tom,' said the Bishop's Bailiff, his voice familiar with a West Country, Winchester burr.

'Hello, old Law,' said Tom.

CHAPTER FOURTEEN

Dead Man's Messages

A bath in London was a rarity. Not so down here in 'the Stews', named for its bathing facilities – and the sexual and medicinal uses to which they could be put. But even down here a private bath was unheard of. The bath at the Elephant was a barrel, a big one, the better part of four feet deep. It was filled from a big copper close by and topped up with water from the cooking fire within. It emptied down a sluice through a solid, brick foundation out into the garden where the boy sang to the amorous couples.

There was a stool at one side of the huge barrel, a three-legged affair made of wood which kept trying to float out from under Tom as he sat up to his waist in the scalding water. There was another bobbing opposite should his mistress care to join him, but Constanza had contented herself by adding perfume, medicinal herbs, leaves of her own precious basil and some violets. Then she had spoilt the aromatic effect by pouring in a quart of white vinegar. Now she was busily scrubbing his neck and shoulders with the cleanest rags she could find, gently bemoaning every bruise, scar and contusion on his body, not least the clear clean wound on his arm from yesterday. A clean linen sheet lay folded, ready to receive him when he pulled himself out, but at least one more cauldron of precious water was heating over the Elephant's big cooking fire to be poured over his head before that happy release.

Poley sat in the corner, by the window through which the boy's pure voice came in. He was fidgeting restlessly. This might have been because Tom and Talbot Law were wasting time on social chit-chat rather than the more pressing matters in hand. Or it might have been because he was due in the steaming barrel next.

'So,' Talbot Law concluded, 'Bess still runs the Nag's Head beside the Bishop's palace in Winchester. But I got bored with tapstering and was glad enough when an alternative career appeared. It was the cage out back that got me into this line of work.' He glanced out of the bathhouse door. Beside the solid lean-to with its tub, stood another one. Like most taverns, the Elephant kept a cage out back with sets of irons to hold drunks, cheats, roughs and those who failed to pay for their food, drink or entertainment. 'It was fortune, really. As an old soldier I got a reputation for running a good house with a strong cage and so when the Bishop needed people held until his court could sit, he came to me. And before I knew what had happened . . .' he shrugged, showing his bailiff's badges. 'I'm only quartered at the Clink these days, mind. My gaol is the Borough Counter, for I've an arrangement with the Borough Watch. My men do their work and they let me use their gaol. Mine at the Clink is full of papist spies and what-not. Hardly room for a good honest felon at all. Borough Counter used to be a church. It's good and solid – and a better house it is than Wood Street or Poultry. But they are City. Borough is mine as the Clink is the Bishop's. But in borough or liberty, I am the law.'

'There are twelve good gaols in London,' snapped Poley.

'Fourteen counting the Tower and the Bridewell,' interrupted Law.

'Are we to discuss the dubious merits of each before we proceed to our business?'

'Ah, yes,' said Law silkily. 'Your business, Master Poley. Your business with me is that you have reported a brawl and guided my watchkeepers. I have taken one man in attack on another and there may be a case toward. I may need to hold you

110

a witness to this assault should a warrant be sworn. Would you prefer Masters Commons, Knights Ward or the Hole?'

Poley rose, shaking with rage. 'You have no hold on me, Sir Bailiff. You get none of my garnish for any of your services. I serve the Council. I am the Lord Chamberlain's man in this matter.'

Law looked at Tom and Tom nodded. 'Both of us,' he confirmed. 'On Lord Hunsdon's own direction.'

'We are carrying his writ,' added the enraged Poley. 'Lord Hunsdon's licence for our action and authority, written in his own hand.'

'Are we?' asked Tom, surprised.

Talbot Law laughed. 'See, Tom? You could have killed all three of them rather than leaving me with two wounded vagrants to find and one loudly calling assault on you from my holding cell at the counter.'

'Sit down, Master Poley. Talbot was speaking in jest. He has no thought to gaol us. Nor any cause. It was the three coney-catchers – ' he turned to Constanza – 'after some revenge for the trick we play'd them last night.'

'Oh, Tom,' she said softly. 'I little thought your help would have been offered at such a price.' She ran her hands across the great purple welt lying athwart his shoulder blades. He hissed.

''Tis not my bones, Bella, but my blade I grieve for.'

'You have the hilts,' snapped Poley again. 'Blades are easy to come by.'

'For you, mayhap,' said Tom. 'But I'd be lucky to have the chance or the money to afford another such as my Ferrara blade. But you are right, Master Poley. We need to move on as swiftly as we may. There are matters here running deep and dark. We need to see what Master Morton has written. We need to hope he has left us some clue as to where his missing contact might be. And some hint as to the reason for his terror and his sense of swiftly nearing death.'

'God's life,' spat Poley. 'Can you hold no curb upon your tongue? These matters are not for the common ear, man.'

'Master Poley,' said Tom, running out of patience and

heaving himself up out of the tub. 'It is your secrecy that has caused much of your trouble in this. We will move faster with a little help. The people whose help we need are here assembled, out at my school and up at the Rose, *valedicet* Ugo Stell and Will Shakespeare. These men need to know what we know and then they will aid us. And at their lips the secret will be sealed, unless we are talking among ourselves.'

'Or unless,' spat Poley, 'they are talking to Rackmaster Topcliffe or his cohorts. The more that know the secret, the more may betray it. This is the law of intelligencing and you break it only at the greatest peril.' As he spoke, Poley was pulling off his clothes. His haste to get into the bath and, like Tom, to have his apparel sponged and dried, arose not only from the relentlessly worsening stink but from the brutal realisation that he dared not open Morton's wallet or any of its contents if there was any risk of him defacing the vital contents with a rancid drip or smear. For once, cleanliness must come before intelligence. In the meantime, as he stripped, Poley went through with Tom at last the details of Morton's death and the present whereabouts of his body.

No sooner had Poley eased his long and none too youthful shanks into the water than a girl arrived from the cooking fire and Will Shakespeare arrived from the Rose. The one was laden with a cauldron of boiling water and the other agog with the news from Bankside about Tom's near death at the hands of three club-men. Neither was particularly welcome. 'Hell's teeth,' groaned Master Poley, fighting to position the bobbing stool beneath his lean arse. 'This is no bathhouse, 'tis St Paul's at high noon. I expect a sermon, a whipping and a hanging at any moment.'

But it so chanced that the kitchen wench who carried through the cauldron was young, plump and comely – and not too shy to help their distinguished guest with his ablutions. And Will had brought his Master of Cypher's commentary on Julius Morton's dying words. So they got their sermon at once. For the whipping and the hanging, they had to wait.

Will rehearsed Morton's last speech, disentangling the intelligencer's extemporised words from those he had written for Mercutio. To Talbot Law and the serving girl, this was all revelation. To Poley and Constanza, less so; and to the others not at all. 'The speech as I wrote it ends here: "Ask for me tomorrow and you shall find me a grave man." Now he goes extempore. I did not write "I am peppered, I warrant . . ." see here? And "A plague o' both your houses." It fits well, but I did not write it. Then we have "A dog, a rat, a mouse, a cat to scratch a man to death." Again, that is new. "A braggart, a rogue, a villain that fights by the book of arithmetic . . ." New again. But here he returns to the play. "Why the devil came you between us? I was hurt under your arm . . ." And then, after Romeo's answer, "Help me to the house, Benvolio, or I shall faint." That is Mercutio's last line. Benvolio carries him off there and he dies in the tiring house. But he has added again, "A plague o' both your houses. They have made worms' meat of me. I have it and soundly . . . Your houses . . ." That is all, but Dick Burbage swears he would have said more had they not carried him off the stage. So those lines, the extempore lines, are the cypher I have been working on.'

'And this work,' asked Poley, his intellect involved now. 'Has it yielded aught?'

'Yes,' said Will roundly. 'I believe that it has.'

'Expound, then, oh Master of Cyphers,' directed Tom quietly.

'By Socratic method, then, for I have not yet plumbed the depths.'

'By Socratic method if you must,' said Tom, glancing across at Poley. Teaching through asking questions seemed to be a popular method among intelligencers, he thought.

'Whose house has received the most pernicious visitings of the plague?' asked Will.

'Most every house in London during the last two years,' answered Tom.

'More than the common run. More than any,' insisted Will.

In the little silence, Tom glanced across to Poley and caught the frown which disfigured his lean, saturnine face. Poley knew the answer, he realised with a prickle of revelation that came close to an icy shiver. 'Master Poley has an answer to your question, Will,' he said, his voice suddenly gravelly and hoarse.

They all looked at Poley and the spymaster's frown deepened. 'The player speaks of the House of Outremer. In the last year almost every person living at his London house at Wormwood in Jewry has died. Lord Outremer himself, his wife and children, servants, cats and dogs. Even the very rats, they say, die in the cellars of Wormwood in Jewry. And that's an odd thing for a family whose fortunes were founded on herbs, medicines—'

'Spices,' added Will. 'Peppers and the like . . . And there you have it,' he cried, so excited that he overlooked the tone in which Poley had described him as a 'player'. 'But you do not have it all. For with old Lord Outremer dead without issue, who is like to inherit?'

'Hugh Outram,' answered Constanza, who had not wasted her year in London without picking up whispers from all quarters, and the juicier the better. 'Baron Cotehel. Third of the Unholy Trinity with Wriothsley and Devereux, Earls of Southampton and Essex. I hear tell the three of them are Raleigh's School of Night reborn, dealing in alchemy, necromancy, all manner of unholy arts. And wait, wasn't Kit Marlowe supposed to be—'

Will cut off her gush of gossip with uncharacteristic rudeness. 'And the London home of Hugh Outram, Baron Cotehel, soon to be Lord Outremer, master of the pepper trade?' he persisted, aglow with febrile, almost frenetic excitement.

But Tom knew this answer, for he had been invited there to give young Baron Cotehel the benefit of his tuition. 'Highmeet House,' he said. 'In the parish of St Magnus.'

'Highmeet St Magnus,' confirmed Will. 'You have it.'

'I have what?' Tom glanced around the steamy little room. Constanza pouted, hurt by Will's rudeness. The kitchen wench rubbed Poley's back, lower and lower, her expression dreamy. Poley himself still frowned, and Tom suspected he saw all too clearly what his dazzling friend was driving at. But Tom had

114

teased him once already. Time to stir his own heat-addled wits. 'Two houses, then, Wormwood already cursed by plague and Highmeet like to succeed it. Literally, if you have the right of Morton's curse. One family, the elder line deceased, the cadet bound to inherit.'

'You have it, Tom. The houses. The names of the houses.'

'Wormwood and Highmeet. Dear God, Will, you're in the right. Worm – meet. 'Tis the two conjoined. Could this be?' he asked, turning to Poley. 'Could Morton have been warning his contact against Hugh Outram?'

'He's the only one of the Three not at Nonesuch,' admitted Poley heavily. 'Essex is Master of the Horse and the Queen needs him to oversee her next move down to Richmond. Southampton is there with Lord Burghley, his guardian, for four more months to the very day. If Morton was caught spying on any of them, then it would be Outram he would have to avoid.'

'If,' said Tom. 'If. If. If. We have too much conjecture and not enough certainty, even from you, Master Poley.'

Poley stood up so swiftly that the steaming water cascaded out on to the rough wooden floor. He stood for a moment, looking around. His clothing was with Tom's steaming in front of the fire and there was no sheet brought by fair hands to cover his loins. But he cared not, it seemed. 'Then we had best look over the letters he had sent us,' he said. 'At the very least your player-codemaster here can reclaim the lines Morton had secreted at his lodgings amongst other, weightier writings. I need a napkin,' he concluded. 'A gown and a private chamber and for God's grace, some peace.'

Poley got his napkin and, soon after, a gown. He and Tom were made free of the tapster's Sunday best. They removed into the quietest of the public rooms, but peace was hard to come by. Will, signally unsatisfied with the mere return of his playsheets, departed moodily, for it was well past ten now and the exigencies of two performances and much brainwork were taking their toll, and his bed in St Helen's beckoned. Constanza, at Tom's request, went off to see whether something more solid than the usual supper could be culled from the ordinary pot below. And so they were, briefly, alone. But before Poley could fall to his urgent inspection of Morton's papers another interloper arrived. It was Ugo.

'They say Alsatia's still alight,' he reported at once. 'But the blaze is dying back, so I'm told.'

'God's death, Ugo, you haven't been waiting there all this time?'

The Dutchman laughed grimly. 'Nay. I've had other business to keep me busy, Tom. Did you know you were followed to Hanging Sword Court?'

'No. By whom?'

'A shiftless scoundrel attired in black.'

Tom shivered, suddenly, and the wound in his arm gave a poignant twinge. He thought of the ambidexter, dressed all in black, looking back up Rose Alley as Julius Morton lay dead on the table, killed at his hand. Perhaps there was more blood to be shed before his account was settled in full. 'This watcher in black,' he said. 'Could you see what he carried? One sword or two? Could he have been of Spanish blood d'you think? A Mediterranean man?'

'I cannot say,' said Ugo in his solid, forthright manner. 'I can tell you little more than I have. But he has dogged your heels like the veriest hound all day.'

'That must have taken some cunning,' observed Poley.

'Cunning indeed, and from both of us. I've never seen such shift to speed out from under a maze of falling bricks and down the very banks of the Fleet with the pair of you bobbing like mermen on the back of your river horse. You kept my guns safe, I trust.'

'Safer than my sword.'

'Aye, I heard tell. And that's the next point of my news. For when my man had followed you across the river – with me scarcely a wherry-length behind – I saw him talking to three ruffians. Solid-looking men, armed with solid-looking clubs. I chose to follow him rather than them and so I think I missed something of your battle. But I did not miss its aftermath, for when all the hue and cry was done, with my man sitting supping sack in the Bear as quiet as you like, a bloody man came running up to him, all distressed. I heard little of the conversation but the pair of them started up again at once and were off through the door like hares at a coursing. I followed the pair of them down to the waterside – a quiet little bank below Goat Stairs – where they hauled me out another ruffian with his leg all torn and his privities on show. After a moment more of talk the wounded birds limped off into the night and my man came back up on to Bankside.'

'Well, God's my life,' breathed Tom. 'And whither went our fight-maker then, pray?'

'Down to the counter, as bold as brass, with his purse in his hand. When I saw that I thought I'd best come here with all good speed.'

'He's gone to buy the third man free,' said Tom, pulling himself to his feet, stiffly and a little unsteadily. 'He'll be done before we can stop it and vanish into the night.'

'Hold, Tom,' said Talbot Law. 'He'll not have bought him out of the counter. 'Tis my prison and I left word. No one can get him out of my cage except myself. And that, I think, I shall do presently. If I'm quick, I'll get the both of them.'

As Tom gave the guns to a tutting Ugo, and Constanza stuck her head round the door to promise a resurrected pottage, then vanished to get Tom her fork, the two men at last found the leisure to turn to Morton's papers.

They started with the letter addressed to Poley, talking quietly as they gingerly opened it and fell to closer scrutiny of its contents. 'It was probably a mere trap,' said Poley. 'Morton must have left it for anyone who knew what he was about and for whom he was working.'

'Men such as he feared the most,' agreed Tom. 'Knowing that of all the papers there they would hasten to open this first, and so fall victim to the Spanish pins. Take care. There is one still left. Here, let me take it and keep it safe. All the uses I have heard of this device require that the pins be poisoned. Do you know an apothecary skilled in poisons?'

'Perhaps,' admitted Poley guardedly. 'But such knowledge is dangerous.'

'Almost all your knowledge seems to be dangerous,' said Tom seriously, and Ugo snorted with grim amusement. 'However,' continued Tom, 'let us consider the letter further. Let us suppose that Morton wrote a genuine letter to you, but had not the means of opportunity to put it in your hands. Could he have relied upon your finding it should anything happen to him?'

'All things being equal,' said Poley slowly. 'I did find it, after all.'

'In that case, the pins are a way of making certain that yours would be the only eyes to see the message. Would you have taken care how you broke the seal, as I did with my sword?'

'Of course. The package was heavy. Stiff. I would have opened it most circumspectly. He would have known that.'

'Then we can assume that he would have written freely to you. This is his parting word. *Quod erat demonstrandum*, I believe. What does it say?'

' "Poley. In haste and in the knowledge that if you read this I am dead. In that case look well to Kate. I have warned Gil Brown to stay close at the Rose for fear of her, but he is not to be relied on for he is slow. My end may be swift but hers would be lengthy and torturous. I fear the Three, though only one is abroad. They have at play not one Don but two, and it is with one of them that the matter of Lathom lies, I fear. They have at play also Phellippes and his crew, I believe, but their object remains obscure. Of one thing I am certain, there are more than are found in Mantua and one such has visited Wormwood in Jewry with what results all the world knows, but with what object and at whose behest? After the play I have told her to ask Master Seyton of Wormwood the manner of things there. I have also given her the name of the Searcher of St Margaret's Old Jewry. But which of the other concerns have been so visited as Wormwood? Kenilworth, or Buckstones, rather? St Augustine's Papey? And what part of the great plan can so many deaths pretend? Such men as you and I must look about us, Poley. Warn Gil Brown. Have a care to Kate, I prithee." '

'I would hazard,' said Tom when Poley had finished reading this, 'that it was Gil Brown who told you of the play?'

'It was.'

'And who lay under the dust pile in Alsatia with his gullet torn asunder?'

'Sadly, yes.'

' 'Tis too late to warn him, then. But what of her?'

'She would not go to Wormwood in Jewry. She would not dare.' But Poley did not sound too certain.

'If she went, she went a day since,' warned Tom. 'And knowing nothing of Morton's death, like as not. But his words on stage would be likely to send her to the house as agreed, if she's of any determination at all.'

'She is My Lady Determination,' admitted Poley.

'Then she has gone.'

'But it is the Lion's den. Death to all who enter there, save only Seyton, the Chamberlain.'

'Then we'd better shift to follow her straightaway.'

'Not without some preparation. And not without some force.'

'We are a force of three,' said Tom.

'Well-armed if we can call in at my rooms to supply our want of guns and blades,' added Ugo, grimly.

'Four if we can tempt the Bishop's Bailiff north of the Thames with us. He might well come exploring on the strength of Lord Hunsdon's writ.'

'On the strength of that I could command the Watch,' said Poley, growing thoughtful.

'If the City Watch are worth commanding, then I'm a Cardinal,' growled Ugo.

'Five indeed,' persisted Tom, all restless energy now, 'if we could stop off at St Helen's and rouse Will Shakespeare. 'Tis hard by Wormwood Street and no distance from Old Jewry.'

'Indeed,' said Constanza suddenly. 'And have you noticed that, when things begin to gather into trouble, at the Rose, at

Southampton House, at Wormwood in Jewry, why there, right at hand, is your Master of Cyphers? And remember, Tom,' she added, sending a darkling glance across at Poley as he spoke, 'Will Shakespeare was as good a friend to Kit Marlowe as he is a friend to you.'

CHAPTER FIFTEEN

Wormwood

T he invasion of Wormwood in Jewry began with a mess of
pottage. The serving girl who had bathed Poley arrived
with two wooden trenchers piled with the thick stew of pork-
belly, root vegetables and beans thickened with oatmeal and
spiced with sage. There was salt, but it never left the ordinary
room, where it sat on the high table. The scrapings of the
ordinary pot were supplemented by two legs of capon, spit-
roast, and a slab of coarse bread broken in two. Poley fell to at
once, using the one horn spoon provided, his dagger and his
fingers. Tom, suddenly ravenous, would have done so too,
though he lacked the spoon until Poley was done with it – and a
dagger come to that. Had not Constanza slipped off to get her
fork, Tom would have been reduced to eating with his fingers
like a beggar. Or, more likely, to waiting like the poor gentleman he was until the implements were wiped and passed. A
bottle of sack completed the repast, and Tom got to the pewter
tankard first.

He was on his second cup when Talbot Law returned. 'I have
your assailant,' he said shortly, 'but his would-be liberator's
gone.'

'Bring him up,' suggested Tom.

'He's coming,' said Talbot, and a rhythmic crashing proved
his words. After a moment more, the door heaved open and two
burly warders hauled the leader of the card-sharps and Tom's

main assailant into the room. Round his neck he wore an iron collar which was attached to two solid bars perhaps a yard in length reaching down between his knees to ankle gyves. From midway on each bar there stood out to right and left another shorter bar ending in wrist-cuffs. The effect of the whole device was to hold the unfortunate wearing it in a painful squat from which position any movement was impossible. It was a brand-new fettering system recently invented by the Warden of the Tower. It was called the Scavenger's Daughter. When the warders dropped their burden he balanced on his feet for a moment, like a goose laying, then he toppled slowly on to his side.

Talbot had said the man had been crying assault on Tom. But that was before his employer had failed to release him and he had begun to suspect just how powerful Tom might be. Also, no doubt, before the irons went on. He was silent enough now.

Tom used Constanza's fork to strip the flesh off his capon's thigh. He did it slowly, lingeringly, threateningly. The coney-catcher had certainly never seen a fork before and its novelty alone was likely to prove unnerving. Tom chewed a sliver of meat and they all sat silently looking down at the silent man. 'Let us begin with you,' said Tom at last. 'Your name is not Paul Carter and you are not a merchant up from Chiddingstone with a load of early apples for the Cheap.'

'No, master. That's true.' The man's words were slow but his eyes darted quickly enough around the room, assessing the situation and measuring the odds against him.

'Then, as the first step on the long road you will need to follow before you are out of the counter and out of those gyves, tell us your real name.'

'I was christened Nicholas Blunt, your worship. Parish of St Mary, Islington, the year of the Queen's sickness, sir.'

'But Islington is a thieves' haunt little better than Alsatia or Damnation Alley. You won't be known as Master Blunt in such quarters, will you? How are you known amongst your confederates, the coney-catchers?'

'Quick Nick, your worship.' The answer came far too swiftly.

A thief's trade name was an important commodity jealously guarded; for upon it rested his reputation and his fortune.

Tom's eyes flicked across to Talbot and his men. Infinitesimal shakes of their heads told him they had never heard of anyone by that name. 'You're lying, Master Blunt. You're a man well set up in your business. You look like a merchant from Chiddingstone. You sound like one and you dress like one. Only a man of established reputation could achieve such things. We will know your name when we hear it. And we will know you are lying in the meantime.'

'We have no time for these courtesies,' suddenly spat Poley. He turned to the kitchen maid who had stayed to make sheep's eyes at him. 'Go down to mine host and tell him I want a rope. We have strong beams up aloft,' he continued as she vanished, 'and I can show you a trick for loostening tongues that was taught me by no less a man than Rackmaster Topcliffe himself.'

Master Blunt had come up with several names by the time that the rope arrived, but he had convinced nobody that he had achieved a state of truthfulness and grace as yet. He had, however, begun to sweat. His words became more effusive, tumbling over each other as Poley slung the rope up over the stoutest beam and looped it around the ankle end of the gyves. 'This is nothing but coney-catcher's cant,' snarled Poley when the rope was tight. 'Take him up, Master Law.'

Tom knelt stiffly at the babbling villain's head. Such sympathy as he displayed was largely feigned, for this man had broken his beloved rapier and had been within a whisker of breaking his skull to boot. But he displayed sympathy nonetheless, to balance Poley's brutality. ' 'Tis only the beginning, man,' he said as the rope creaked over the beam and the gyves began to rise. 'We have an infinity more of questions and you are like to meet an eternity of pain if you equivocate with us. I was lately talking to a friend called Kydd, a scholar and playwright racked more than a year ago in the matter of Kit Marlowe's death, and he was scarce able to walk since. A broken man after an hour or two's examination; not long for the world. And what Master Poley has in mind for you is worse than ten rackings, I can see that plain. Be straight with us, man, or you'll be Blunt the Beggar, crutched or crawling, with your limbs askew and your business gone, your sons in the Islington brick kilns and your wives and daughters turned to bawds. There are houses here,' he persisted, 'as will take a girl from eight years old, for the gentlemen that like them young.'

Blunt's legs were in the air now and the weight of his thighs and backside was working on the fulcrums of his ankles. And the moment his shoulders left the floor he saw that Tom's words were literally true. Something cracked, the sound explosively loud in the little room. It might have been the beam, the rope, the gyves or any of the bones they gripped so cruelly. The hanging man screamed. 'Nick o' Darkmans. They call me Nick o' Darkmans.'

Tom's eyes met Talbot's and the Bishop's Bailiff, pale and wide eyed, nodded. Tom's hand went up and Nick o' Darkmans came down. 'The Bishop's Bailiff knows you, man. And that means hanging or burning like as not. Unless you can give us other game to skin. What was your latest business with me?'

'Not to kill you, Master. Never to kill you.'

'What, then?'

'We was to break your sword, then your arms and your hands. Then your skull if we wanted. But we were to leave you alive, Master, I swear it.'

Constanza screamed, choking the sound off with the back of her hand. Tom looked across at Poley and Talbot. 'Not dead, but crippled. Who would want that for me?'

He was addressing the question to his friends but Nick o' Darkmans was falling over himself to answer it. 'His name is Baines. Richard Baines. He tried to hide the truth from us by calling himself Henry Carey. Said he came from Berwick and spoke with a Northern voice well enough. But we saw through him all too quick, though we never told him aught. 'Tis a law of the trade – always know your employer.'

Now it was Tom's turn to look surprised, for he had been certain in his own mind from the moment Ugo warned him of the man in black that he was being followed by the two-sworded ambidexter who had murdered Morton; the Spaniard staying in the Earl of Essex's household. One of two Spaniards waiting there for my Lord's duties at Nonesuch to be done.

But no. From the moment Blunt had admitted he was Nick o' Darkmans, the truth had flowed from him, as pure as Jordan's stream. Tom would just have to find out more about this Richard Baines and fit him into the widening web of the puzzle. He suddenly remembered what Poley had said about Morton's murder being like the pinnacle of a pyramid of Egypt and the full massive truth lying buried in the sand far below.

'Is Baines a name that means anything to you?' he asked Poley and received a curt, negative shake of the head in reply and a speaking look around the company – from which he assumed that Poley might pass on information as soon as they were alone. The next step would require more time and teasing out of information from the man. Time they did not have to hand now. 'Take him away,' he ordered Talbot's men, 'and keep him close. We have work to do which calls urgently on us now; but, like so much else that we have gathered today, Nick o' Darkmans will bear closer scrutiny when our leisure serves.'

Then, as they began to pull their own clothes back on, Tom managed to clear the room at last and Poley began to speak of Richard Baines. 'When Master Secretary Walsingham died, the company he had gathered together began to fall apart. While he was still alive, there were a goodly number of us working on such matters as the Queen's cousin Mary of Scots, dealing with such as Babbington and his traitors, as you know. It was the same company that Sir Francis had created over the years to guard Her Majesty against plots from Cadiz, from Rome, from much nearer home. I was the head of the active section. My duties were to contact, examine, report. Work on the streets, in the stews, the counters and gaols, anywhere sedition and treason were brewing. But, equally important, was another section. This was the dealers in Codes and Cyphers. It was led by Thomas Phellippes. Richard Baines works for him – or used to do so. Even Masters of Cyphers need protection sometimes –

and that was what Baines was there for. He's a roaring boy, a bully, a quick man with a knife.'

'And where does your ancient intelligencer owe his loyalty now?' asked Tom quietly.

'Wherever Thomas Phellippes owes his – or so I would believe.'

'And where does this code-master Phellippes roost?' Tom glanced up from the task of pulling up his sodden boots.

'At Essex House.'

'So,' said Tom thoughtfully, tightening his belt at last, 'the company of Sir Francis, his secret servants, have fallen into two camps now that Master Secretary is dead. You and those few of your men left alive seem to be working for the Council, reporting to Lord Hunsdon, looking into the deaths of a shocking number of important men. Phellippes and his crew work for the Earl of Essex. And these are the men that are set to kill us all if they can.'

'That would seem to be the bare bones of the situation.'

'But you have no idea why this should be.'

'I have ideas in plenty, Master Musgrave. But none for the common ear – or even your own at present. Come. There have been enough confidences. We have work at hand and an ounce of proof is better than a tun of speculation.'

Tom and Poley's clothes were still damp but – to begin with – warm. And they smelt of vinegar instead of ordure. Had either man been particularly worried about their state of dress, the bustle that followed their re-clothing would have distracted them. For there was to be no further hesitation. Pausing only at Blackfriars to gather Tom and Ugo's best, they were off to Old Jewry and Wormwood House.

Talbot had agreed to join them, pronouncing himself weary of the simple tasks of being Bishop's Bailiff and keen to see real action once again of the sort he had enjoyed with the Master of Logic at Nijmagen. His men declined the opportunity to risk a moonlight flit from one end of the city to the other, armed to the teeth under the eyes of the Watch – this leading only to the opportunity to search in secret darkness through a cursed house full of madness, demons and death. 'You can hardly blame them,' said Ugo solidly. 'I could do with some Dutch Courage myself.'

It was a breathless, overcast night. The moon was just rising as Tom tore himself away from the delicious farewells of Constanza and ran out of the Elephant, across Bankside and down to Molestrand Dock. A couple of wherries took them swiftly across to Blackfriars Steps and a link boy guided them swiftly up Water Street, for it was not yet ten. Up in Tom's rooms they gathered swords and daggers, making sure that each of them was well supplied with cold steel before Ugo began to pass out his own special wares. Poley's wheel lock and Tom's snaphaunce revolver were out of commission. Ugo kept his own revolver and replaced Poley's with a single-barrelled weapon. 'We'll need to prepare for silent work as well,' said Tom quietly, and for himself and Talbot he pulled off one of Ugo's shelves a pair of small cross-bows which were carefully designed to fire either from shoulder like a small musket or hand like a big pistol. With each came a belt-full of slim iron-headed bolts. Thinking ahead, and dismissing the bulk of what Poley had told him earlier, Tom took a second rapier and slung it across his right thigh for when they summoned Will to join them. Then, with Tom armed like the ambidexter Spaniard, they were off into the night.

As they ran out of Blackfriars into Carter Lane, the great bell at Bow rang out. The bustle in the dark roadway ahead of them began to thin out almost magically. Link boys began to run home to their beds, taking their blazing torches with them. By the time the four companions reached the end of the long thoroughfare and crossed into Maidenhead Lane, the only lights still on were the torches by the doors of civic men slow to extinguish their civic duties. The bustle had died to the extent that they could hear the Bellman in the distance calling, 'Remember the clocks, look well to your locks . . .'

By the time they had followed Maidenhead Lane into Friday Street and run northward into Cheapside, all the mighty heart of London seemed to have slowed in sleep. Under the incon-

stant moon, the roadway – widest in London with the Cheapside Market packed away until dawn tomorrow – was a silver
river running between great black cliffs of shadow. And it was
the shadows that claimed them, for in spite of Poley's bravado,
they really did not want to show Lord Henry's commission to
the City Watch – most of whom were illiterate and many of
whom were ill conditioned and ill tempered.

They paused at the corner of Old Jewry and held a breathless
conversation, the burden of which was that Tom should run on
to call Will if he so desired. The rest of them would wait for
them here for a count of a thousand. If Tom had not returned
by then – or if anything served to disturb them in the meantime
– they would proceed to Wormwood House and all would meet
there in any case. It seemed a sound plan.

Tom ran off up Old Jewry. The swiftest way to Will's
lodgings would take him past Wormwood House and then
up Lothbury, Throckmorton and Threadneedle. He had it all
planned ahead in his mind, knowing every twist and turn;
hoping Will would not mistake him for a hooker when he
tapped on the window and call down the Watch on him. But
thoughts of the hooker's long hooked pole designed to pull
valuables out of unlatched windows – indeed, thoughts of Will
and all – were driven out of his head as he came close to
Wormwood House itself.

The house stood on the corner of Old Jewry and Lothbury
Street. It was a great old mansion, built the better part of a
century since when men such as the first Lord Outremer were
opening up the great trade routes in spices and herbs such as the
one that gave the place its name. It had been added to by the
lord lately deceased and it now stepped out into the air, storey
overhanging storey, to blot out the moon-blue sky. There was a
maze of rooms within, by all accounts, a wilderness of corridors. There was even, at the inmost corner of the place, a tower,
so Tom had heard. The swift patter of his footsteps slowed as
Wormwood House reared its shadowed head over him. He was
no more superstitous than the clearest thinking humanist of his
time and yet he could not help a shudder at being so close to the

place alone. But then his fears were set aside by circumstance.

For, deep within the stygian darkness of the place he saw a pinprick of light. The fact of it stopped him in his tracks. His shoulder was already brushing the sill of the window where the light shone. He pressed his ear against the ancient glass, squinting to see where the pinprick of brightness was coming from. And the instant that his ear touched the icy pane he heard the moaning. His hair stirred and for a moment he thought it was alive, seeking to crawl from his very head. But if his hair was stirring it was the only part of him that was. His heart seemed to have stopped and his very blood was frozen in his veins. The moaning went on and on. Hoarse, desperate, as though uttered by a throat long past the necessity of breathing. Something within Tom associated the sound with the light – perhaps because they were both so ghastly and unvarying. And once his wits had stirred themselves that far, he was able to drag first his mind then his body into motion. It seemed that he had found Master Seyton, the Chamberlain of Wormwood – but he had found trouble into the bargain.

Down Old Jewry he stole, his eye enthralled by the way the light blinked out and on again as he passed along the deserted roadway. At the corner of the two grand old streets stood the main door of the accursed place, and it stood wide. Out through the black throat of it there issued that almost silent moaning. Had he not known of it, had he not been listening for it, Tom would never have heard it. Those few – like the Watch, perhaps – scurrying past this haunted and accursed place, would never have heard it. Would probably never have stopped to see the door standing wide open. But Tom could hear and Tom could see. And Tom was going to investigate.

There were two steps, hollowed by a century's busy traffic, up into Wormwood House. Tom took them a'tiptoe. Then a low sill separated the outside step from the inner flags of the hall. Here, on the very lip of the threshold, Tom hesitated. Should he close the door? He thought not. The only people he was like to be keeping out were his friends, due in a count of five hundred or so. Whoever had been here to leave all unguarded was gone, apart from the moaning man they left behind. And the Watch were hardly likely to be a trouble in this place – in this place least of all, in fact.

Ten careful steps took Tom into the centre of that cavern of darkness – a place confirmed only by his ears registering accoustics far beyond his comprehension. But in the coaly darkness of the place, the thread of sound ran true, guiding him under a bulk of greater darkness into smaller, more confined environs. And here, distantly, but blessedly, he got his first flicker of that distant, golden light. The sight of it betrayed him into confidence and he strode through an open portal into a passageway, walking as though that distant star were a sun on midsummer day. He crashed into a toppled chair and nearly tripped headlong. Then, feeling ahead of himself at knee height, he soon realised that the whole hallway was filled with the wreckage of smashed and scattered furnishings. He piled it against the walls, worrying only about clearing a passageway through to the light and the gathering sound.

At last, he came into the source of both. It was a great wide parlour with a kitchen area two steps below it. The whole place looked like the hall and he had to toss wrecked furniture hither and thither as he fought his way across to the only piece of furniture in the place still standing. It was an ancient table. At it sat a man whose face seemed to be in like condition to the rest of the house. It was puffed with beating and seemed so black with shadows and bruises that it might have been the face of a blackamoor. The jaws were wedged wide and the cheeks puffed by a gag forced immoveably between his jaws, round which the unvarying moan seemed to be his loudest cries for help. All that seemed to be holding him erect was the great candle which stood between his hands, into the searing heat of which his face would have fallen had he moved. At first, Tom could not work out why the old man – battered and blood-bespattered to be sure – did not simply pick up the candle and either toss it aside or use it to light his way to the Watch. But then Tom noticed the old man's hands, where they lay half engulfed by molten wax from the candle.

They were nailed to the table.

And that, in fact was only the first part of a series of revelations. The old man could not move the candle because of his hands. He could not blow it out because of his gag. He could not use his face to blot it out at the price of a burn and some wax-scalding because the blackness on his skin was not bruising – it was gunpowder. And the great gag, dribbling black spittle down the old man's chin, was a bag of powder too. He could not pull back from the searing heat because of the way his hands were nailed yet he dare not rock forward at all or the candle would ignite the powder and blow his head off there and then.

Tom rushed forward, hurling a shattered stool to one side, just as the old man's face fell forward into the candle flame. The searing pain and the shattering noise jerked the swollen eyes into a narrow glare. The ancient body heaved until only the hands held it grotesquely in place. The candle-light spread to reveal a skinny chest and brutally abused shoulders.

Tom swung round the table and caught the mouth of the powder-bag gag, easing it out of the old man's mouth. It was a solid bag of the finest leather, swollen to the size of a fist with the powder. On it were embroidered in fine gold thread the letters S and D all interwoven in a strangely ornate fashion. But Tom had no great liberty for examination, for at once the moaning choked into words. 'Bring her back, *señor*. She will harm no one. She says nothing and lives as quiet as the mouse on my master's arms. She has not stirred abroad this five year, *señor*, and speaks no word to any. I did not lie when I told you. Never a word. Never a word to any. I have kept her by the book with kindness and never needed the whips. Oh do not take her to Bedlam sir, I beg you in my master's name who gave her charge to me.'

Tom stood by the old man, thinking nothing of his raving for the time being. 'Master Seyton,' he hazarded. 'Is it Mistress Kate you speak of?'

'Oh, you cannot trick me, you Spanish devil,' spat the old man, full of fire and choler suddenly. 'You know we talk of

Mistress Margaret whom you have stolen away from me. Burn down the house as you burned down Mousehole. Burn it down around my ears and have done.'

Tom knelt on one knee and looked up into Chamberlain Seyton's ruined face. 'I am no Spaniard but Tom Musgrave, Master of Defence. I have come to aid you and yours, Master Seyton, but I must know what has gone on here and I must know of Mistress Kate if you have news of her.' His hand went up the old man's back to the shoulders, supporting him as he crouched on the three-legged stool they had left him on. Seyton gave a great shudder and leaned back, no longer having to hold himself erect, no longer having to save his crucified hands. He looked Tom in the face and something moved in the blood-red slits behind the blackened ruins of his eyes. Tom wished that it had been sanity and recognition; willingness to impart the information that he needed, but it was not.

'If you are not the whoreson Spaniard,' whispered the old man with a lunatic's cunning, 'then why do you wear his swords? You are a creature compounded of lies. You and your crew and the bookseller's boy this morning whose volumes brought my lady no peace. No peace . . .'

Tom only half heard the end of this diatribe for he was looking down, thunderstruck, at the hilt of his own sword on one side, and the hilt of the second one he'd brought for Will on the other. And he realised with a lurch like a body-blow what the old man had been talking about. But when he looked up, the ancient chamberlain was dead. Still leaning back against his shaking hand, still staring with those mad red eyes. But stone dead for all that. Tom had seen enough death to know. The weight of the frail old body became well-nigh unbearable.

With the reverence due to such simple bravery in age, Tom moved the candle forward and laid the ancient head between the tormented hands, then he put the bag of powder in his belt and set to searching for some other light. He had only just begun when a crash from the end of the corridor informed him that the other three had arrived. He went with the candle and guided them through. Then they shared the table with the ancient corpse and held a swift council of war. The bag of powder that had served as a gag was examined in as much detail as the candle would allow, but even Poley could make nothing of the ornate initials D.S. or S.D. And so they proceeded to do what they had actually come to do.

They searched in pairs, starting in the wreckage of the parlour and spreading out into the devastation of the rest. Dining chambers, reception chambers, galleries and sleeping chambers all were smashed and shattered. Public rooms and private, owners' quarters and servants', living rooms, working rooms and storage rooms – it was all the same. 'Such destruction,' whispered Talbot Law, awed, to his partner, Tom. 'It bespeaks great madness or great rage.'

'Or a great search for a small thing,' said Tom. 'But how could this much have been done with no one coming to investigate or offer help? Where was the Watch?'

'Where are they now?' asked Talbot. Then he answered his own question. 'Paid to look the other way.'

But search as they might – exchanging information when their paths crossed – neither pair could find sight nor sign of Poley's Mistress Kate nor Seyton's silent Margaret, one or the other or both of them carried away by the Spaniard who always wore two swords. And, thought Tom grimly, if the Spaniard had exercised such fiendish cruelty upon a harmless old man and left him like the Inquisition just for amusement's sake, then Morton's fears for Mistress Kate's lingering, torturous death were well founded indeed, and he held out no great hopes that the lady Margaret would fare much better.

CHAPTER SIXTEEN

The Mad Room

Tom found the doorway first, though it hardly lay hidden now. Obviously it had once stood in a secret corner of an apparently little-used upper gallery, covered by a tapestry; but now the tapestry was torn asunder and the doorway gaped like every other doorway in the ravaged house. 'This place is like Nijmagen was, when we had looted it and left,' he whispered to Talbot. The old soldier gave one grim nod, and side by side they stepped over the rags of tapestry, through the ravished portal and into the stairwell of the tower.

Round about the outer walls the circular staircase wound, up the shaft of the ancient stone keep and into a turret room. The room was entered by a trap that stood as open as all the other doors. Candle high in one hand, and sword in the other in spite of the oppressive silence of the place, Tom went first. Like Leviathan arising from the depths, he rose into a circular room whose thin, leaded windows nevertheless gave a sight of the moon and stars on every hand. But it was not the heavens beyond those walls that held the secret agent rapt. It was the realisation of what a hell had lain within them. For this was a mad room. Like any public chamber in Bedlam, just outside Bishops Gate, not so far north of here, where the good folk of London could go on a Sunday to see the lunatics chained, stripped, abused and whipped, this was a room designed to hold a lunatic. There were straps and manacles secured to the heavy wooden frame of the bed – though the bedding itself seemed soft and clean – or it must have been so before it was torn asunder and strewn. The posts at the bed's foot were particularly strong and both bolted to the floor. There were manacles and iron belts secured to both of them. The cuffs and waistband, Tom noted automatically, were set for the slimmest of figures.

By the largest of the windows, looking down over the bustle of Stocks Market and Dowgate to the river beside the Steelyard, was a standing lectern half the size of a table. No chair or stool. The books that might have lain upon it or on the little shelf beside it were all strewn in tatters on the floor. Around the bare and brutal walls hung a range of medicinal whips and scourges which ranged from a few light cords such as might be used on a child to the sort of instruments usually reserved for the cart's tail, Tyburn, Paul's Churchyard and Bedlam itself, to whip out the madness as prescribed by medical wisdom for the benefit of the patient. They were all dusty, however, and clearly wanted use.

And what made the room doubly sad in Tom's eyes was the scrap of rag that Talbot was holding now. It fitted so well with the settings of the manacles and the lightness of most of the scourges, for it was a piece of a woman's dress. This, Tom realised, was where Mistress Margaret had lived, until the Spaniard had come with his men, torn the house to pieces searching, tortured the ancient Seyton and spirited poor mad Meg away.

But where was Poley's Kate in all of this? Why had Morton sent her here? What had she seen when she came – and what had she learned? What did she know and where was she now?

What had Poley called her? Tom thought, as his mind raced. My Lady Determination. If Mistress Kate had been here then she would have contrived to leave a message somehow. Yet the old man had not known the name – unless he was just too taken up with Mistress Margaret, whom he must have tended and shielded for at least a year since the rest of the family died. In such circumstances who would give a second thought to some woman but lately arrived when such a trust had been broken in such a manner?

'We must get Poley up here,' breathed Tom to Talbot, but the instant that the Bailiff looked down through the trap he said, 'He's on his way.'

A moment later the mad room was more crowded than it was likely to have been in a long, long time. Poley looked around, his expression much as Tom's had been. 'Mistress Margaret,' he said, his voice dull.

Tom nodded. 'But what of Mistress Kate?' he mused.

'What indeed?' wondered Poley, clearly shaken, looking around with a vain attempt to mask his confusion and anxiety.

'Think, man. Morton must have sent her here a day since. This was done tonight or the old man and the candle would have died long since. If she came, would she have lingered?'

'Surely that would depend on what she sought,' chimed in Talbot.

'Aye, but Master Poley here does not know what she sought. Do you?'

'No.' Against his inclination, belief and usual practice; clearly under the greatest duress, Poley followed Tom's more open approach, certain that all here were confederates and there was none to overhear. 'Morton had discovered something he wished to impart to me but he was killed before he could do so.'

Save that he wrote the import of it in a letter, thought Tom, but he said nothing for the moment.

'Since that time,' continued Poley, 'almost all the men he worked with have died too. Everyone who might have known what he discovered is dead or under threat – including Tom, as we know, and myself. What Kate knows only Morton knew, and why he sent her here perhaps even Kate did not know. It is something about this house and how and why all who lived here died. It might even have been to do with that poor old man downstairs and the mad woman they held up here. I do not know. And I do not know how long Kate would have stayed for I do not know what it was she sought. And I do not know whether she was here when Morton's assassin arrived with the other men who did this. I hope she was not, or she will be beyond all help now if they have taken her.'

'Well enough,' said Tom. 'But we have not yet reached the limit of where logic might take us. Master Poley, if we know nothing about why Mistress Kate came, can we at least guess how she came?'

Poley frowned – as did the others. Tom expounded. 'Would she have come as herself. *Per exemplum*, we know Master Nicholas Blunt of Islington had little enough business on the Bankside; but Nick o' Darkmans was like a Drake or Raleigh among the thieves' brotherhood working there. Is the same true of your Kate? Would Mistress Kate So-and-so have had reason to call at Wormwood House? Or would she have come in disguise like an actor or a coney-catcher? And, if so, was there a disguise she favoured? One she would most likely have used?'

Poley answered at once. 'For herself, she would have had no business here. Therefore she would have come disguised. I have often met her at Paul's Churchyard, and I have seen her at play there as though she were at the Rose with Master Shakespeare. I have seen her be the country maiden of Puritan bent, up to hear the sermons. I have seen her pretend to be the courtier of fashion jetting in the walk – almost to the bawd, though I have never seen her whoring. I have seen her act the earnest young assistant to the myriad booksellers there. But that is all. I have never seen her singing "Cherry Ripe" nor bearing a milk yoke such as country wenches do. Only of the better sort . . .'

Poley's voice trailed off, for he had clearly lost Tom's attention. While the others stood gaping, Tom had fallen on his knees, candle aloft and sword cast carelessly aside. And he was gathering up the scraps of paper on the floor. The remains of the pamphlets and the books such as were sold in their hundreds every day at St Paul's Churchyard.

'The old man,' he explained. 'With his dying breath he talked of the bookseller's boy. It must have been your Mistress Kate in disguise, Poley. She was here today, and some of these at least must be her wares.'

Talbot Law held the light high; the Bishop's Bailiff, apparently, being above such common pastimes as scrabbling on the floor. The other three gathered the scraps of paper together. 'These have just been wantonly destroyed,' said Tom. 'There was surely no design to find any message hidden in them. And yet they searched for something small that might be hidden anywhere. Even in a book or pamphlet such as these.'

'Particularly in a pamphlet,' said Poley grimly, 'if we may judge from the state of these. As you find them, pass them to me and I will try to piece them together if I can.' After a while, he continued, in Tom's fashion, 'They searched for more than Mistress Margaret, then. But did they find what they sought once they had discovered her?'

'No,' said Tom roundly. 'Had they found what they sought, then their destruction would have stopped. It did not stop – therefore they did not find it.'

'*Quod erat demonstrandum*,' said Talbot. 'You should still consider Bartholomew Fair if they close the theatres again.'

'But stay, there is more. I rival Doctor Dee tonight. For the thing they sought might have been concealed anywhere – or they would never have broken everything. In a padded chair-seat, behind a picture, even in a mad girl's bedding; in a pamphlet. Most especially in a pamphlet. It is of paper, then, and written or printed. Some document of legal weight and import.'

'A map of the route to Cathay?' hazarded Ugo, unexpectedly romantically, thinking no doubt of how the Lords of Outremer had made their enormous fortune.

'A chart of the Spice Islands,' Talbot took up the theme.

'I'd hazard something more immediate and practical. What about you, Master Poley?' asked Tom. Poley merely grunted in reply, consumed with trying to rebuild the ruined books upon the lectern by the window.

Tom sat at more ease on the edge of the bed. 'We have a house recently bereft of its lord and his family,' he said. 'A house about to fall into the hands of the next in line, Hugh Outram, Baron Cotehel, friend to the dazzling young earls of

Southampton and Essex, desperate to keep up with the brightest and most dangerous stars at Court. But within the death-house, what do we find? An ancient chamberlain who remains in spite of all; remains against all reason. And why? To tend a mad woman in the tower. Who should this woman be? Who could ever garner such loyalty in the face of her insanity?'

'The daughter of the house,' spat Poley over his shoulder. 'Half a wit could see it clear, but that you obscure all with your exercises of logic.'

'The daughter of the house,' agreed Tom cheerfully. 'The last of the dead lord's line. Beloved daughter of a father richer than Croesus, the ballast of whose very ships is gold instead of stone, or so the story goes. And what might the Spaniard and his cohorts be searching for among the writings of the house, therefore?'

'They seek the old man's will,' snapped Poley.

And Tom swung round then, his lips thin and his level brows twisted in a frown. 'Right, Master Poley. The will. And they do not have it. You see how swiftly and clearly we can move forward when you say what you think and tell us what you know instead of equivocating with half-truths and secrets. If we sit atop a pyramid of mystery and murder, as you say, then you above all others hold the plans to the place and we need to see at least a part of them. Can you begin to imagine what they will do to Mistress Margaret, mad or not, if they think she might know where the will of Lord Outremer might be hidden?'

'There,' said Poley, and this time it was his turn to let his rage have rein. 'There. In that very question lies the reason I will never share the whole truth with you. You would charge off to save the fate of one mad girl in the face of the plague of treason and assassination that holds us in its grip. You exercise your logic well, Master Musgrave, but you exercise it on a trifle, on a toy. Did you not listen when I read Morton's missive to you? Have you no idea what he suspected?'

'Aye,' said Tom. 'Well enough.'

'Then expound again, O Master of Logic, whom nothing ever escapes. Cut this Gordian knot of black satanity for me with the shining sword of your reason.'

Tom, sitting in the wreckage of the mad woman's bed, looked up at Robert Poley then, his sympathy stirred by the man's frustrated rage. 'Very well,' he said. 'Without the cant and rigmarole, in plain blunt terms. Your intelligencer Morton feared that one of the Spaniards currently kicking their heels at Essex House is an assassin. A man who can kill by blade or knife or more darkly subtle means. He believed that this man or another like him has found employment here regularly in the past five years, working at the behest, perhaps, of Essex or Southampton or Outram or some other of their dangerous circle. The assassin's employment has been political and personal. He has added his dangerous wisdom to the ravages of the plague and so the senior line of Lord Outremer's family have all died out – all but the mad girl in the attic.

'But, feared Morton, and fears Master Poley, all too clearly, there have been others dying suddenly over recent years, dying mysteriously before their time, suddenly clearing paths to power and wealth, as Hugh Outram's path is now so clear to Lord Outremer's titles, houses and fortune.

'But his investigation did not begin here. His suspicions were not aroused here – but at Lathom House. So, I surmise, he and you – and the Council – fear that Lord Strange, who died two months since, died of poison and murder. And, said Morton's message to Master Poley, one such also died at Kenilworth, or rather at Buckstones. That could only be Lord Robert Dudley, the Earl of Leicester, the Queen's own darling and strong right hand, at the end of Armada year. And another died less than a league up the road at St Augustine's Papey hard by Bevis Marks, halfway between this place and Bedlam. To wit Sir Francis Walsingham a little more than four years since – Mr Secretary Walsingham the secret councillor, unmasker of plots and master of intelligence, for whom, I guess, Master Poley here has worked. If

Morton has discovered that even such men as those were not safe, 'tis no wonder he beset his house with traps and sought to hide himself behind an actor's mask, as poor Kit Marlowe did before him.'

Poley was white. 'Do you know what you are saying, man? Do you not see where your precious logic has led you? You talk of treasons so terrible it is treason even to think of them. A breath of such thinking goes outside this room and we are all fodder for Topcliffe and his monstrous machines. We would die to a man like Babbington, choked to the very edge of death at Tyburn but watching our guts and private parts burn in the hangman's brazier. Forget your Master Marlowe blinked out on a summer's evening like an ant beneath an impatient heel, here and gone in the blink of an eye. I saw it done to Babbington and his crew of plotters slowly and by the book and I tell you young Chidiock Tichbourne was still alive and screaming when the horses ripped him asunder into quarters.

'Yes, I worked for Mr Secretary Walsingham and it was I who brought down Babbington and his traitorous confederates; I who brought down Mary Queen of Scots and led her to the headsman. But in the face of this, even I am helpless. And so, I fear, are the Council for whom I work.'

'Master Robert,' said Tom gently, using the man's Christian name to call him back from the horrors he was all too clearly reliving. 'What is truly dangerous about this is that you believe it to be true and yet you fear even to talk of it. You fear to talk of it even to us who are your best help, your only hope. Because of this, secret treasons and unsuspected murders done in the past are starting to happen again and Morton somehow has used the deaths of this poor family to prove that the earlier deaths were in fact assassinations. People are dying, now – this very day – all around you because you believe what Morton believed to be true, and you cannot seem to call a halt to the slaughter because you cannot get your grip upon the heart of it.'

'That at least is the truth,' said Poley, more quietly. 'It is a monstrous thing. It has grown slowly, unsuspected and in secret. When Master Secretary Walsingham and we dealt with Ridolfi, Babbington and all the rest, we had a view of the plot like hunters hounding the hart. We were able to take action, to cause the plots to misfire under our eyes and within our own control. But this is different. This has become a monstrous thing with its roots and branches twisting from the stews to the throne room; yet it is a hydra without one single throat to cut, one single head to lop.'

'Then we must find that throat and that head,' said Tom. 'But in the meantime we must also look to Mistress Kate and Mistress Margaret if we can, before their deaths are added to the growing list.'

'So, Master Poley,' said Ugo, solidly, practically, unshaken in the face of such terrifying treason, 'have you found any messages hidden in the books?'

And Poley himself looked quite surprised when he answered, 'Yes, I have.' Then, in the face of Tom's cold stare, he added, 'I was about to tell you when the Master of Logic tempted me into a forbidden conversation, like Mephistophilis in Master Marlowe's play.'

Tom put that sinister little aside into the purse of his memory as he crossed to look at what Poley had laid out on the lectern. It was a copy of an old pamphlet newly reprinted, a popular text about the treatment of madness by Dr Andrew Boorde, called 'The Second Book of the Breviary of Health'. 'You see how it opens?' asked Poley, tracing the writing with his finger across the rags of paper he had carefully fitted together. ' "First, in the chamber where the patient is kept in, let there be no pictures or painted cloths about the bed or the chamber . . ." You see that? Now, observe how these marks signal and add to words within the writing. Your Master of Cyphers now abed would appreciate this, Tom. For see how the pamphlet goes of sweet savours and study and merry communication before threat of fear and punishments, but warm meat and cassia fistula and epithyme. But see how another message is pricked out and added to with a mark here and a cross there.'

'I see what has been done,' said Tom. 'I do not yet see what the cypher says.'

'I will translate: "b patient m i goe about to seek the srchr but i fear one man and go where he is punished armaddia man".'

CHAPTER SEVENTEEN

The Searcher of Jewry

R obert Poley lived in outside the northern wall in Hog
Lane, where he lodged with Master Yeomans, an elderly
cutler with a trade in the city, and slept with his buxom wife
Mistress Joan, as inclination and occasion arose. Tom found
him alone next morning when he arrived unfashionably early,
showing precious little evidence of having gone to bed at all and
threatening to return to his old untrusting ways. But Tom had
gone back to Blackfriars after the business in Wormwood
House had come to a close, for he had managed at least to
change out of his damp and offensively odorous clothes and
was willing to put up with Poley's thin lips and dark looks.
Also, he brought with him a gallon of ale, a loaf of new bread
and a cheese for breakfast. 'I got these from a stall outside
Bedlam Gate on the way here,' he informed his tired host
cheerfully. 'I came along Old Jewry and up through Bishops
Gate. I was hard put to push past the crush outside Wormwood
House. The Watch discovered the old chamberlain dead within
just before the City Gates opened this morning, apparently. No
one has any idea what's afoot there, so I am told. What sense
have you made of the messages, many and various – starting
with that from Mistress Kate?'

As he talked, Tom had been tearing up the bread and
breaking the crumbly cheese. Poley made no verbal answer,
but accepted a pile of food in exchange for a page of close

writing and looked for a couple of tankards as Tom read Kate's message fully transcribed.

> Be patient, Morton. I go nearby to find the Searcher at first. But I am frightened of one man and I will go to where he is held. (That will be to Bridewell for) he is an Armada man.

Tom looked up. 'All this in so few words?'

'I add a little commentary, here and there, knowing the lady and the situation.'

'So she still thinks Morton is alive,' mused Tom. 'Were they close?'

Poley shrugged. 'I think not. They worked together because I put them together like horses in harness. But they came from different worlds and Morton was never like to climb up into My Lady Kate's for all his pretty smile and winning ways.'

Tom decided to follow that line of enquiry later. After he had met My Lady, perhaps. In the meantime there were more important aspects to the lady's message. 'Are there any prisoners from the Armada still being held in Bridewell? I had thought them all dead long since.'

'A few. Desperate and hardy men, too full of the Devil to die. Dangerous and friendless. Too risky to release, too little thought of in Cadiz to warrant diplomacy or ransom.'

'Such men as our Spaniards might wish to contact. With information or wisdom to share?'

'Perhaps. The elder of our Spaniards is well enough known here and there and at Court come to that. It is Don Antonio Perez. You know his story, I am sure.'

'Yes,' said Tom shortly. 'But such a man as Perez who has been Secretary of State to Philip of Spain and an acknowledged poisoner and spy, would be just such a man as to consort with the ambidexter assassin, S.D., and with desperate, secret survivors of the Armada, since all are Spanish.'

'Perhaps. But he is an acknowledged traitor to Spain, has sold Philip's secrets to Henry of France and will tell anyone that listens any secrets that they list. He sits high in Essex's eye at present. He is shortly to publish a book of his relations, I understand, and will dedicate it to Essex, Southampton, Outram and the rest. But I still have no knowledge of your ambidexter other than his initials. His lover, like as not.'

'It is not their inclinations that disturb me. It is their intentions. And their abilities. Perez is a poisoner, or a man that consorts with poisoners. Morton mentioned poisoners in his letter to you. It was a reference to the play at the Rose. The Man in Mantua is an apothecary who sells poisons to the lover Romeo.'

'That play's a thing that disturbs me. Rapiers and poisons and public disorder. It would be bad enough if it was all simply on stage; but it is spreading out too readily into the world at large. And more than two thousand saw it yesterday alone I am told. It is all the rage. If I had my way I'd close it forthwith and let Master Shakespeare pass the time of day with Master Topcliffe.'

'You distract yourself, Master Poley. We need to find the Searcher before we close the Rose. And we need to look for Mistress Kate and her sinister Don in Bridewell. How in God's name does she propose to get into Bridewell?'

'I sometimes wonder how in God's name she keeps out of Bridewell. But you are right. We must follow her footsteps if we are to track her down safely. To the Searcher of Jewry, then.'

'At the very least, we should be able to learn what it was she wanted to know, even if she never got to learn it for herself.'

The Vicar of St Margaret Lothby, through whose parish Old Jewry ran, was an arrogant, opinionated and unpleasant man. He was very much of the new Protestant stamp, with no sense of the structure of Society and his responsibilities to his betters therein. He had direct communication with God's truth and that put him far beyond any responsibility to man – except to lecture and bully him towards his very doubtful salvation. With women he had no truck at all, being vessels of lust and pools of filth, causes of mens' downfall. Angels to the girdle, perhaps; but very devils beneath. And on the rock of this little man's petty obduracy, clearly, the vessel of Kate's investigation had foundered.

'Aye,' said the Reverend Word-of-the-Lord Parris, 'there was a woman here. A very trull from her dress and manner, demanding I tell her where our Searcher is to be found. I sent her on her way to church in her own parish, wherever that may be, and recommended her to her knees weeping and praying for marriage and motherhood according to the Word of the Lord.'

'A tall woman, well-set, with red hair and brown eyes. Fashionably dressed, like as not and softly spoken?' asked Poley quietly, while Tom shifted from foot to foot, thinking that a sound thrashing might bring this young jackanapes swiftly to the better.

'As to her person, it was as you describe. As to her attire, it would have shamed the veriest bawd. As soon as she left I called the Watch and set them after her. An arrant, jetting bawd with all her wares on display like a trull with her oranges on a tray. A compound of lust and whoredom, all frills and furbelows with the breast uncovered, a veritable valley of the shadow . . .'

'The very dress Her Majesty wore but last week,' whispered Poley, his voice like sand on silk. 'Uncovered, as befits a maiden lady. And as we have Her Majesty in mind, you should be aware that My Lady Kate Shelton, of whom you speak, on whom you set the Watch in God's name, is second cousin to the Queen. Her family has been wardens of Hunsdon Hall for generations and she could have your Brownist cant lashed or racked out of you tomorrow, did she so choose.'

'I fear neither she nor you. I serve a greater—'

'Call not your God down on my head, man, or I will have you at Paul's Churchyard – and for whipping, not for preaching.'

'You mistake me, Master Poley. I meant that I serve the new Lord of Wormwood himself. Baron Cotehel has been here to talk to me now that his title to the lands and possessions of the late Lord Outremer has been agreed. I have his ear at Court, sir, and he has that of Lord Essex. And my Lord Essex has the Queen's ear I am told. So I fear neither you nor Lady Shelton, if she is indeed a lady. But I will help you out of charity. The woman you seek is Hagar Kinch. If you would find her, ask first at the Poultry Counter, for she lives hard by.'

Poley turned to go at that, having had his belly-full of Master Parris. But Tom lingered. 'Was it recently you talked to Baron Cotehel?' he asked.

Parris enjoyed boasting of his influential contacts, clearly. He was much more forthcoming with Tom. 'Indeed. But two days since. He came in the evening, for evensong, and afterwards we talked, almost until the Bellman stirred. Such an earnest and well-conditioned young man, mindful of what is due to the Ministry of the Lord. He promises well in himself, and promises much for this parish when he comes into his own.'

'And he mentioned the Searcher?'

'In passing only. It was she of course who took away the body of my predecessor here as well as the corpses of the family at Wormwood during the Great Visitation a year since. He wished to ensure, he said, that she too received her just desserts.'

'It is as well, perhaps, he told Kate nothing,' said Tom as they pushed their way through the lingering press outside Wormwood House just as the Watch carried an ill-wrapped corpse out across the road, heading for the church they had just left and the tender mercies of Word-of-the-Lord Parris. 'Or she might well have been inextricably involved with the way the Searcher gets her just desserts from Baron Cotehel. We'll be lucky to find her alive.'

'Aye,' said Poley. 'From the sound of it we will.'

'And did you notice the timing of My Lord's visitation? He must have been sitting passing the time with this foolish young cockscomb while his Spanish cohort was nailing that old man to the table and carrying off the girl in the attic. But here is Poultry. Now where is the counter?'

They were lucky. The Searcher of Jewry was alive and easy to find. She was old, more than sixty years by her own calculation, for she claimed to have been born before the Queen, in the heyday of Good King Harry. Her body was twisted with age but her hands were big, square and capable. Her face was wizened, worldly-wise and toothless, but there was no doubting the wisdom and strength shining from her clear eyes. She took to Tom, for he was young and good looking and not too grand to flirt with her a little. And that was lucky, too. Poley began the conversation the instant they entered the broken-down shack behind the counter that she called home, having once been married to a long-dead bailiff.

Even before they began to speak, Poley produced a golden angel. The old woman looked a the coin calculatingly. 'It's information, then,' she said. 'The time's long past I could earn an angel any other way.'

Poley opened his mouth, but Tom spoke first, lightly. 'Mayhap, mistress, but I'll wager there was a time you could have called down more angels than sing in Heaven, had you a mind to it.'

The Searcher grinned and winked. 'For such a lad as yourself, I'd have opened Heaven's gates with no mention of an angel at all.'

'Still and all,' persisted Tom, 'angels of any kind must be few and far between with Word-of-the-Lord Parris at St Margaret's.'

'Nary an angel in sight up there,' she said. 'He's a hellfire man. And like to get to spend eternity in one of his own sermons, if I have any say in the matter. Which of course I won't. But ask away, gentlemen, and we'll see whether this old head has anything in it worth your precious gold.'

'It's there,' said Poley. 'But you may be hesitant to let it out. So remember, Mistress Kinch, that after the angel comes the stool at St Mary's Steps.'

'You'd never cry witch against me,' whispered the old woman.

'If I had to. With no more second thought than the Reverend Parris.'

'But there will be no need,' said Tom swiftly. 'My friend simply warns that we deal in the darkest matters here. There have been throats cut and rack-wheels a' creak over the matter so far. We need what you can tell us to cast a little light into some dark, dark rooms. You have heard what was done at Wormwood House a day since?'

'I heard old Master Seyton's been taken dead,' she said shifting uneasily. 'Found by the Watch, they said. I'd a mind to go there later myself—'

'No need,' said Tom, his mind leaping like a greyhound at the gate. 'Master Seyton was murdered last night and the house all but wrecked.' He paused a moment to let the information sink in. The woman's eyes widened as the implications hit the Searcher's mind. 'And those that did it ravished Mistress Margaret away with them.'

The broad hand rose shakily to the lined lips. The wise eyes bulged in horror. 'The information that you can give us will help us find her,' said Tom, quietly. 'Help us get her back before they hurt her.'

'Ask, then.'

Poley took over at once, switching from days to years past. 'It was you who took out the bodies of Lord Outremer and his family?'

'Aye. I've been Searcher here since Nell Field died the summer before Armada Year.'

'You registered their deaths and the cause of their deaths.'

'I registered their deaths with Master Scrope the Parish Clerk, God rest him. I said nothing of the cause.'

'It was not the plague, then?' asked Tom, latching on to the momentary equivocation.

'It may have been, for they were swollen up and black. Even the little boys. But that could have been because they had lain dead a week and more before Master Seyton came to find them. Midsummer it was, and all hot and wet, like this year. But I found no marks or special swellings upon them. No sores or buboes, such as cry out the plague. Master Seyton it was who found them, like I said. He'd been a week away and it seems they all died the day after he left. All in the house, except poor Mistress Margaret in the tower. He'd found them and laid them ready, tidied them up and such, before he called me and the parish. I checked, though, for it is my duty, before I reported to the clerk. But all I could tell him was what Master Seyton told me. They were dead and they had run mad before they died. I could see that of course because of the state of their fingers and their clothes. Mad the lot of them, mad as poor Mistress Margaret; and only she alive. Mad before them, Heaven send her grace, and mad long after.'

'Seyton away when they all died, you say?' said Poley, narrow-eyed. 'That was a monstrous piece of luck.'

'Ill luck for him, poor man. Coming back to that horror near addled his wits. Them all stark dead – his beloved master and mistress; his own wife and sons as was among the servants. The lord's four children, on whom he doted as though they were his own. And poor Mistress Margaret up in the tower a week with only the scraps he had left her and the pitcher of water to sustain her, near famished to death. And she must have heard it all going on, for it can't have been that they died in silence nor anything like it. He never left the house again.'

'He left it an hour since,' said Poley. 'Carried over to the church. They'll be calling for you soon, no doubt, to lay yet another body out.'

'This one won't be pretty either,' warned Tom gently. 'He died hard. And if he was a friend . . .'

'Aye, it makes it harder. When it's a friend.'

'Run mad, you said,' continued Tom after an instant's pause. 'He told you they had all run mad.'

'So he said. They had all run wild, convulsing, tearing themselves and each other, ripping away at clothes, walls and doors but none of them strong enough to go into the street and call for aid. Last summer, mind, they'd have never found any for the place was a forest of crosses. With Seyton back, they were planning to go to the country, he told me once. They were only waiting for him before they left the accursed place. More crosses than doors, it seemed sometimes, and the dead cart out every night. We took them up to the Pardon Yard from here, hard by Barbican. And that's where My Lord Outremer and all his household went. Death's no respecter of titles or power.'

'But you've helped Seyton look after Mistress Margaret, haven't you? During the last year?' persisted Tom.

'Lord love you, sir, how could I not? He was only a man after all. He knew nothing of women and their ways. Married a score of years and a father twice over, but the first time she had her monthly bleeding he was round to my door crying death and destruction. For I'm known as a wise woman locally. Wise woman, Master Poley, not witch.

'And I had been midwife to her in any case, all those years back when the little boy came. I'd brought in the new and laid out the old. Of course he came to me.'

Revelation sang in Tom's head like the Heavenly Choir itself. Poley pounced while the Master reasoned. 'A child you say? The mad girl had a child? A boy?'

'Yes. Early in Armada Year. She was run mad already and they had her locked up in the tower even then. A little boy it was. She doted on it and they let her keep it. Her mother and father would never look on her nor on the child, for there was never any father named for it – nor banns read nor vows exchanged. So it was Seyton and me as looked to it, poor little bastard mite. She was her own wet-nurse, though a lady born and should have been far above such things. And she doted on the babe. I'd watched her with it, or one of the serving girls would, for we never let her have hold of it alone. But then last summer my lord decided the child should go away and that's where Seyton was. Away with the child. Though it was a lovely lisping boy when last I saw him, five years old and sharp as a pin. None of his mother's madness there. He'll be turned six this summer. I don't know where he is, God love him. And never am like to now.'

Ten minutes later, Tom and Poley walked slowly past the great water cans outside the Mercer's Hall where Poultry ran into Cheapside. They were deep in conversation. 'We had best take this to Lord Hunsdon,' said Poley. 'And he'll need to take it to the Secretary. I dare not move and must not stay.'

'Nor even hesitate,' said Tom. 'They sought a will. I supposed it was a will that named a poor mad girl. A daughter to the dead lord, yes, but nothing of import. A botch in the plan; a roughness to be smoothed away. But now it is all changed. The mad woman has a sane son and the dead lord has a living heir and Baron Cotehel is suddenly second in line for the title, so his dogs are out again.

'They knew about Morton and his fears for the family. They know about you and me; they know about Kate and the Searcher back there. They must know about the boy or Seyton would still be sitting in Hell. If we do not act, we die . . .'

And even as he spoke, a white-faced apprentice came past at a run, crashing almost blindly into them. 'Where away so fast, lad?' asked Tom.

The wild-eyed boy swung round. 'I'm to run for the Watch. There's murder done.'

Tom caught the boy by the shoulder. 'Who?' he demanded. 'Where?'

'Mistress Kinch the Searcher,' he answered breathlessly. 'She was called to St Margaret's to lay out a corpse but as she crossed into Old Jewry a man walking past her reached over and cut her throat. Cut her throat in broad daylight, just like that and vanished before any could call hue and cry. A man all in black, they told me, and I must find Master Curberry, the Captain of the Watch.'

CHAPTER EIGHTEEN

The Raid on Bridewell

Tom and Robert Poley ran back at once, their eyes everywhere as they went, knowing that the Spaniard must be somewhere about. It had to be the Spaniard's handiwork – the swift execution had none of Baines's brutal stamp about it. If they saw him they would take him, hue and cry or no; whether the Watch were present or not. But there was no sign of him. Instead there was a bunch of onlookers crowded round the corner where the boy had said the murder had been done. With the necessary brusqueness of high office, Poley shoved the crowd around the body aside. Tom knelt by the Searcher as she lay, white as wax in the midst of a great puddle of blood. Typically, thinking to the end, her hands were clasped around her throat, trying to hold her blood in to the last. Her eyes stared fixedly into his as though trying to communicate some last, vital message. Some men believed, thought Tom, that the image of her murderer would be there, engraved upon the back of her eye, available to any who knew the correct necromantic spell. But he needed no magic to see who had done this. He eased the grasping fingers and laid bare the exact opposite to the last cut throat he had seen. The body under the rubbish pile outside Morton's lodgings had had his throat torn out as though by a wild dog – the work of a dull blade, of inferior quality, roughly wielded. Baines's work, thought Tom now, beginning to see clearly the differences between his opponents' handiwork. Here, however, lay a masterpiece of the assassin's art. Like Tom himself, like Will, like Morton, she would scarce have felt the blade slip in behind her Adam's Apple and slit through on its swift way out. The first she would have known about the serpent-swift bite of death was that first great spray of blood which soaked into the rags at her breast now, and the fact that when she tried to scream, nothing at all would come.

Tom glanced up at Poley. 'There is nothing we can do here. Let us haste away now or we will waste the morning talking to the Watch.'

Poley nodded and the pair of them shouldered their way back out of the crowds and turned south for the river at once. Poley was bound – more urgently now than ever – straight to White-hall in the hope that Lord Hunsdon was still there. But that hope was increasingly faint – for Lord Hunsdon was also Lord Chamberlain, responsible for running the Queen's household – as Essex, Master of the Horse, was responsible for moving it. And if the Queen was growing restless at Nonesuch Palace, then her Chamberlain had best be close at hand. Tom was bound for Bridewell, armed with Poley's commission from My Lord in his purse. They separated at the Steelyard steps, Poley's wherry-man unwilling to break a long westward run at Bridewell Stairs and Poley's urgency supporting him in this.

They were to meet by noon, however, back here at the Steelyard, though Tom had no idea why. He knew that, whatever their business there, they would have to be quick. His first student of the day was due to be in Blackfriars at one – then his time was full once again until six tonight.

The keeper of Bridewell's Black Book was so impressed with the commission that he did not even ask whether Tom was the Master Poley so trusted by the Lord Chamberlain and Her Majesty's Council. Together they looked through the admissions register, noting the names of the men and women brought here during the day, checking the times of their arrival and their destinations within the massive place. There had been no one called Shelton admitted at all. Caught between relief and concern, Tom was just turning away, when a thought struck him. 'May I see the book again?' he asked. And, while he checked through the names to see whether any bore the mark of Mistress Kate's peculiar brand of code, he fell into conversation with the man. 'I suppose you see most of the people you record here?'

'Most, aye. They stand before me to tell me their names for the book and wait while I assign them to their quarters. It is a huge place, this, and we are not a huge company to run it. It was a palace you know, until poor King Edward gave it to the city. 'Tis a weighty responsibility, recording all the comings and goings.'

'And you do it well. I shall mention it to the Council, rest assured. Do you call to mind a woman brought in earlier today? Brought by the Watch from St Martin's.'

'One of Vicar Parris's trulls? He's always calling whore on some girl or another. Then, often as not he's here to see 'em whipped in. We do it on the bare back here, sir, all clothing pulled down. And no telling where the whip will wander.'

'Aye, aye . . .' Tom's mind was elsewhere as his eyes scanned the columns of names recorded in handwriting that only served to make the spelling more impossible to decipher. 'Did you see any such today? A tall, well-set woman with red hair and clear brown eyes. Modishly dressed.'

'Oh, aye, I saw such a one and no mistake,' said the book-keeper roundly. 'Gave me the benefit of her wisdom, too – though as nothing to what she was saying to the poor men from the Watch. Hair like a fox and the tongue of a shrew. Now what did she call herself . . .'

But Tom had found her. 'Mistress Catherine Poley. Bawd.'

'You have it. Why, but that's . . .'

Tom had an instant to think. 'My wife,' he admitted, shame-facedly.

'Well, you're not the first, Master Poley, and you won't be the last. 'Tis quite the fashion, I am told, for ladies of the better sort to go whoring around the town these days. But if you're here to buy her out, you must see the governor, or better still the treasurer—'

'No, no.' Tom rose quickly. Mistress Kate had been here several hours – but she planned to try and make contact with a Spaniard in the Armada dungeons and that would likely take time. 'Let her stew for a little longer, eh?' he said to the book-keeper, man-to-man. And was rewarded with a large wink in return.

'They're all trulls at heart, Master Poley. You leave her with us and she'll learn to repent her ways. Come back at six this evening if you want to leave her that long, and see her whipped in with the others as I said. Fifteen lashes on their bare backs to welcome them. Then, if you'll take a homely man's advice, sir, you'll take the lady home and repeat the dose below the girdle that we have given her above. Then she'll mend her ways, doubt it not. "A woman, a cur and a walnut tree, the more you beat them, the better they be." '

Tom left without further comment, mentally swearing by all he held dear that he would be back for Kate before six. With or without the real Master Poley.

The Steelyard was a great maze of buildings on the riverside a couple of hundred yards upriver from the Bridge. Here the smaller boats and barges docked, having transferred part cargoes in the Pool below the Bridge or in Deptford where the big ships docked when they came in from Germany and the North. It was the headquarters in London of that great pan-Germanic political and trading empire called the Hanseatic League. Since the times of Harry the Great and his movement away from Rome and into the Protestant camp, the Steelyard had been the gateway to a wonderland of artistry and invention slowed only during the Catholic excesses of Bloody Mary and her husband Phillip, King of Spain, and, briefly, of England.

Tom could have been meeting Poley at the Steelyard for any of a thousand reasons – but the true one was the last he would ever have guessed. As Tom explained what he had discovered at Bridewell, Poley led him purposefully through a maze of corridors. His hurrying footsteps faltered only once – when Tom told him Kate's current alias. 'God's my life, she goes too far. I will leave her to the post and the whip. On my life I will. Catherine Poley. What of my good name now?'

'Your good name . . .' said Tom, carefully – for no one is more careful of his reputation than one who has been to prison. Poley had first been there for using a Catholic priest in a plot to seduce Mistress Joan Yeomans. He had needed neither priest nor prison to repeat the offence on a regular basis, by all accounts. 'Your good name will by no means be enhanced by having her stripped and whipped under the common eye. The Bookkeeper tells me that like as not the Reverend Parris will slip up there after evensong to see it done. Purely for spiritual reasons, I am sure.'

'Well, we must go in after her. And here is the best place of all to begin to make our plans.'

As he spoke, Poley pushed open a little door and swept Tom into a small shop. Behind a table stood a rotund man in a leather apron and thick spectacles. '*Guten tag*,' he welcomed them courteously. 'And how may I serve you gentlemens?'

'As you might expect,' said Poley, apparently to both of them, 'we are here in the Steelyard to buy a yard or two of steel.'

'Ah,' said the German with solid satisfaction.

'The best. The very best,' said Poley. 'For the Master of Defence, here.'

'Please to stand up straight, *Mein Herr*.'

Suddenly short of breath, like a boy at his first play, Tom stood.

'You use the right hand, *ja?*'

Tom nodded, and followed the German's instructions to the letter. He stretched out his arm and was measured from shoulder to fingertip, from armpit to wrist. He picked up and balanced a series of weights and hefted a series of rods while the German made careful notes. When it was all finished, the little man bustled off into a stockroom behind the shop. A moment later he returned with a length of steel. White as silver, it gleamed with wicked brilliance as it lay on the dark wood of the table. At one end there was a spike of steel stretching little more than a hand's breadth of slightly duller roughness down to the brightness beneath. Then it was a finger's width of icy silver reaching down along a yard to the finest of points. At the spike-end, where the blade was thickest, in black chasing there was marked the figure of a running wolf. Tom reached out, entranced.

'*Nein*,' called the German. '*Mein Herr*, please to wait.' He pulled on a leather gauntlet and reached back into a cupboard behind him, then he lifted the blade with the utmost care and slipped the spike end into a plain steel hilt. A moment more of fiddling, then he handed the sword to Tom, holding the blade in his gauntleted hand. 'Take care with the blade,' he warned as Tom took the thing. 'It is so sharp it will cut to the bone and you will never even feel it.'

'I know,' said Tom. 'I've had one through my arm and scarce noticed it. And I know a man who was run clear through the breast with one but only felt it when it also pierced his hand . . .'

Tom made a series of passes, watching the lethal beauty of the thing, utterly entranced. But more than his eyes were ravished. Even with this common steel handle – hardly to be called a hilt – the balance of the thing was wondrous. It exuded almost God-like power. Or rather, a Satanic power, for it whispered to him as he held it; wielded it. Like Marlowe's Mephistophilis it said, seductively, 'Kill before you put me up. I will only sleep if I have drunk enough of blood.'

'This is a wondrous, terrible thing,' he said. 'Even my Ferrara blade was nothing compared with this . . .'

'It is a Solingen blade,' said Poley, redundantly, 'like my own. And it is what the Spaniard wields, as you have said, I think. This is to replace the blade snapped by Nick o' Darkmans and his men.'

'A thousand thanks, Master Poley . . .'

'It is not from me,' said Poley shortly. 'I could never afford the like of this. But Lord Hunsdon wants you properly armed for the tasks we ask you to undertake.'

'You saw him today, then? I had thought Nonesuch Palace called most urgently.'

159

'Not today, no,' said Poley thoughtlessly, then checked himself.

'You have hilts for this blade?' the German interrupted, with a pointed glance at the workaday rapier Tom had borrowed from the school.

'I have some hilts of Ferrara make,' answered Tom, distracted, entranced. The German nodded approvingly. 'And,' he continued, 'I have a Dutchman who will fit them for me.'

The German smiled. '*Sehr gut.* But you will wish this to make the match, *ja?*' Where the blade had lain he placed a naked dagger – the very match of the rapier except that it came with a hilt. The blade alone was fifteen inches of razor sharpness almost impossibly slim and narrow. As Tom looked at it, he saw it in his imagination, sliding in through the Scavenger's throat and slitting its way almost painlessly out of the front. 'Aye,' he said breathlessly. 'I'll take that too, *Mein Herr.*'

'But,' said Poley quietly, 'we are only halfway through our business. Put that blade down, Tom, and let the Steelmaster of Solingen here measure your left arm too.'

By the best of good fortune, Tom's last pupil of the day – filling the full hour from five to six – was Will. As soon as he arrived, Tom explained what Poley and he proposed to do and the playwright was happy enough to join the enterprise. Raids on Bridewell were an occasionally popular sport with young gentlemen, for the keepers of the prison were notoriously reluctant to put up a fight, and the whores who were rescued were famously grateful. Then Tom and he spent a quarter hour exercising with extreme care so that Will could test his technique and Tom could try out the Solingen blades that Ugo had set in the finest Ferrara hilts. As he warned Will about the properties of the blades, Tom reminded him about the almost painless wound the Spaniard had given to his side, and repeated his worrying theory that Julius Morton had not felt the same blade – or its sinister companion – pass through his body; only his hand.

Ugo came out of the workshop at last and Tom pulled up his blade. 'Time to go.'

'You're not wearing them?' said Ugo as Tom completed his preparations.

'I am.'

'Both?' The Dutchman was frowning, worried.

'Both,' said Tom decisively, 'and the dagger in the belt at my back.'

As they shouldered their way along the foot of City Wall, Tom explained. 'Half of the Spaniard's power comes from his two blades. Poley and I have discussed the matter and I agree. We face up to the Spaniard, Baron Cotehel and whoever else works with them, and we make ourselves the stronger. And how better can we face up to the Spaniard than in this way? My swords are the equal of his. My cunning is the equal of his – better, forsooth – in my right arm and my left. Let the Spaniard and Master Baines and Master Outram be afraid therefore – Tom Musgrave will meet them beard to beard.'

'Take double care, and more, even so,' said Will, quietly, as Ugo nodded agreement. 'The man who declares a war is often the first to die.'

The City Wall led them directly to the Bridewell Bridge over the River Fleet. Then they were on familiar territory hurrying south along the stinking bank down to the Bridewell steps and the Bookkeeper's entrance. They arrived in the midst of a stirring bustle. Men of all sorts were pushing in through the gates. Tom paused, looking around, well aware that it must be near six already – though he had not heard it struck. There was no sign of Poley and the men he had promised to bring with him. Instead, there was the Reverend Word-of-the-Lord Parris, his face folded into a frown and his eyes focussed solely ahead. He pushed rudely past, safe from the danger of challenge at his rudeness behind the reverend sobriety of his clothing. He was far too distracted to notice Tom.

Tom met the eyes of his two companions. 'In,' he said quietly. 'We'll mask our faces when we act but until then we are simply part of the audience.' As he spoke, the bells of all the local churches began to chime the hour.

The great court of Bridewell was busy. Men strolled or sat in a rough circle around the raised stage on which there stood the whipping post. There was an air about the place which was, to Tom's mind, vicious and unhealthy. It was the atmosphere he had experienced on the rare visits he had made to Tyburn, but there was an undisguised lustful element added to it – and by no means a lust for blood.

Tom's narrow eyes raked the faces of the men there, looking for Poley. He did not see him, nor anyone else he recognised. Except for Will and Ugo, every man there avoided his gaze, until he began to wonder whether he would need to mask after all, for it seemed that he was hardly here at all. The feeling of invisibility was suddenly compounded by the throwing open of a large double door. Every eye in the place was suddenly fastened on the entrance of a column of girls and women led by the pompous Bookkeeper out into the yard. The women were of various ages and various aspects. They wore a range of clothing from the courtly to the ragged. They all wore chains. Cuffs closed around their wrists and were joined with fetters to each other – and to the ankle gyves they also had to wear. Tom used the collective sigh which whispered around the place to cover a swift check – still no sign of Poley. He narrowed his eyes, his mind racing. He would be prepared to act without the spymaster's help, but the risks were higher and the options for wider action limited. He moved sideways so that he could get a clearer view of the line of bawds. There were a dozen or so of them. Closer inspection showed them by and large to be a sorry lot, bedraggled and dirty, with a couple of cleaner, better-dressed exceptions. They were all round-shouldered and downcast except the woman who led the sorry troupe – led in every way, as though she was their spirit, their pattern and their commander. The first of the line walked tall, with her red head set as high as the Queen's at a state occasion. There was no mistaking Mistress Kate Shelton. And no mistaking just how little time he had in which to free her if she was going to escape a whipping.

Already one of the three guards accompanying the women was leading the first fair victim up on to the platform. The Bookkeeper and another two men stood waiting. The first of these was clearly the cell keeper, for he carried a chatelaine of keys and was reaching forward to unfasten the woman's wrist shackles as she mounted the stage, looking down her nose at him with undisguised disdain. The second man, having shaken out a whip of five lashes about a yard in length, accepted the woman had hooked her fetters up on to the top of the whipping post. Then, to another communal sigh from the increasingly excited crowd, he pulled open the back of Mistress Kate's dress, which she had wisely enough left unlaced. Beneath the finery of her bodice, she wore a shift of the snowiest white. The flesh of the bare back beneath it was exactly the same colour.

The executioner pushed the edges of the shift wider sliding his fists under the woman's upstretched arms. He was brutally rough, perhaps to please the crowd or perhaps to revenge some failure by the beautiful, proud young woman to bribe or seduce more gentle handling out of him. The laces and straps across her shoulders tore allowing the whole of her top to fall down over her belly like an apron. There was a ragged cheer as her breasts were bared, and the executioner stood back with a leer, ready to send the first stroke broadly across back and front.

But then Tom was up on the platform between the whip-master and his victim. Somehow, without his even realising he had drawn it, his Solingen blade was out and resting on the gaoler's throat. 'I cry clubs,' he bellowed, invoking the universal call to riot and revolt against authority. 'Clubs and freedom for the ladies.'

There was an instant of silence, then, 'Clubs,' cried Will and Ugo both together, each standing almost magically behind an official on the platform, daggers out and tickling ribs. Tom noted wryly that they at least had had the wit to pull up their masks. His eyes raked over the crowd of men, and a good number of eyes met his now. The line of whores waiting to be whipped, suddenly lost their hang-dog expressions and started looking speculatively around. There was no doubt that a hot reward awaited anyone who saved their backs and got them out of here. But on the other hand, the three remaining guards looked threatening: their backs were at risk here too, for if the women went they would likely replace them at the whipping post. The situation teetered on the point of a dagger for an instant, then, 'Clubs,' bellowed a familiar voice, and Poley, masked but well-armed, appeared behind a guard and the crowd went wild.

Tom turned and unhooked Kate Shelton from the post. He did so with his left hand, holding the gaoler at bay with the rapier in his right. Left-handed, he caught the key Will tossed, and he handed it to her so that she could free herself. She took off the wrist-locks and the ankle-locks before she began to pull up the front of her dress. And all the time, her eyes were fixed on his. Wide, excited, burning.

When the clamour in the courtyard died sufficiently for them to exchange a word or two, she asked as she gathered the cherry-tipped creaminess of her bosom and tucked it back within her bodice, 'And who do I have to thank for saving my tender back? Master . . .'

'Musgrave,' he answered, his mouth feeling dry of a sudden. 'Tom Musgrave.'

CHAPTER NINETEEN

Kate

A ll the other women in the whipping line, accompanied by a good number liberated from the Whore's dungeon, were heading out past the helpless guards, borne by the largely exultant crowd. Tom and Kate were running in, deeper into the inner corridors and recesses of the place. Not for an instant had she seemed to doubt who Tom was – or what. They had become confederates as suddenly and as absolutely as had he and Ugo, long ago and far away. Ugo, who made the two of them a threesome, bringing up the rear. Will had vanished with Poley, his associates and the rest.

'I have not yet met the Spaniard, but I know which one he is,' she said as they ran.

'How?'

'I have seen the Black Book. It records visitors as well as everything else. And you can imagine, I am certain, just how many Armada men have had visitors of late.'

'And how did you get to see the book?'

'Vanity. The Bookkeeper's. He believed like most men that there is something irresistible to women hidden under even the most repulsive and disgusting exterior. And that a full under-standing of the weight of his great responsibilities would make his personal qualities utterly irresistible. I allowed him to live with his arrant self-deception until I had what I wanted then I roundly disabused him.'

'That nearly cost you dear,' observed Tom, thinking of the brutal manner in which she had been prepared for her brutal flogging.

'When I think of the alternative he had in mind,' she said, 'ten times the whipping would have been a Cheapside bargain.'

Kate knew the inside of the Bridewell as though she had walked every corridor. Hence, thought Tom shrewdly, the vengeful anger of the gaoler with the whip. And they said that Vanity's true name was Woman. 'Hist!' she said, slowing her purposeful rush. 'Down here. And there's a guard.'

Tom went first, tip-toeing down a narrow flight of steps into a fetid little tunnel so low he had to stoop. The tip of his high-held rapier scraped along the stony roof. It would have struck sparks from the flinty stone of the place except that the whole tunnel was oozing water. Some twenty feet down the running tunnel was a narrow doorway into a small guard-chamber. The disturbance aloft had not yet made itself known down here so the guard was sitting at their ease – or rather they seemed to be so. Tom froze, scarcely breathing, and watched the three men grouped around the table. A trencher of food was piled in front of them and scraps of it lay on the table before them, but none of them was eating. Instead they were hunched, heads close, as though in the midst of a whispered conversation. And yet they were not talking. A lamp close beside them was flickering, almost guttering, and the dancing shadows from it made them seem to be moving. And yet, he realised, with a tightening of his stomach, they were not moving. And were never like to do so again. Feeling the silent stirring of Ugo's arrival at his shoulder, he stepped into the cramped little chamber. None of the guards looked at him.

'They're all dead,' he said to Ugo, and Kate coming in behind the Dutchman caught her breath. Tom crossed to the nearest, seeing the great key hanging from his belt. Ugo caught up the candle. Kate led the way down the corridor to the door at the end.

As the heavy portal creaked wide, Ugo stepped in and Tom followed at his shoulder to be confronted with the strangest of sights. A tall, gaunt man, chained and dressed in rags, knelt astride a trencher piled with food, frozen in the act of fighting off four equally gaunt, equally famished-looking prisoners.

'Help me,' he said in thickly accented English as he turned and glared into the light. 'Help me whoever you are. They must not eat this. It is poisoned and they are too famished even to care.'

Kate darted in and caught up the trencher, whirling it back out of the door. The four starving men seemed to sag. 'You were wise, master, and you have saved your friends,' said Tom. 'The guards stole the best of your repast by the look of it and they have paid with their lives for their greed.'

Kate was back. She held more keys. 'Don Diego de Villalar?' she asked.

'I hold no rank, *señorita*, but yes, I am Diego de Villalar.'

'Then I have come to set you free.'

'At what price?'

'Life, for a start. These four are like to kill you if you remain when we go. Perhaps you have all had enough of living, though. And advice. You are after all, an expert in some black arts are you not? Known to Señor Perez?'

'His friend who carries two swords,' added Tom. 'The friend who sent you the food.'

'Yes. Young Señor Domenico Salgado. I would enjoy another little talk with him.'

And so, at last, the mysterious assassin D.S. had a name.

And Tom had another ally to add to the list below Poley, who also wanted constant watching.

The central courtyard of the Bridewell was deserted as the four figures stole across it, but there was wreckage speaking eloquently of a riotous mob chased hither recently by a number of angry guards. 'What has happened here?' asked Villalar as he limped through the debris borne between Ugo and Kate while Tom led the way with his rapier out.

'To come down and rescue you,' said Kate, with something of a laugh in her voice, 'our brave leader there led a riot and released half the bawds in London.'

'It is not that I am not most grateful,' said the Spaniard. 'But could you not have saved one for me? Just one flawed jewel? It has been six years and more, and the *señorita* here, even though she serves but as a crutch, is setting my blood afire.'

'Indeed?' said Kate. 'I had heard much of the gallantry of the true Dons. And now I experience it for myself. A crutch. A crutch, forsooth. I'd rather have taken my whipping and let the old goat rot.' And yet, for all her words seemed shocked and bitter, she still held him firmly and led him surely. But the wry words were scarcely out of her mouth before their luck ran out.

'Who goes there?' called a raucous voice, and a sturdy body thrust itself into the gape of the gate. Behind the solid outline of his shoulder glinted freedom in the vision of the glittering river at the foot of the Bridewell Stairs. The four of them could hardly have looked more guilty. The trull who caused the riot, the roaring boy who led it, a Dutchman and a Don but lately taken from the Armada Hole.

'Shoot him,' said Tom to Ugo.

Ugo pulled out his wheel lock under cover of Diego's sagging body and cocked it against the pull of the wheel lock. He brought the pistol up, but just at the very instant he did so, the Reverend Word-of-the-Lord Parris appeared at his shoulder, calling, 'Here. Here they are . . .'

'Shoot him,' said Kate in a vicious undertone. 'Oh please, my brave pistoleer, shoot Parris. Right through his cod-piece if you can take the aim.'

Inevitably, Ugo hesitated, and the moment was gone. Parris's shouts brought half a dozen guards back and suddenly even the sparkle of the Thames was blotted by their forms.

But then, almost miraculously, Parris's shouts brought others back as well; for suddenly both he and the guards were swamped by a wave of men and women. 'It's Will,' cried Tom. And so it was. Will, Poley and his men, together with the more spirited of the girls they had rescued, had been waiting for Kate, Ugo and Tom. The guards, bested twice in one evening, broke and ran at once, leaving the Reverend Parris alone and badly outnumbered. He remained, dazed and stumbling at the top of the Bridewell Stairs as Tom led his little band out on to the low wooden platform. There they were welcomed with a rousing cheer which almost drowned the sound of Kate shoving Parris over the low rail on the east side and down into the slime of the Fleet Ditch. And Tom's wry words to the Spaniard. 'There, *señor*, you spoke too soon. It seems that we had saved you not one flawed jewel but an embarrassment of riches.'

The lads who rowed the wherries fell in with the adventure with an alacrity that was part of the tradition and the clocks had scarcely struck seven before the band – a dozen or so in all – were crowding up the Goat Stairs on to the Bankside where most of the girls lived their professional lives. Tom, Kate, Poley, Will and Ugo took the Don Diego to the Elephant and it was, perhaps, fortunate that Mistress Constanza had taken her Italian cards elsewhere for the evening. But the Elephant was only a stopping-off point where Diego was given the chance of a wash, a shave and a change of clothes. And if he needed the lingering help of two of the girls to assist him, why no one begrudged him, as long as he had the strength.

Will departed almost at once. 'We've a replacement now to double as Mercutio and the Prince,' he said. 'The play is doing roaring business. Two houses a day, the better part of three thousand souls – I've never seen the like – and Master Henslowe's saying he is thinking of a full ten-day run. And in the meantime I'm to get the next play down. It's an old piece about Sir Thomas More he wants me to fix as swiftly as I can and then I'll try something new again. But in the meantime I must write and write and write . . .'

Then Ugo became restless. 'I never like to leave the Rooms for too long,' he said, his voice low. 'And there's too many know about the gun-smithing for me to sit easy. If you've no objection, Tom . . .' and off he went. But for all his virtuous, sensible talk, one of the brightest and liveliest of the grateful girls followed him out through the door, and Tom smiled, thinking Ugo would be lucky to see his own bed in Blackfriars tonight. Or would that be *unlucky* . . .?

Poley leaned in close. 'When the Don gets back we've one more call to make before they close the City Gates.'

169

'Does it need all of us?' asked Kate, to whom bodily risks and high adventure seemed to have lent a considerable appetite – one that even the shock of hearing Julius Morton was dead couldn't quite drive away. She stuck Tom's new dagger in her pottage and speared a chunk of beef which she proceeded to nibble daintily – she had become very dainty after he had showed her what the German blade could do.

'Aye,' said Poley. 'I've a man the Don must meet and I need Tom to see what they do and to guard our backs and although I know you would be better at Scadbury House or Hunsdon House – or even, God save the mark – at Nonesuch, I doubt you'll leave us alone this night.'

'You have the right of it,' she said. 'But now we have a little leisure and not too many ears, Poley, can you whisper something of this man I risked my back – and a good deal more, I think – to rescue? He says he is nameless and of little or no account. And yet he carries himself more like a courtier than a commoner.'

'And speaks English after his fashion,' said Tom. 'Not many Spaniards do that.'

Poley hesitated, looking round. Then, in the face of the combined enquiry of their four wide eyes, he began to give them details in a most unaccustomed fashion. 'He was Perez's man. When Perez was the King's personal advisor. He was landed then, and wealthy. But when Perez needed a poisoner, it was to Diego of Villalar he turned. And when Perez was forced to flee, Diego would not leave his family. For which crime he was brought to court, stripped of rank and honour and made a galley slave. There were many slaves in the galleys of the Armada and many of them were Spanish criminals. Our justice made no discrimination between the captains who laid the plans and the galley slaves that pulled the oars. And so he is here now and at our beck. The Master of all the Masters of Spain in the art of poisoning . . .'

Kate laid down the dagger at that, and Tom thought the information must have stopped her appetite at last. It may have stopped it for pottage, but the rich stew was followed by warden pears preserved in syrup and served with a syllabub.

'But Perez like as not knew of his old friend's fate,' said Tom, thoughtfully. 'And when he looked over the lists of the Armada men – no doubt at the Council's own request, and if not their's at Lord Essex's – he knew the name at once. And so he has called upon Don Diego in the past, to discuss matters of health, security, herbs and poisons. And sends his new young Master in the Dark Arts to see the old man, and perhaps, to bring him a timely rest from the sad burdens of living.'

'The old man's worked that out,' said Kate. 'And has a score to settle with Perez now; and with his creature Salgado of the two swords. And, perhaps, with whoever is currently employing him. So our old enemy is now our new enemy's enemy. And our enemy's enemy is our friend.'

'For as long as it suits him,' said Tom. 'Have you read much of Machiavelli?'

'Who?' asked Kate, all innocence. She wrinkled up her nose in apparent distaste at the perfidy they were discussing and Tom thought the conversation must at last have stilled her appetite. But instead she caught up the horn spoon she was also sharing with Tom. She dug into the fragrant richness of the pears and syllabub ecstatically. Then she saw Tom looking at her and grinned. 'Heart and stomach of a man,' she said. 'Though not, like Her Majesty, of a king.'

If Kate regretted her titanic supper later, she never said so. And she had good reason to regret it. As soon as Don Diego de Villalar returned, Poley swept them out of the Elephant and into the gathering darkness. The Spaniard persisted in leaning upon Kate and indeed he had need to. Years as a galley slave followed by years in fetters were like to have crippled any man – but a fierce, independent intelligence burned behind that lean, angular face, and it was clear to Tom at least that the old man had used every opportunity to keep his strength and vigour up. Vigour, he noted, that not even the attentions of the two bawds who washed him had done much to dissipate. And, of course, a good measure of the Elephant's best pottage and finest claret had gone some way to strengthening him into the bargain. And someone in the depths of the fine old inn had found him a stick, for Spaniard or no, he was clearly a fine, witty, kindly and grateful old man, with a range of respected and popular friends.

They found a wherry at the Goat Stairs big enough to accommodate all of them, and the wherrymen rowed them across the river to the Cold Harbour Stairs. These stairs were unusual among the city's stairs for they mounted into a narrow doorway instead of a broad street or landing place. Poley went up first, as intimately acquainted with this place, clearly, as he was with the ant's nest of the Steelyard. Through the Cold Harbour Gate he led them, past the warehouses that did their best to contain chilled and fresh goods with ice and cold stores, into the rabbit warren behind. Here were the spice merchants whose wares preserved the meats that the ice could not protect. And, behind them, the dyers and others whose trades depended on plants and potions of all sorts from all sources. Here, rubbing jowls with each of them, there sat a little apothecary's shop.

What seemed small on the outside was in fact deep and cavernous within. The smells in the street were heady to say the least, nutmeg and clove and cinnamon wafting in an instant away to be replaced by urine, acid, indigo and woad. In the apothecary's they were overpowering – not least because among the herbs, tinctures, tisanes and compounds the apothecary and his assistants made and kept in here, there were also cages of assorted birds, mice, rats, cats and dogs.

The apothecary was a tall, bright-eyed old man whose hair and beard were almost as long as Diego Villalar's. He recognised Poley at once and waved his assistants away into the depths of the shop. His eyes raked expressionlessly over the unusual collection Poley had brought with him, but his eyebrows almost vanished into his white hair when Poley, apparently thinking nothing of the courtesy, introduced Villalar.

'Don Diego de Villalar is dead,' said the apothecary, his voice surprisingly strong, issuing from such a seemingly frail body.

'Not so.' Don Diego was well able to speak for himself, though Poley had begun to answer. 'A recent guest of Her Majesty at Bridewell Palace. That is all. And who do I have the honour of addressing?'

'Master Apothecary Gerard,' the old man bowed.

'So now,' said Poley, brusquely, 'we have together two fine minds for answering some questions that have been taxing some important intelligences. And ours as well, come to that.' He pulled out a satchel that had been appearing and disappearing through the evening, and threw it open. Out of it on to the boards of Apothecary Gerard's table tumbled a series of bundles, large and small. All were carefully wrapped and labelled – except one. 'That looks like the present of food but lately sent to me,' said the Spaniard.

'Mistress Kate reserved it,' said Poley. 'She has a subtle mind.'

'Ah,' said Diego. 'Now I see which way the game goes. Had I not already been awash with suspicions.' He glanced up at Master Gerard. 'I would hazard merely your mice to begin with, Master Gerard, for there is a great amount of death wrapped up in all of these little parcels, I would guess. Then, perhaps, your cats and dogs to test the strength.'

The first mouse that tasted a crumb of the Spaniard's food lasted a few seconds. The Masters of Apothecary watched its spastic twitching into a frozen stasis of death with fearsome concentration. 'Hemlock,' said Gerard, and Diego nodded. They tested it on a cat and then a dog. The dose was massive; the diagnosis unvaried: hemlock.

'That's the closest those ignorant buffoons of guards ever came to understanding Socrates,' Diego observed dryly over the rigid body of the dog. 'But I expect Salgado meant it as a compliment to me.' He picked up the mouse and looked deep into its wide eyes. 'They say the mind remains alive, locked in a dying body, unable to cry out,' he said. 'At least that's what Plato said of Socrates after he drank it.'

'It's also what those who found him dying said of Sir Francis Walsingham,' whispered Kate into the hollow of Tom's ear. His blood ran cold, for he remembered all too clearly Morton's letter and the manner in which he had expounded it to Poley and the rest.

They sorted the little piles according to the labels Poley had put upon them, being very careful to touch them only with

Master Gerard's wooden spoons and sticks. The one Spanish needle rescued from Morton's letter had a very different effect when another unfortunate mouse was scratched with it. The poor little creature writhed in agony, spraying various liquids from various parts of its body before it froze into juddering stasis. 'Monk's Hood,' opined Gerard.

Don Diego was nodding sagely. 'Aconite,' he said. 'The effect is the same if you eat it.'

'And the end is the same as the Earl of Leicester suffered on his way to Buxton,' breathed Kate as Gerard, gauntleted, reached for a cat to scratch.

Tom tore himself forward, as much to escape the terrible weight of her knowledge as to add to the dread weight of his own. 'And which,' he choked, 'which of these hell-born things could cause a whole family to run mad and fall screaming into swollen death? Which of these poisons could do that, my Masters?'

And the two men looked at each other, frowning with shared knowledge. Then Don Diego turned to Tom and answered for them both. 'What you describe is poisoning from the most terrible poison of all, more dreadful even than the black hellebore or deadly nightshade. It is mandragora or mandrake you describe. Only mandrake takes the reason as well as the life. That is why they call it "the insane root".'

And even as Tom turned away, brow folded in thought and horror, Poley silently pulled something out of another little package. Half rotten and blackened, it was, of all things, a strawberry.

Tom and Kate walked silently up towards Blackfriars as the Bellman said goodnight.

> 'Remember the clocks,
> Look well to your locks,
> Fire and your light,
> And give you goodnight
> For now the bell ringeth.'

'The bell has rung for too many of late,' said Tom.

'It has,' agreed Kate. 'So we should be glad we are none of their number.

'You have the right of it, I suppose,' he answered. 'But Kate, how is it that you come by the terrible knowledge you possess? Who are you that you know such people and such things?'

'I will tell you it all, in due course,' she said. 'But nothing more tonight. Tonight there is no more Lady Catherine Shelton. There is only Kate of Bridewell, the bawd who escaped a whipping because of your bravery and your gallantry. Who is hot to express her thanks.'

Up they ran, into the rooms above Master Aske's haberdashery, and Tom was overjoyed to discover that Ugo had not managed to make it home after all. He had managed to do no more than to dash a handful of cool water in his face and set light to his bedside lamp when he turned to find Kate of Bridewell slipping lithely out of her skirts. 'Hold,' he said, and raising the light above his head he took her through into the fencing chamber and stood her like a female Narcissus in front of his great mirror. Then as he stripped, she stood, awed by the wonder of her reflection, caught between lamplight and moonlight and shadow, a thing of marble curves and russet tints and black velvet deeps. Never, not even at Court, had she seen a mirror to equal this. 'I burn,' she whispered. 'Oh, I burn to thank you.'

Then Tom came up and wrapped his arms around her, looking over her shoulder at her form in the tall cold mirror while, with trembling fingers, she showed him where she burned. And how.

CHAPTER TWENTY

Highmeet

They greeted the morning with Kate still full of gratitude. She straddled Tom's loins and held him within her as she told him of her family and background. This was a ploy to prolong their passion, and so far it had lasted well. He, ever the scholar, had suggested quoting from the classical masters to distract his mind at first, but she had hardly suggested '*Nam concordia pavae res cruscunt*' ('Harmony makes small things huge') than he misquoted loudly, '*Praeparetur corpus contra omnia*' ('Prepare your body for the unexpected') and even arid, Stoical Seneca undid them both.

Now, however, as she eased herself ever so slightly forward and back, her husky voice held him entranced, even as her glorious body held him enraptured. 'The Sheltons have been the wardens of Hunsdon House since the days of Harry the King. We're related to the Careys and the Boleyns and the Howards of Norfolk. When Queen Anne fell out of favour with the old man, soon after Elizabeth was born, the child was sent to Hunsdon House, and my family looked after her while Queen Anne went through the trial and execution while the old man prepared the way for Jane Seymour to become his next queen in her turn. And incidentally mounting Queen Anne's sister Mary Boleyn as his mistress while he was at it, the old goat. But Elizabeth came to us at Hunsdon and we raised her. And so in due course, the Sheltons fell into something like friendship with her. The eldest, Mary, was her maid in waiting until she married in secret, and the Queen boxed her ears for her. My elder sister, Audrey, is down at Scadbury at the moment, with her lover, Sir Thomas Walsingham, soon to be her husband. And I whirl around the edges of our family and round the edges of the Court, trying not to get my body mounted or my ears boxed.'

Tom eased his hips, using sensation to maintain his ardent physical interest while his enquiring mind was tempted away from the carnal. 'I promise not to box your ears at least,' he promised.

'It's not you I'm worried about,' she parried.

'But you whirl around the edges of this dark world as well,' he continued, more seriously. 'How is that?'

'Did you not hear? Audrey has been Tom Walsingham's lover since he worked as a spy for Sir Francis, the Queen's Mister Secretary. She has worked for them both. Like any family where such things happen, the game has been played by one sister and then another.'

'Tom Walsingham was Kit Marlowe's patron, was he not?'

'Patron and lover, if I dare mention such things without risking another crisis.' She moved playfully, in just such a way as would precipitate one.

But Tom held hard. 'As Wriothsley was with Will,' he said.

'The Earl of Southampton? Some say he still is. Both patron and lover. You'll have to ask Will if you want to know more.'

'I was just thinking, though, about how much there is in the play of Romeo not only about swordplay, but about poisons and drugs. Morton mentioned that to Poley in his letter, which I think was no coincidence. And Will wrote most of it, he says, when he was with Southampton and his circle last summer. Poley said that also, but it's only just begun to made me think . . .'

Kate began to move more urgently. 'Well in that case it is time to stop thinking, Tom Musgrave. Wasn't it Seneca who said, "*Cogitatum maximae dilabuntur*"?'

'Jade,' he gasped. 'You misquote. It was *discordia*, not

cogitatum. Discord, not thought, makes huge things small . . .'
But Seneca, once again, had undone him.

Later, as they rinsed themselves off and began to pull on
some clothing, he pushed his line of questioning into deeper,
darker areas. Areas that she herself had referred to at the
apothecary's late last night before Poley had dragged Diego
de Villalar off to his hovel in Hog Lane and the pair of them
had come back here. 'Had you known,' he asked delicately,
'that Lord Strange was poisoned not two months since?
There seems to have been much work done to keep the fact
a secret.'

'I knew nothing until the mouse ate the strawberry,' she said
with a frown. 'And the cat ate the mouse – and the dog ate the
cat. But looking back now, I am sure Julius Morton suspected.
I think he wrote to Lord Strange only a week or so before his
lordship's death. Or rather, I think he and Will wrote to Lord
Strange.'

'Telling him what?'

'Again, I am not certain. Something he had overheard somewhere. Not enough to pass on to Poley, perhaps, but enough to
send to his lordship because they were his men – Morton, Will
and the rest. The company were Lord Strange's Men.'

There was a tiny silence as Tom began to digest this information. Then Kate added, her fine brow furrowed in
thought, 'Or, if Will wrote the letter, perhaps it was something
that Will overheard.'

'But I was one of the company myself,' said Tom thoughtfully. 'Yet I suspected nothing.'

She shrugged. 'They are actors. They act. Is that so strange?'

'But Will has his feet in two camps here. He has his own
patron, the Earl of Southampton. Why could he not take it to
Southampton?'

'If it concerned the events in Wormwood in Jewry and
Essex's poisoner Salgado, then of course it could not go to
Southampton – he is bosom friend to both Essex and Cotehel.'
Kate fitted her reasoning to Tom's as though they had worked
together for years.

'And yet Morton was hesitant even to take it to Poley, for whom he worked,' said Tom.

'Like Kit Marlowe,' she observed.

'Like Marlowe? Why do you say that?'

'Because Marlowe was the last of their number that worked for Poley. His fate might give a man pause if he was carrying dangerous information. There is still a deal of speculation as to what in all creation could have brought together a man who works in secret for the Council, another that works for Essex and a third who works for Tom Walsingham, to do a man to death in Deptford.'

'It happened while I was on my way back from Italy,' said Tom, feeling the response to be somehow inadequate. There was a slight pause. Then Tom pushed on, changing to a slightly different tack. 'I suppose,' he said, calculatedly, 'that it was your sister and her contacts who told you the detail of the Earl of Leicester's death?'

' 'Tis common knowledge. He felt unwell after the great festivity at Tilbury that he had organised after the crushing of the Armada. He went off up to Buckstones to take the waters. The Queen, ever mindful of his welfare, sent some medicines after him. He took them. He died. He died as the creature died last night, screaming of agony in his belly. The surgeons said it was disorder of the stomach and the bowel. But some call it poison.'

Tom sat. He was utterly stunned. He felt in full the shock that Poley warned of. That simple association that had Topcliffe, the rack, the fire and Tyburn at its heels. The Queen sent him medicine. He took it and he died, his stomach cramping in agony, his belly and bowels in revolt, bellowing his agony. Not gripped by terminal illness. Poisoned.

The Queen sent him poison. Monkshood. Aconite.

But no. Such a thing was impossible. The world would need to be flat and sitting still at the centre of the universe and the Pope descended straight from God for such things to be true. Go to work, Tom, go to work on this, he thought; for there is something you are missing.

But then Kate turned and he saw no earth-shattering revelation in her eyes. Her gaze was open, quizzical perhaps, caught between amusement and wonder at his expression.

'What ails you?' she asked.

'The Queen sent medicine. He took it. He died. Poisoned.'

'No.' She smiled. 'You ask the wrong question. Ask not who sent the medicine. Ask who delivered it. For who's to say that he delivered exactly what Her Majesty had sent.'

'The Queen sent the medicine. Who took it to the Earl of Leicester, then?'

'Why a servant to the Master of Horse, of course. The Master of Horse arranges everything to do with the movement of the Queen, her Court, her missives and her messages.'

'But Leicester was the Master of Horse.'

'Leicester was sick. He asked his ward and godson, whom he had trained up so well, to take over the responsibility for him. Responsibility he holds to this day.'

'The Earl of Essex,' he breathed.

'The Earl of Essex.' She nodded.

'But who was the messenger? Who did Essex send? Does anybody know?'

'Morton knew. And he told me. But he told someone else as well, and now Morton is dead.'

'Not Poley.'

'Probably not Poley. But with Poley, who can tell? Perhaps someone else – even someone innocent who mentioned it at the wrong time, who knows?'

'But the knowledge was deadly.'

'To Morton, yes. To Lord Strange if that is what they wrote about. To me if they can catch me. To you if you care to share it.'

'Of course. Tell me his name.'

'Essex sent a creature of his own. A man dressed all in black, apparently. A man I am told called Baines. Richard Baines.'

Tom laughed aloud.

'It is well that you quote Seneca. You are of the Stoic disposition indeed if you can hear the announcement of your own death with a laugh.'

'No. You do not understand. I laugh because your dreadful doom is no added fate to me. Master Baines has been trying to kill me these past two days at the least.'

'Then he hasn't been trying very hard,' she said, a little tartly.

And his laughter died a little. What had Nick o' Darkmans said? To break his hands and arms and head. That's what Baines had ordered. Hands and arms, but leave him alive. Of a sudden his blood ran cold.

'But still,' he said, 'what good could the Earl of Essex hope to gain? All he had to do was to wait and it all would come to him.'

'Perhaps he did not want to wait,' she said, fiddling with the torn straps of her shift as though she had two minds whether to put the thing on or take it off again. 'Have you met Robert Devereux?'

'No.'

'He is not a man in whom patience is predominant.'

'Even so, there must have been something more to motivate him, other than impatience.'

'Perhaps,' she said, her fingers suddenly busy with the knot that would secure her shift.

'And Walsingham? Master Secretary? It was the hemlock for him, you said.'

She shrugged. 'I have talked with one who talked with one that saw him die. It was as the Spaniard Don Diego said. His body ceased to function of a sudden. But not his mind. His mind remained alive for days, they said. Trapped silent and helpless behind his eyes. A judicious draught of hemlock might do that. His doctors said a seizure, of course. But again . . .'

'And who would dare to send Mister Secretary hemlock? Who in all the world, let alone in the Court?'

'Someone desperate, impatient, mad for power. But again, you ask the wrong question. Not who might want it done – but who might have carried the tincture.'

'Only someone trusted by Walsingham and all those around him. Someone at the very heart even of Poley's circle. Someone apparently beyond the shadow of a question.'

'There you have it.'

'But do you have a name?'

'Perhaps,' she said and reached over for her dress.

Just as the door opened. In the doorway stood Ugo Stell, his fair eyebrows raised in an expression of shocked amusement that went far beyond anything required by their dress or compromising position. But then a long, dark hand thrust him aside and the reason for his concern made her presence plain.

'I have come,' spat Constanza, 'to bring you this letter. It was left at the Elephant for you last evening. A man dressed in black said he had tried to deliver it to you here but could not get in.'

That is what her words said. But their tone said I hate you you inconstant pig and I hope you rot in hell. Which may have been closer to the Italian woman's thoughts, for all their arrangement had become a little ad hoc. But then, Constanza's sweat was hardly dry on his skin before Kate had added hers.

'Dressed all in black?' asked Tom, his eyes steady on hers.

'I have said.'

'Not your Spaniard, not Señor Domenico Salgado with the two swords?'

'Not Señor Salgado, no,' she said, his name just a little too familiar in her mouth. 'One of your common Englishmen. But a hard-faced man for all that. He is your enemy?'

'He is. Therefore if you see him again, Constanza, stay clear of him.'

'If I see him again, Tomas – ' she spat it with the Italian inflection which had been part of their most intimate love play – 'I shall do just as I please.'

Constanza threw the letter she had brought on to the bed and Tom flinched, thinking of Spanish pins dipped in monkshood. Then, quick as a flash, he had snatched it up before Kate could touch it. When he looked back at the doorway, Constanza had gone.

In a comic dumbshow of embarrassment worthy of Kempe himself, Ugo also left the room. The intelligencers sat in shift and shirt, and looked at the letter left by Baines, the man who wanted them crippled or dead.

Five minutes later, the letter was on Ugo's workbench and, at arm's length, using his Solingen blades, Tom was easing the blood-red seal off the back of it. He was certain there were no pins concealed within it ready to spray out in a hail of aconite-tipped death. But his time and studies in Italy had made him privy to such murderous mysteries as powdered arsenic and strychnine, dusts made of white henbane and black hellebore.

But no. The letter contained only an ornate script in a florid if unfamiliar hand. He read it aloud from a distance, however; breathing shallowly.

> Hugh Outram, Baron Cotehel, soon-to-be Lord Out-remer, wishes that Thomas Musgrave, Master of the Science of Defence, will forgive the cancellation of our lesson tomorrow afternoon at Highmeet, and hopes the said Master Musgrave, with any retinue he cares to bring, will follow Baron Cotehel to Elfinstone Castle at Rochester on Saturday next, to celebrate with a festival of feasting, music, theatre and swordplay, the Baron's assumption of his legal title to the lands and possessions of Outremer.

Tom stood for a while in silence, deeply immersed in thought, for this was such an unexpected development that it required the most careful consideration. Kate crossed to the letter where it lay beside the window and read it through again, distracting him unconsciously by the way the light shone through her shift. She distracted him further by giving a delicious gurgle of laughter.

'What?'

'Retinue. You have a retinue?'

'I have Ugo, if he'd care to come.'

Ugo looked up. 'After what I've heard about Elfinstone, I would be mad to refuse. The lands down to the river are packed with game. The hunting is beyond compare. The food is legendary. Even the lowliest kitchen maids are among the comeliest lasses in Kent . . .'

'I have a retinue,' said Tom.

'And I have a thought,' said Kate.

'What thought is that? That of a sudden I have an afternoon at liberty?'

'Not quite. I think that Highmeet House is likely to be closed and empty, if Baron Cotehel, soon-to-be Lord Outremer, is entertaining at Elfinstone, and we might be well employed in visiting the place in secret before you and your retinue go gaily into the lion's den.'

Like the raid on Wormwood in Jewry, the raid on Highmeet St Magnus began with pottage in the ordinary at the Elephant. Here Tom brought Kate, and hither Ugo sent Poley and Diego Villalar when they came down to Blackfriars from Hog Lane a little later. Here too came Will Shakespeare all aglow with excitement with the news that the Rose Company had been employed for a performance of *Romeo* on Saturday before the Earl of Southampton. Will could – would – talk of nothing else, not even his letter to the ill-fated Lord Strange. In the playwright's desperation to repair the finances of the company, there was simply nothing more important in this world or the next than putting on a performance before the Earl of Southampton that might get them all recognised at Court and put on a sound financial, social and legal footing before simple beggary gulped them all down and condemned them to the horrors of a vagrant life as masterless men, literally being whipped from pillar to post. If Tom or anyone wished to discuss Shakespeare's past rather than his future, they would have to wait a while yet.

But long before such things had to be addressed by Tom, Kate, Poley and the rest, of course, there was the matter of Highmeet House in St Magnus's parish, lying as unprotected as a sleeping virgin. 'We need another charm,' said Poley. 'A picker of locks,' he translated automatically for Don Diego. 'But the only man I knew who practised those black arts we left pinned to Morton's door. Do you know any such?' he asked Tom.

'No, but I know a man who may do,' answered Tom. 'Two in

fact. Nick o' Darkmans and the man who holds the key to his fetters.'

Nick o' Darkmans came himself. He would have been mad not to, given his state in the fetters in the Borough Counter. But he had his professional pride, near to being his downfall though it was. He was not for breaking in during daylight – Darkmans, his thief's name, meant 'darkness', and that was when he worked. And he was taking along no trulls. Not even those that looked like Her Majesty God Bless Her and was easy on the eyes like Mistress Kate.

'Take someone else with you. Someone with a gun,' advised Talbot grimly. 'And I'd be happier if we were holding a hostage here that we were certain he'd come back for.'

'Like his wife or perhaps his daughter?' suggested Kate.

'Like his purse if he had one, or failing that, his stones,' said Talbot, tapping Nick o' Darkman's codpiece suggestively as he stooped to loose his gyves. 'I still hold your mittimus,' he said to the thief as he stretched stiffly to his full height. 'You let these men down and I'll be after you. Hell itself will be too hot to hold you, Nick o' Darkmans.'

Nick took them to St Paul's first, though it was nearing six when they got there and the bustle was beginning to ease. There in the great walk, the thief made glancing contact with a little ferret of a man who followed them out into a quiet section of the churchyard beside the currently untenanted gallows where Nick introduced his friend as 'Kit Callot, the deftest charm and master of the black art of lockpicking'.

'At your service, gentles,' said Callot, bowing particularly low before Kate and leering with all the effect the black stumps of his teeth were capable of exercising. 'The name of the ken you want cracked?'

Before they got too deeply into practical talk, Nick led them to the Lion in Pissing Alley, between St Paul's and their eventual destination. Here, over a blackjack of ale – which even Kate shared – they began to talk their dark business.

'Highmeet. It's an evil place,' said Callot at once. 'Cost you

185

extra bite to have the black art practised on those locks. Less o'
course your doxy here'll make up the difference. Fair difference, mind,' he said, exposing Kate to another of his gallant
leers. 'Difference between Heaven and Hell for me, as I
shouldn't wonder.'

'You will have to continue to wonder, Master Callot,' said
Kate sweetly. 'Nothing you have ever stolen, not even the sum
of all you have stolen, buys one light kiss from me.'

Callot shrugged philosophically. 'Hope one of you rufflers
has a weighty purse at his belt, then.'

'If I did,' said Tom, glancing around the Lion. 'I'd never dare
admit it in this company.'

Callot showed his teeth again in a smile that stopped well
below his eyes.

'Come along, Kit, I'll stand surety for them,' said Nick. 'Get
us into the place and I swear you'll not be the loser.'

Unlike the last charm who worked on Poley's business,
thought Tom grimly.

'Well,' said the charm, 'if the trull ain't going to occupy any
of us then she don't come neither.'

'She's been told,' said Nick. 'She's off to this gentleman's
ken as soon as we're on the move. But does we have a deal in
this?'

The lock-pick spat on to his hand and offered it to the thief-
master. They shook over the blackjack. 'Done deal,' they said.

Highmeet was one of the oldest houses in London. It was
named from the belief that, during the years between the
Roman withdrawal and the French invasion, the Saxons had
held their High Moot, or parliament, in its great old halls. Just
where its more sinister reputation had come from was more
difficult to assess. Unlike the companion house at Wormwood,
there had been no family wiped out here – by plague or poison.
But the place had an atmosphere, Tom had to admit that. It
wasn't by any means just a piece of imaginative extortion from
their low company. In the gathering darkness under a lowering
sky as the Bellman began to stir, the huge old house sat

brooding. The streets near it were deserted, as though no one else wanted to be nearby when the full darkness came and whatever nameless evils within might be released. They had stopped off at one or two other establishments in various unsavoury locations after they had left Pissing Alley. Callot had supplied them with dark lanterns. They had supplied themselves with weapons and all four of them were armed to the teeth. Perhaps against any unexpected occupants of the house, thought Tom; perhaps against each other.

As they followed the thin beams of gold light under the glooming eaves of the place, Callot tested all the doors. All seemed to be secured by solid locks on the outside. The trick was, he whispered, to know which were likely to be bolted from the inside as well. But a series of judicious experiments – largely consisting of rattling the doors and feeling how firmly they were secured, led Callot at last to the back door in a tiny alley off Bottolph's Lane. Here the charm practised his black arts to good effect and the lock soon snapped open.

The door swung silently inwards on well-greased hinges, ushering them into a corridor leading between storerooms into a wide and ancient kitchen area. Grouped into a close-spaced file by the corridor, here they spread out, sliding the darkening doors of their lanterns wider.

'We are here to look,' Tom warned the two thieves. 'To look, not to lift.'

Together they followed his careful lead out of the main kitchen into other, smaller, food-preparation areas. The corridors between these were something of a maze but Tom led the way with increasing confidence as the widening of the corridors they followed led to more and more stately chambers. And, at last, out into a main hall. From this great area, stairways reached up on right and left, the walls above them laden, as was the tradition, with family portraits. Tom crossed to these at once and shone his lantern up amongst them, regretting poignantly the fact that he had agreed to Nick o' Darkmans's ban on trulls and sent Kate away. For the faces in the family portraits were oddly familiar. The two lowest in the range, the most recent by the looks of things, were strangely, almost disturbingly familiar.

One showed the idealised portrait of a fair young man, book in hand, fist on sword, gazing with martial frown into the distance while behind him a town seemed to be exploding. Fascinated, Tom climbed the stairs and narrowed his eyes against the glare of the lantern's light reflecting off the varnish on the oil. The young warrior was not holding just any book. He was holding *The Practise of Fortification* by Charles Ive.

Frowning as he wrestled with the relevance of that, Tom stepped down to face the man in the second portrait. A young man whose sneer and curling mustachio simply served to emphasise the fact that he had a harelip. Whose extravagant curls, swept in the fashion of the Earl of Southampton's, could not hide the star-shaped scar right in the middle of his forehead.

Tom turned, looking down into the blaze of Ugo's wide-doored lantern. 'I know them,' he said. 'I know both of these men.'

There was a great revelation there, just at the back of his mind, just beyond his grip, if only he could put his finger on it. But then a black-clad figure stepped out of the sea of shadows behind the three hooded lanterns. He pointed up at Tom and a flash of light came with a clap of thunder and a concussion against his temple that stopped everything Tom was trying to think and say as instantly and effectively as a blow from a headsman's axe.

CHAPTER TWENTY-ONE

Topcliffe

Tom awoke to piercing agony in his head and his arms. The pain was such that to begin with he thought he must be making those screaming, babbling sounds himself. But then he began to register that the screams were too distant to be his own. And, come to that, of far too high a register ever to issue from his gruff throat. The suspicion that someone must be torturing a woman stabbed through him like a rapier made of ice and did much to jerk him awake. The last rags of unconsciousness were stripped away by the repetition of one name in a deep, flat tone among all the screaming. 'Kate,' said the voice gruffly. 'You know that another turn or two will render you a crippled beggar for life—' The conversation vanished below a renewed bout of weeping and pleading.

Only the wildest extremes of agony and terror could have rendered Kate so pathetically incoherent, thought Tom grimly. He began to look about himself, seeking an escape for himself and a rescue for her. Things did not seem too hopeful. He was hanging against a high stone wall. A twisting movement allowed him to glance up and he saw that his wrists were cuffed at the end of a yard or so of fetters and these were held by a huge hook set in the rough stone nearly ten feet above the floor. His ankles were also fettered and the massy chain between them just failed to touch the damp flags below. A couple of feet beyond his pendant toes there stood a little table across which lay his rapiers. The room must be two yards square but four yards high at least, for Tom had to look up to see the ankles of people scurrying past a grating just below the ceiling.

There seemed to be a market of some kind going on out there, where the screams of a tortured woman might blend in almost unremarked behind the screaming of dying calves, sheep and birds. Newgate Market, he suspected. And that made this place a cell in Newgate gaol. And that was very bad news indeed.

'Very well, Kate. Another notch,' came the gruff voice. 'You have brought it on yourself. If you are fortunate, the joints of your shoulders will slip back into their sockets in time. I have seen it happen . . .'

The voice vanished beneath another wave of helpless pleading, only to rise again, sharply. 'No, Master Baines. I will turn the ratchet. 'Tis my duty. I am the Rackmaster.'

Five years of fencing and practice in the Science of Defence had given Tom massive strength of arm, shoulder and chest. Strength lent an added power by desperation as the screams from the neighbouring chamber attained a new intensity. He heaved his whole body upward on his right hand and caught at the chain with his left. One hook, he thought, and no thought of separating his wrists gave Tom a double-length of fetters stretching directly up to the hook. And, one thoughtless – unconsidered – element gave him a further hope. Immediately in the crooks behind his knees a pair of shackles were set in the wall. His plan was simple – this was no time for anything complex. He would pull himself up the double chain above him until he could set his heels in the shackles against the wall. Then, leaning back and taking care, he should be able to straighten and stand tall enough to lift free of the hook above his head. He heaved up on his left hand and his right caught the icy links immediately above it.

Now, Tom reckoned, the only way for such an escape attempt to be effective was if it came unsuspected. Surprise was all. Therefore he breathed shallowly and moved with all the silence at his command. And because of this, he was able to hear more than he might have done of the conversation in the torture chamber next door.

'This one knows little enough, Master Topcliffe,' said Baines as the renewed screams died to a broken sobbing. 'God knows, if there was any information in that stubborn heart, your rack would have loosened it by now.'

'Even so, we must persist. There is no telling what little titbit might lie as yet undiscovered under this sorry tongue. And we need what we can glean from her. When we replace this broken creature with the Master of Defence next door, we have to be more careful. This one we may break. That one we may not. Do you see that? The Earl's warrant is very precise. The information is less important than the damage. It is unusual I allow . . .'

'Not so, Master Topcliffe. The damage there has always been paramount. Even were we to prove beyond a shadow of doubt that Musgrave was seated at Lord Strange's shoulder when the strawberries arrived, even then we have no warrant to rack him until he breaks. He must be fit to walk – fit to fight a little – before he goes screaming down.'

' 'Tis a great risk, however. If as you say he has a mind well schooled and gifted in logic, he may well have a tongue that will wag before his race is run.'

' 'Twill wag to no effect, then. When we are finished here, I am to take him straight to Elfinstone and there he will end his days. And it will matter not one jot who he can talk to in the meantime, for there are none there that will listen, except for the others marked for death in any case. No, I tell you, at the opening of the next new week we shall look to have a brave new world.'

'Well. So it may prove. But in the meantime, this one does not lie under the Earl's edict. This one we may rack until the arms and legs tear off. So, now your pleading has quietened, tell us, what does the Master of Defence know of the matter of Lord Outremer? What does he know of the will?'

'Come,' snarled Baines's brutal voice. 'The will, while your legs are still in place at least . . .'

Tom had the hook now. He was breathing in great shuddering gasps, feeling up the rough wall with his boot-heels, seeking for a purchase on the solid step of the wall-mounted shackles. He was awash with sweat. Apart from the fierce concentration he was forcing into his heels as they explored, all his mind was filled with the vision of his swords. Calculatedly so, for the sounds from the rack room next door had gone almost to the realms of madness. He could not tell – and would not begin to speculate – whether the creak and tear he could hear were coming from the terrible machine or from its tortured occupant. He bent his arms slowly, lifting the whole of his weighted body upwards, thews threatening to tear as though on the rack themselves. The howling of the victim ceased sounding even human. He had heard sounds like that at the bull-baiting when one of the dogs got gutted.

There! He had the shackles under his heels. He began to straighten his legs slowly, easing the muscles in his arms and shoulders. Lifting the shackles out of the hook, he straightened his arms and, falling forward at once by the weight of them, he leaped forward and down.

The arm-shackles slammed across the table, sending it skittering over to slam against the wall beneath the window even as the rapiers jumped and juddered atop the wood. The ankle fetters fell on to the stone flags of the floor. The sound was like the thunder-machine which hung behind the stage at the Rose. As though someone was battering on the door to the cell with all the vigour and power at their command.

Tom did not hesitate. He grabbed his nearest rapier and slid his hand into the basket of the hilts, catching the hook with his thumb and hurling the scabbard aside as he spun, blade high and wickedly naked, to face Baines and Topcliffe as they came crowding into the torture chamber door. Tom hurled himself forward, his movements hampered by the weight of the iron attached to wrist and ankle, but deadly still. This was no fencing match, this was a proposed slaughter where speed and elegance were irrelevant.

Topcliffe froze, thunderstruck. Baines hurled himself back into the rack room as Tom's blade hissed towards the Rackmaster. Topcliffe was a big man, ill-kempt and ill-shaved. Nothing to look at for a man who boasted of the way his rack stories ignited the Queen's blood and allowed him shocking licence with her person. He was a lucky man, however, in that the blade missed his throat, pulled awry after all by the swing of the fetters. Through the top of his shoulder it hissed and he leaped back with a scream almost as high as those of his victim.

Then Baines was back. He had discharged his gun to knock Tom senseless earlier and had not seen the need to reload. Now he was pouring powder into the nozzle with trembling speed and tamping it home. He half hid behind the stumbling form of the wounded Rackmaster and both of them fell back into the larger area of the torture chamber. Tom followed them slowly and relentlessly, until he had a clear view of the rack and its well-stretched occupant.

And it was not a woman but a man whose body lay prone and whimpering before him. Not Kate but Kit. Not Shelton the spy but Callot the charm. The relief was so intense that it made his head swim. His sword-point wavered and fell. There came a decisive, final *snap* as Baines cocked his pistol.

'Earl's command or no,' said Baines quietly, 'put down your sword or I'll kill you where you stand.'

'Shoot him in the leg, fool,' suggested Topcliffe viciously, his hand failing to staunch the blood seeping from his shoulder. 'I can still rack him with a shattered leg.'

But before Baines could follow his own thoughts or the Rackmaster's advice, there was a thundering on the outer door. 'My name is Robert Poley,' bellowed a stentorian voice. 'I hold a warrant here for Thomas Musgrave, Master of the Science of Defence. It is a warrant from the Court of Star Chamber to deliver the body of the said Thomas Musgrave whole and unwounded, to me forthwith; and I warn you, Baines and Topcliffe both, that it bears the signatures of Lord Henry Carey and Sir Robert Cecil and of Lord Burghley himself.'

*   *   *

Tom, relieved alike of his foils and his fetters on the swift journey from Newgate to Westminster, looked around the Court of Star Chamber. The chamber after which the court was named earned its own name from the designs on the ceiling and floor. It earned its fearsome reputation under the two great Henrys when it had been a fearsome engine of state repression. Enough of that reputation still remained for even the usually iron control of Tom Musgrave to soften a little. For this was in many ways the highest but most secret court in all the land. This was the most powerful court in all the kingdom – except for the court of the Queen's own will. This was the court, composed of the ministers of the Privy Council, that dealt with matters too great or too secret for all the other courts. Those matters touching the Throne too nearly. It was the great exception to the fatal rule for any man such as Tom himself to face the Court of Star Chamber and ever to be heard of again. The last man to do it was Kit Marlowe, summoned to court in May last year and dead in Deptford within the month, murdered by Robert Poley and his men. Tom looked across the room at his only friend there – Robert Poley. But Poley was looking at the court.

It was not a fully convened Star Chamber Court – rather a committee. Still and all, thought Tom, there was the Archbishop, to whom he had delivered Henslowe's dead dogs as a pretext to hide Morton's corpse. There was Henry Carey, Lord Hunsdon and Lord Chamberlain, whose wrath was the last thing he had heard. There was Lord Howard, the Lord Admiral, familiar from the Armada celebrations, last of the old warhorses now that Leicester was gone. There was quiet, sinister, crook-backed Robert Cecil, Mister Secretary in the late Sir Francis Walsingham's shoes. And there, in the central chair was Cecil the elder, Robert's father, Lord Burghley, King in all but name.

So, thought Tom, his mind racing like a hound at the hart's flank, these were the old guard. Where were the likes of Essex, Southampton, Cotehel, who would be Outremer within the week? Never allowed on committees such as this one. Closed out. Lacking real power. Forbidden access to any of the levers of civil power, forbidden everything except access to Her Majesty which could not be denied even by men like this. Like Southampton, like the late Lord Strange, forbidden even the distant dreams of a Catholic succession to keep their impatience in check. Dreams so close – in distance and time, for there were Catholics just across the Channel and Catholics who had held thrones both here and in neighbouring Scotland within the Queen's own lifetime. Dreams but one monarch and one plot-damned pretender – both called Mary – away. Dreams running hard against the walls of inevitability now – of an old woman whom they would outlive but with whom their hopes of power would die. Of a Scottish succession when King James would come south out of Edinburgh to London and these men, and their sons, would be set to inherit all.

One such son leaned forward. Sir Robert Cecil whispered into the ear of Lord Burghley, his father.

'Master Musgrave,' said Lord Burghley. 'You have been busying yourself in the affairs of this court and of the Council.'

'I have, my lord.'

The son spoke, before the lordly father could. 'You do not deny it?' snapped Sir Robert Cecil.

'To do so would be stupid in so many ways, my lord.' Tom continued talking to Lord Burghley, for the white-haired old man was the senior justice of the Star Chamber, the Principal Secretary of State to Queen and Council. The time spent at his uncle's knee and in conversations with the Lord of Bewcastle when down from Glasgow University had none of them been wasted, thought Tom now.

'How so?' asked Burghley.

'Although the matter began for me with a petty deception and a poor attempt to unmask the murderer of an actor at the Rose some three days since . . .'

Sir Robert Cecil leaned forward and whispered in his father's ear again. His eyes rested on Tom reminding him suddenly of Will's eyes, for they were heavy with intelligence. This man, Kate had said and Poley had confirmed, ran the remains of

Walsingham's intelligencer service and slept with her older sister Audrey who was set to marry Tom Walsingham, his predecessor's adopted son.

'This court has no record of such a murder.'

Tom continued to talk to Burghley but his eyes remained fixed on Sir Robert Cecil's eyes. 'I hid the body, my lord, for reasons I have explained to Master Poley, who is, sometimes at the least, an officer of the court; and to Lord Henry, here also. And, I believe, of Sir Robert, your son. It was only during my conversation with his Lordship and subsequently, working with Master Poley, that I came to realise that my little murder had anything to do with secret matters of state. But since I came to that realisation, reading Julius Morton's letter two days since in Alsatia, I have known. Yes, my lord.'

'And yet you saw fit to continue?'

'I stand to be corrected, my lord, but what I was doing seemed rather to be of help than otherwise. Always assuming that Master Poley's continued life, health and work were your lordships' principal method of investigation.'

'And why should they not be?' demanded Sir Robert Cecil, his eyes never leaving Tom's.

'I have Master Poley's word, my lord, and that of Lord Hunsdon. Both of course are sufficient in themselves. On the other hand, at no time has Master Poley made me privy to the full scale of the matter. In this case I am a veritable Pandora, my lord, and each time I open a box some greater evil leaps out of it. And opening boxes, my lord, is what I have been doing for the last three days; in the sure and certain knowledge that there are bigger boxes yet to be opened and Master Poley persists in keeping the keys concealed.'

'Were you a Pandora in truth,' observed Sir Robert dryly, 'then keeping the keys concealed would be a work of wisdom.'

'Then, my lord, if the truth is always to remain hidden from me then perhaps I should be hidden away from the truth.'

'Master Poley?' asked Sir Robert. 'How do we untangle this coil? 'Twould be easy enough to take him at his word. There are cells within the Tower that could accommodate him until the outer bounds of patience and convenience. Always assuming we wish to keep him above ground or in the city.'

Tom's heart clenched within him. But, just as Sir Robert had asked the question without looking away, so Tom awaited the answer with his eyes steadily on the secret Secretary's.

'I have tested this man in many ways,' said Robert Poley quietly. 'And have yet to find him wanting. I am slow to trust and with good reason as you know, but I have come to trust this man as my Lord of Hunsdon does. Except in the matter of the body, everything he has told me seems to have the stamp of truth. And even though, when I checked at the Plague Pit on the night of our first meeting and found it untenanted as I reported, there may have been a body as he says. Others I have subtly questioned agree. And it may have been spirited away. Both Phellippes's man Baines and my Lord of Essex's man Salgado have been busy behind our backs. But the nub of the matter is this. As Phellippes and Will Shakespeare are with codes and cyphers, so is this man with logic, Sir Robert. If I asked him to expound the entire matter now, like as not he would do so from the start, missing out little of import in spite of what I have kept locked away from him. He has saved my life. He has done much to slow the massacre of my people. Chance, Fortune – or Divine Providence – has fitted him for the task not only with the sharpness of his mind but also with the genius of his fencing arms and the position in which we find him, acquainted with Kate Shelton, friends with Will Shakespeare, allied with the Bishop's Bailiff. He has played Moses to Baines's subtle Pharaoh and has vanquished him at every turn. And – and this is most important, though I cannot yet explain it – he holds an invitation to go to Elfinstone for Baron Cotehel wishes to see him – and he alone, none other but he – fence with the Spanish assassin Salgado before the Earls of Essex and Southampton.'

'Not merely to fence, my lord,' added Tom quietly. 'To die. Whoever is Baines's master in this, the Earl of Essex or no, he has been ordered to ensure my arms are hurt. By rack or by bludgeon. I am to go there crippled if possible so that I may be seen to fight and die.'

'But if you are crippled,' asked Sir Robert quietly, 'how will they make sure that you go? That you fight against such fearful odds?'

'I have no idea,' said Tom quietly. 'But I know that it will be so.'

Henry Carey, Lord Hunsdon and Lord Chamberlain, shook his head, brows folding in that familiar frown. Both Tom and Robert Cecil were fooled into glancing towards him. 'It sits ill with me,' he growled, 'that Cotehel be allowed to enter into his uncle's castle and estates before due process of chancery law. Even by a day or two.'

'Your concern is noted, my lord,' said Lord Burghley. 'But what are your thoughts as to the matter before this court?'

'Oh, aye. Let the boy go. If he can survive, he's like to learn what lies at the bottom of this. And it'll be something foul, I'll wager, rather than something fair. And, now I think of it, I'm more than a little worried about the part played in this by those actors. Most of them are masterless men since the murder of Lord Strange and there seems little limit to the mischief they get up to if there's no eye kept upon them. I'll take Strange's men under my livery. It was Strange's Men that Morton and Shakespeare worked for was it not? Yes. I'll take them. Anyone like to stand surety for the rest?'

The Lord Admiral looked up. 'A good thought, Lord Hunsdon,' he said. 'I'll take the rest. Where are they playing now?'

Tom opened his mouth to answer, but it was Robert Cecil who said, 'They're playing at the Rose, my lord.'

They probably would never had believed it if anyone else had told them – certainly none of them would have credited it from the lips of Poley, who stood at Tom's side in the middle of the Rose's stage. 'Those that were Lord Strange's men may call themselves Lord Hunsdon's,' he told them. 'And the rest of you the Lord Admiral's.'

'But when is this to start?' demanded Dick Burbage, his face aglow.

'Not before the week's end,' said Will with an unexpected

frown. 'We play before my Lord of Southampton on Saturday. We cannot bow to another livery before then.'

'True,' chorused one or two others – the younger men eager to sample the delights promised by a weekend at a great house.

'And we cannot split up the company,' added Philip Henslowe, powerfully, 'before the end of our run with *Romeo*. We had planned to replace *Romeo* in the midst of next week. Let us wait until then and all part friends.'

And so it was agreed, and the company went off to prepare for the first house of the afternoon. Except for Will; he went off into the tiring room to work through some ill-hewn pieces of *The Play of Thomas More*. Tom followed, deep in thought, with Poley like Marlowe's Mephistophilis at his shoulder. 'Will . . .'

'Aye?'

'This Saturday . . .'

'What of it?'

'You play before Southampton, do you not?'

Will turned. There was a glow of excitement – perhaps of something more – in his face and eyes. 'We do. What of it?'

'But where do you play? Not Southampton House? For . . .'

'Ah. I see. No. We play before the Earl away. We are part of the merry evening he has planned with his friend Lord Outremer. We play at Elfinstone.'

'Would that be enough to get you down to Elfinstone, broken arms and all?' asked Robert Poley as they sat at the ordinary table in the Elephant. They had discussed Poley's fears on discovering no body in the plague pit and the manner that this had slowed his trust. But things were becoming clearer between them now.

Tom spooned some brewis into his mouth, savouring the way the salt-beef broth had softened the bread and filled it with flavour. There was a sallet of herbs on the table beside it and he took a mouthful of breath-freshening leaves, thinking of Constanza and her basil – both now gone. And of Kate, not yet reappeared. 'No,' he answered roundly enough. 'There would have to be more. What do we know of Baines and his present whereabouts?'

Poley chewed on his eel pie. 'Nothing. He'll have taken his warrant back to the Earl of Essex like as not. He's Star Chamber business now. The Fleet is the Star Chamber's prison and that's where he'll end when his foot slips. Or back with Topcliffe.'

'Aye. But in the meantime, he's still likely dogging our heels. He and Salgado both.'

'Then you had best watch your back as you go down to Elfinstone tomorrow.'

'Little need for that,' said Tom with a lightness he did not feel. 'I have a retinue to guard me.'

Whatever other confidences the two men might have been about to share were rudely interrupted by near pandemonium at the tavern's main door. Both men leaped to their feet and crossed decisively to the gaggle of people gathered loudly there. 'What's amiss?' demanded Poley.

An ill-looking man tugged an oily forelock, his broad, stubbled face folded in almost vacuous concern. 'There's terrible trouble at the Clink, your worship. There's mortal sickness abroad and even the Bishop's Bailiff stricken down and like to die.'

CHAPTER TWENTY-TWO

The Golden Hind

Talbot Law was dying. Neither he nor Tom doubted that for an instant. The Bishop's Bailiff lay on the table in the cramped little watch room of the Clink Prison, his head cradled in his friend's arms, his body gripped by racking convulsions. And yet he refused to die. Instead, between bouts of gasping and vomiting, he was choking out his confession – or that part of it that might pertain to Tom.

'Seven years back. At Nijmagen. The day the walls fell. Remember?'

'I remember, Old Law. What of it?'

'Weighed heavy on my conscience ever since. Time to un-burden now, I guess. You call to mind the tent? Lord Robert's tent? The rape? Aye. I see you do. Think on that Tom, where was the Master of Logic then? Think on the girl. And the boy you cut down.' Talbot's eyes begged as his face twisted in a grimace and his racked body heaved again.

Tom remembered. The scene had visited both memory and dreams often enough since, but he had never really thought about the incident. Truth to tell, he had always tried to avoid thinking about it. But as Talbot requested, and from the heights of much more worldly experience, he thought about it now. And saw at once what his friend was driving at. 'The girl had been ravaged. Thoroughly and brutally so. But not by the boy I fought. He was at a point, sure enough, and ready to push his rapine home – but he had yet to do so or he could never have faced me as he did. God's death, there was another man there. Hidden from us, letting his companion face us down!'

'Two lads, aye. Young but vicious enough, in all good faith. Hell-born, the pair of them. I held them there in spite of all their threatening and caterwauling. And I sent word to Lord Robert too, while Bess tended the poor maid as best she could. Lord Robert came out of the battle at my call, for the whelps had been eager enough to tell me who they were while they threatened what they would do to me unless I let them go – and Lord Robert was responsible for one of them at least. As you'd suspect, given where they were.

'The long and the short of it was that the Earl of Leicester himself came back from the battle like the wrath of God. He took one look at the situation; listened to what we all had to say. Then he whipped the pair of them to within an inch of their lives – there and then, in the tent, in front of the girl. He swore they were lucky he did not do the same in front of the whole of the army. Then he swore us all to silence and secrecy and we went on about the war.'

Tom sat, awed by the patterns that the simple revelation set forming through his head. 'The boy I fought was Hugh Outram, before he became Baron Cotehel,' he whispered, remembering the picture in Highmeet House. The hare lip, the star-shaped scar in the forehead. 'I marked him for life.'

'You marked his face,' whispered Talbot. 'But the Earl of Leicester marked his arse a good deal more.'

Tom gave a grating laugh. 'His arse wasn't in his portrait. But wait. The portrait that hung next to Cotehel's portrait. It showed the dead engineer. Captain Ive's messenger who died delivering the code.'

'That would be young Lord Henry. Cotehel's cousin. Son and heir to Lord Outremer of Wormwood in Jewry. Died like Sir Phillip Sidney in the service of his country. You'll have been in Siena for the great outpourings of public grief in London. Then the Armada came and we all forgot. Then the plague came and Lord Outremer's family all joined poor Lord Henry, leaving Hugh Outram, Baron Cotehel, Sir Rapine the Ravisher, to inherit it all.'

'And what of the girl?'

'Who knows? Bess tended her for a while, but she was a broken reed. A spirited, independent lass before, by all accounts, she simply became a kind of puppet. To lose her maidenhead and her brother in the one day addled her wits, poor thing. Especially as it was her cousin that she had grown up with since the cradle that was set to rape her too. And from what I could gather, her father, who was there supplying the army and had brought her because of her own flighty insistence, blamed her for the matter. Though he was broken in his own way by the death of Lord Henry his son and by the perfidy of his nephew Sir Hugh.'

'A heavy day all round,' mused Tom, thoughtfully. 'But tell me, Law, who was the second boy? The one who did perform the rape?'

Talbot convulsed, his face working. Tom leaned forward into the cloud of foetid breath reeking from his friend and pressed his ear to Talbot's lips. 'It was Robert Devereux,' whispered Talbot, his voice ghostly already.

And that was lucky, for at the very instant that Talbot spoke, Tom felt a heavy hand clap him on the shoulder. He glanced up to see Robert Poley looking down at him. 'Your friend is fortunate,' said Poley. 'I have managed to find both Señor Villalar and Master Gerard. If it is poison and anything can be done, these are the very men.'

Tom straightened slowly, his eyes on Talbot's, the weight of his friend's confession threatening to stoop his shoulders, but its relevance shining through the darkness of his thoughts like a summer's dawn. Like a man in a trance he walked up the steps out into Clink Street and stood with his back against the wall looking over a low fence, past the water mill and across the river to the Steelyard. He was still standing like a mooncalf when Villalar came up beside him some time later. 'Fear not,' said the Spaniard. 'They were not poisoned. They were purged.' He held up a sodden plant for Tom's inspection. 'Cassia fistula,' he said.

'More powerful than senna pods. It was in the drinking water.'

Tom simply gaped at the Spaniard, wrestling to bring his mind to a sharp focus on this. Of all the questions that came tumbling into his mind, the most urgent was: why? And the answer to that seemed all too plain.

Tom pushed past Villalar and stumbled back down the steps into the reeking place. Poley was there, in frowning conversation with Gerard. Talbot had swung round on the table and was half sitting up. He was looking stronger. His eyes skated away from Tom's gaze and the too-early breaking of his promise to the Earl of Leicester lay between them like a shadow. Tom had no leisure to dispel it now. 'Poley,' he said. 'This was done on purpose and the Bailiff was not its main object. I was. And this has held me here, while some darker business has been toward in Blackfriars, I am certain. Shall we go and look?'

Poley took a deep breath and choked upon it, then he gave a terse, frowning nod.

The four of them went together, crossing from St Mary Overie Stairs to Blackfriars and running up the bustle of Water Street. The little crowd that had gathered outside Master Aske's haberdashery confirmed Tom's worst suspicions. The haberdasher himself was seated on a stool immediately outside his shop door, talking to the City Watch as Mistress Aske mended his broken crown with one of her good Spanish needles and some thread. 'I saw them pushing out of Master Musgrave's door,' he was saying. 'A band of ruffians carrying a half-smothered woman . . . O Master Musgrave, thank the Lord you are here, sir. Your rooms are robbed, sir, and the lady ravished away. I tried to stop them in the street, sir, and am lucky to be able to tell the tale.'

'Has any been up to look?' demanded Tom, mentally swearing to thank his good neighbour more fully and formally when the opportunity allowed.

'None.'

Tom was in motion at once, shouldering through the crowd and pushing in through the vacant gape of his doorway. Eyes everywhere, wide in the gloom of his stairwell, he ran up the stairs. Poley was hard at his heels and Villalar not far behind. Tom erupted on to the landing and kicked the door to the long room open. The place was a mess – but his mirror stood unscathed. He turned and more gently pushed at the door into Ugo's workroom.

The room seemed empty; stripped. Except for Ugo himself. The Dutchman was seated, lashed securely, on his work stool. Movement was clearly difficult, perhaps impossible. Out before his rigid body stretched his right arm, reaching towards the bench immediately in front of him. Here, his right hand was clamped in his work vice, its fingers spread like the arms of a starfish and his thumb standing rigidly upright. And deeply into the tip of the upright thumb there was plunged a Spanish needle.

Tom thought he was dead. 'Ugo!' he called, his throat tearing.

But the Dutchman's head swivelled round towards him, dragging eyes reluctantly away from the needle. His face was a mess, eyes swollen, nose flattened, ears crusted with blood. 'He has her, Tom,' said Ugo, his voice slurred and his tone dead; defeated. 'He took her half an hour since by the chimes of Paul's bells. And he left a message for you. Señor Domenico Salgado extends his compliments to Master Thomas Musgrave and expresses his keen anticipation at the thought of meeting him blade to blade at Elfinstone. Until that time Señor Salgado salutes Master Musgrave and is happy to inform him that it will be his pleasure to entertain Signora Constanza d'Agostino and Mistress Katherine Shelton, who is currently accompanying him into the country . . . There was more, in the same flowery vein, but I cannot call it to mind now. The burden of it was that if you try to follow now, and be lucky enough to overtake him on his way, he will simply cut Kate's throat before he lets you take her back . . .'

As Ugo was speaking, Tom crossed to the bench and gently loosened the vice, lifting his hand free, as carefully as though it were Venetian glass.

Poley, at the door, observed dryly, 'Now at least we know

how they plan to get you to Elfinstone tomorrow, broken arms and certain death or no.' Then he joined Tom in untying Ugo, slipping the ropes off with exquisite care, for the Hollander was swaying with pain and fatigue – at the very least.

'The needle's poisoned,' continued Ugo conversationally as though Poley had not spoken. 'He said it will kill me sometime tonight. He suggests you do not wait to bury me before you start out in the morning.'

'Arrogant puppy! *Madre de Dios!*' Villalar spat from the doorway, where he had replaced Poley. 'Master Musgrave, bring your friend to myself and Master Gerard here, and we will undo what the poison has done, be it never so venomous. The quickest poisons are the surest. A lingering tincture like this will be more easily overcome. Señor Stell, can you stand? *Excellente!* Now, can you walk? *Hola!* We are on the way to making you well again, are we not, Señor Gerard?'

Tom would have gone with them but Poley stopped him. 'Tomorrow morning you must go to Elfinstone. It may be that you will have to go alone, or it may be that Villalar and Gerard will be as good as their word. I will be close at hand but I dare not come into Elfinstone itself – no disguise would hide me from some of the eyes that will be there. It may be that you will be able to rely upon Will Shakespeare and his men if your need becomes great. But the long and the short of the matter is this, and you know it. Only you can stand against Salgado and the men he works for. Only you can free Kate – and Constanza if you wish – from the toils that have them bound down there. And only you can see us clear through to the black heart of this thing.'

'And I can only do that,' concluded Tom, 'for as long as I remain alive.'

'There will be no lessons this afternoon,' said Poley. 'None of your lordly pupils would come pushing past the Watch at your door. I will put up a notice of warning and leave you be while the Master Apothecaries see to Ugo. And you, for the love of God, must practise. Practise to the top of your bent.'

When the rooms were quiet once again, Tom went through

into the long room, stripping off his doublet and pulling on his black fencing gloves. He kicked aside the mess on the floor and picked up the wooden dummies marked with all the target areas, using the effort of heaving them back into position to bring fire and suppleness to his muscles. Then, having arranged them in a row alongside the end of the mirror, he cleared a line in front of them so that a glance to the side revealed his reflection. He loosened his sword belt and pulled out the swords. Then, slowly at first, he began to fall into a series of poses. One after another, he rehearsed all Capo Ferro's opening positions, and then added his own favourite variants. Right hand leading, with left curled like the tail of a scorpion; left hand leading with the right held low. From the *Posta del Falcone* on high, to the *Porta di Ferro* below. From the fourteen *postas* or positions, he began to move into his attacks on the four openings, wounding the wooden opponents more and more fiercely on the right side, left side, right below the belt and left below the belt. And time after time, breaking from the rigorous inevitability of the chess-like fight sequences, to thrust with all his power, giving the great bellow of, 'Hey!' Knees and hamstrings, thighs, groin, hip, belly, wrist, elbow, shoulder, chest, heart, heart, heart, lung, throat, mouth, nose, cheek, eye, brain, all the targets felt his points repeatedly, unerringly, more and more swiftly, as he slid back and forth along the line of attack, ever glancing at himself in the mirror, coldly noting the perfections of his stance.

Darkness gathered until Tom was little more than a shadow moving in the shadowy mirror like a deadly fish deep in a still pool. The targets began to splinter, gouged into perfect little hollows by the repeated, relentless probing of his unerring point. The cool of the evening stuck the billowing lawn of his shirt to his sweating torso. His hair wound itself into dripping coils and hung burning in his eyes. His mind soared free, like the falcon that gave its name to his first high stance. Refusing to speculate about what might be happening to Ugo, Kate or even Constanza, he let it wander freely looking down at the patterns this active day had shown him. As Poley had asked him to, so seemingly long ago, seeking for the one throat to cut, the one head to lop whose fall might bring the whole coil to an end. It was like a quartering after the hanging and drawing. First the limbs and then the head. First Baines, then Salgado, then who? Who? Who?

Tom had no knowledge that he was shouting the question '*Who?*' instead of the fencer's '*Hey!*' at the completion of each attack, until Ugo called gently to him, 'Master?' Breaking his terrible concentration just at the moment that Poley brought in the light. Then all three of them stood staring, simply appalled, at the relentlessly focussed devastation he had visited on the crippled, man-shaped targets.

Exhausted on every level, Tom plunged into a sleep every bit as deep as the one Villalar's healing potions induced in Ugo. So that it was Poley, coming down from Hog Lane laden with plans and breakfast, who awoke them in the morning. As they ate and drank, Villalar arrived, fresh from Gerard's apothecary. He carried a black box the size of a church bible. Inside it he revealed and then described some half dozen jars containing remedies to various poisons. 'And this last, it is most sovereign but most dangerous. It is a tincture of aconite, good for treating most poisons, according to the ancients, as fire can cast out fire. But it must only be used in the last extremity, for it is as like to kill as to cure. Here you see a bleeding bowl and surgeon's knife, tourniquet, syringes and a jar of leeches.'

While their guests finished Poley's breakfast, Tom and Ugo both went through what was left in their ransacked rooms. Ugo pulled the snaphaunce revolvers from their hiding places and gathered sufficient gunpowder and lead to load them both, a laborious procedure largely completed left-handed. Then he looked to some clothing impressive enough, he hoped, to make the legendary chambermaids overlook the ruin of his face and the bandages on his right hand. Tom, meanwhile, saw to the tending, scabbarding and packing of his Solingen blades, then sorted out the best attire his years in the cockpit of Italian fashion could afford.

They set out for Elfinstone mid-morning, starting at the

Blackfriars Steps and shooting the Bridge on a falling tide, before they transferred to one of the larger ferries which jostled along the length of Deptford Strand. If Tom suspected that the big house up above them there was the house of Mistress Bull where Kit Marlowe had died bleeding over Poley's hands, he said nothing – beyond giving his directions to the boatmen. The boat dropped them at Greenhithe little more than an hour later and Ugo, narrow-eyed and practical, hired them four good-looking horses. One of was them black as night – a fine gelding entirely suited to the swagger of a Master of Defence called to perform the mysteries of his science before the richest and the noblest in the land. No one argued when Tom took that one.

An hour's leisurely travel, enlivened by the deepest, darkest conference, brought them along the south bank of the river to the village of Gravesend, with its crossing to the grander town of Tilbury to the north. There the Earl of Leicester's last public responsibilities had been accomplished mere days before his death. Then they turned south through the balmy afternoon, into the gentle Kent countryside, following an ancient roadway wandering past tiny hamlets to the crossroads at Higham where they meandered eastwards to the inn at Wainscott. Here they tethered their horses and gathered in the coolness of the tap for a final, almost whispered conference.

The land to the south of them gathered up and fell away, Rochester on the far face of the rise overlooking the River Medway and King Henry's Dockyard at Chatham. Along the eastern stretch of the cliff, well outside the town itself, stood Elfinstone. Had any of them cared to stand up on the old inn's thatched roof, they might have seen its upper battlements from here. At Wainscott, finally, Tom and Ugo invested an hour in gorging themselves with the finest the old inn had to offer. 'For remember,' said Villalar urgently, as they left at last, 'eat nothing. Drink nothing, if you can. Any drop or morsel that passes your lip might be death.'

'Our very bedding might be deadly,' said Ugo lugubriously, half an hour later. 'Clothing can be primed to kill. I am no scholar and master such as you, Tom, but I know well enough the way even mighty Hercules was killed with a poisoned cloak, by his wife Dejanira at the bidding of Nessus the Centaur.'

'My life at least is like to be preserved until the fight after the play tonight,' said Tom. 'My life, if not my limbs.'

This last observation served to take them under the great gate that stood astride the main entrance into the walled grounds of Elfinstone. On this side they were walled, to stop the deer in the park from wandering away, but further east, as the ground settled down to the River Medway, there was no need for walls and the great hunting grounds swept away almost unlimited towards Cliffe and Hoo St Werburgh. To the west, the cliff on which Elfinstone itself sat, gathered into such precipitate wildness that only the most desperate hart or hind would dare attempt it.

The gate stood wide, inviting Tom and Ugo to follow the broad roadway down to the castle, but the pair of them turned aside into the wooded sward on their right hand, preferring to come upon Elfinstone unannounced, from the wild side, having spied out the time and the land. The woodland gathered rapidly and the hillside gathered beneath it until Tom slowed the black gelding to a careful walk. 'There's a cliff edge hidden in the undergrowth nearby,' Tom said quietly. '' Tis time to turn and see how we can reach Elfinstone from here.' But the instant that he spoke, the quiet of the summer's afternoon was shattered by the baying of hounds. Away, further right still, at the very cliff edge hidden in the woods, a hunt was in progress. Tom's horse danced uneasily, and Tom himself rose in the stirrups, looking around with a frown. 'There looks to be a pathway down here,' he began, sitting again and nudging his nervous mount forward.

No sooner had he done so, however, than a wild figure hurled out of the undergrowth beneath its very hooves. The gelding reared and Tom fought for a moment to settle it down again. By the time it was still, Ugo was down, had knelt, and was standing again. In his arms he held the slight figure of a woman. She seemed to have fainted or been caught by the plunging horse's hoof. Her hair was a tangle of dark gold badly in need of a wash and comb. Her clothing seemed to consist merely of a solid bodice and the rags of a skirt. As Ugo lifted her higher, Tom saw that she was wearing a thick belt with short-chained manacles designed to hold her hands at her sides. Frowning, he reached down and caught her up out of Ugo's arms. The rags of skirt fell away from long, lean thighs, but Tom's eyes remained entranced by the pattern instead of the nudity. He knew the cloth she was wearing. And he knew her, therefore.

Her eyelids flickered. 'Mistress Margaret,' he said gently. 'Mistress Margaret, I have followed you here from Wormwood House. I bring greetings from Master Seyton . . .'

Her eyes opened, as though she had been in the deepest sleep. The bright blue of her gaze swirled around huge black pupils which seemed to gulp him down like the River Styx washing into the deeps of hell. He felt her tense, fighting like a hind indeed to be free of her relentless hunters. 'Margaret,' he said again, with all the gentleness at his command. And the writhing of her body stilled. A kind of recognition entered those wild eyes. Recognition and a kind of trust. She nestled against him and he saw, in the wild riot of her hair, half covering her naked and abused body, this same girl, seven years earlier in the Earl of Leicester's tent near Nijmagen, falling fainting at the feet of her would-be ravisher, the Baron Cotehel.

The dogs burst out of the undergrowth then, with the huntsmen hard behind them. Surrounded by baying hounds, Tom's gelding simply froze; and much to his relief the Lady Margaret did the same.

So it was that he was able to confront his host, straight-backed and eye to eye. Baron Cotehel reined his mount to a plunging stand as half a dozen wild bucks did the like behind him, and his huntsmen ran forward to whip the dogs away. The two men knew each other at once as though they had been adversaries fighting face to face over the last few deadly days. Over the shrinking form of the shackled, half-naked woman, Tom made his most courtly bow. 'My Lord of Cotehel,' he said quietly. 'May I congratulate you on your accession to the titles, lands and chattels of Outremer, when they come to you tomorrow.'

The sneering boy had grown into a sneering man – aided by the damage Tom had done to his lips. He had lost nothing of the temper or the arrogance Tom remembered so well. His face went purple now as he saw the terrified object of his hunt held safe in Tom's strong arms. The scar upon his forehead burned red like a new brand. He opened his mouth to reveal smashed and blackened teeth.

'Out, you whoreson . . .' he began, and two men spurred up to sit beside him. Domenico Salgado sat tall, and every bit as deadly as Tom remembered from his fleeting glimpse at the Rose, though he wore no swords when hunting, of course. On Cotehel's other side sat a tall, long-faced gallant a year or two older than his friend. He had a long face with high cheekbones and steady brown eyes astride a long nose. The long hair and the wisp of moustache were at the pinnacle of fashion. Beneath the moustache the thin upper lip twisted in a smile that barely stirred the sensuous thickness of the lower and reached nowhere near those steady, chilly, chocolate eyes. 'Come now, Hugh,' drawled Robert Devereux. 'You said whoever caught her could have her. And Master Musgrave has her, never a doubt. It is Thomas Musgrave, Master of Defence, is it not?'

'It is, your grace. Though how you come to know me I cannot begin to tell.'

'Oh I know you, Master Musgrave,' purred the Earl of Essex coldly. 'Though I regret that our acquaintance shall be sadly short-lived.'

CHAPTER TWENTY-THREE

The Point of Death

A ny attempt to spy out the land in secret was now at an end.
With the half-naked woman sitting, shrinking, across his
saddle-bow, Tom turned the black gelding's head towards the
main gate and the thoroughfare leading down to Elfinstone's
grand entrance. All along this open, public way were the marks
of earlier celebrations. A cart of deer hunted to death yesterday
trundling inwards for tonight's table. The blackened, smoul-
dering craters of huge bonfires, the scars of the blazing,
showering and exploding of fireworks. An empty pavilion
down by the castle's wide fishponds, a gilded barge pulled
on to the sloping sward beside it. What looked like a mermaid's
tail, eerily empty. An antique tomb lying open, blasted wide,
apparently by some pyrotechnic accident. The atmosphere of
dissipation spinning into wild excess closed relentlessly around
them as they approached Elfinstone's craggy walls.

Tom, Ugo and the silent Lady Margaret passed through a
lengthy series of rituals as they were guided deeper and deeper
into the cold grey heart of the place. In the granite-flagged
courtyard inside the huge portcullis, they were relieved of their
horses, which were led away by Lord Outremer's grooms. They
were assigned servants to take the baggage that the horses had
carried and to guide them through the maze of the massive,
steely keep to Tom's chamber first, then Ugo's bed in the
servants' hall. As a guest of the chamber, Tom fell under the

sway of my Lord's Chamberlain, and that assured him of elevated status in accommodation, of service and at meals. And, indeed, he was to be flattered with one of the most commodious chambers, on the outer wall above the midden, with its own private garderobe, four-poster and wide ewer of fresh water. From its one tall window, it commanded a view across the western grounds, over the blasted tomb towards the forested cliffs. Ugo was destined to sleep in the hall, pitched in with the retinues of the other visiting dignitaries; but even he took precedence over the lowlier servants of Elfinstone Castle itself, many of whom had been dragged in from farms and smallholdings on the estate and nearby for the occasion.

This was just as well. Ugo bore no indentures and was a freeman in a guild of his own. Only his association with actors over the last few months allowed him to move out of his real self, forget what respect was due to him, and assume the person of the Master's man he seemed to be. Tom, of course, had taken to duplicity as though it had come to him with his mother's milk – though had he been the man he pretended, he would have been wet-nursed.

Now he gazed deeply into the wide, trusting eyes of Lady Margaret as she sat, rigid on his bed. Ugo finished loosening the straps that had pinioned her arms. She moved them stiffly, as though unused to having them free. Such was her fierce concentration on Tom's face that all else seemed blotted out to her – not least the utterly revealing nature of the few shreds of rag that were all she wore beneath her waist. Hesitantly, like a virgin lover, she reached out to Tom. Tom, all but entranced, reached out to her in return. Gently, she took his hand and pressed it with fearsome strength to her bosom. Through the stiff bib of her bodice Tom could feel the pounding of her heart, the urgent swell and fall of her breasts. She looked at him, frowning with concentration, her mouth wide and working, but silent.

'What is it, my Lady?' he asked gently. 'What would you have of me?'

Frowning more deeply still, she crushed his hand to her

softness, but he could not understand what she was trying to tell him. His kindness and concern were focussed upon her, but in truth his mind was not. He wished to see her properly dressed, and wondered how to go about that. He wanted to explore the castle – to find out where his enemies were, and where they held his friends. He ached with impatience to assure himself that Kate and Constanza had not been harmed. And yet he was held here by the wild eyes of this poor mad girl, the strength of her grip and the burning softness of her bosom.

The door to the chamber opened behind him. He turned, hearing a quiet step and the swish of a skirt. 'God's my life, Tomas. I cannot visit you these days but I find you sporting with some naked trull. When you wish to end an *amour*, sir, you certainly go about it hammer and tongs!'

'Bella!' he cried with relief. 'Are you well?'

'Why should I not be well?'

The simple innocence of the question gave him pause. He had supposed her ravished away; and yet, apparently not. 'You are a guest here?' he asked.

'Of Señor Salgado, the Spanish Maestro, friend and advisor to His Grace of Essex.'

'He is your lover, then?' asked Tom with some relief.

'Tomas! Not in front of Signor Stell, whom I know well, and certainly not in front of some doxy I know not at all! Why does she press your hand to herself in this manner? What in all the world is that mess she is wearing?'

Ugo rose to the occasion while Tom was caught between framing a lie that would cover it all and trying to recover his hand. 'She is a maudlin woman we found in the woods, *madonna*. Master Tom wishes to take care of her and was trying to find out about her when you came in.'

'So, she has her past engraved on her heart, has she? Well, her future must involve some bathing and some dressing. Maudlin, you say. Is she new escaped from Bedlam then? Does she rave? Is she dangerous?'

'The opposite,' said Tom. 'She has been ill-used beyond imagining and yet she sits silent as a puppy.'

'Well, I will tend to her,' decided Constanza. But her simple plan was lent unexpected complexity by Lady Margaret's intractable refusal to leave Tom's room. Constanza swept out to get her maid and some clothing. Tom sent Ugo out to look for the servants' hall and reconnoitre as he did so.

The instant they were alone, Margaret let go of Tom's hand. He stood back a little, frowning down at her, all too aware that her presence here was a responsibility and a handicap he could well do without. He glanced at the door, crossed to it and exchanged a nod with the servant standing guard outside, closed it again then turned back to the bed – and found Margaret stark naked. Above the scratched and battered paleness of her body, her eyes claimed his again. There was nothing of carnality in them; little enough of madness. Simply an absolute, child-like, overwhelming trust. Out above the mottled moons of her breasts, she was thrusting the verminous wreckage of her clothing at him, the bodice of her gown spread taut. He took it automatically, and the moment that he did so, he realised what she had been trying to tell him. The layers of material crackled stiffly between his fingers. He brought the bodice up closer and looked at it. There was layer upon layer of neat stitching around the edge where layer after layer of extra cloth had been sewn on to the inside. He slid out his dagger and slit the cloth with all the care of a barber surgeon. And pulled out Lord Outremer's missing will. One glance at the ornate writing on the official-looking parchment was enough. This was the document Wormwood in Jewry had been torn asunder to find. And she had carried it next to her heart all along. Constanza's jibe had been true enough after all. His eyes met Margaret's over the top of the document and both of them smiled.

The door opened and the fleeting moment of intimacy was past. As was the tiny instant of sanity. The naked woman's eyes were blank, fathomless. 'Tomas!' cried Constanza. 'What now?'

He stood between the women, using his body as a shield while he folded the will into the breast of his doublet. 'I think Lady Margaret is ready for a wash,' he said. Then he wasted ten more minutes explaining to Constanza how he knew the lady's name and title all of a sudden, what little he knew of her – what little he dared reveal to Domenico Salgado's new *amour*.

The Great Hall was a wild bustle. It was a room large enough to have contained the Rose, tall enough to have held two of its three galleries. And it was galleried indeed, on three walls, with tall windows standing high above. Below, the east and west ends of the room were distinguished by the Great Door and the Lesser Door and along the walls to north and south stood suits of armour holding huge swords such as might have been wielded in the heroic days of old.

Above the Great Door hung the coat of arms of Lord Outremer. Through this door, beneath these gilded arms, all the guests would process to table tonight. Above the Lesser Door to the west stood a gallery like the minstrels' gallery at the Rose, which would indeed be a minstrels' gallery tonight, until the play transformed it into Juliet's bed chamber, and her tomb.

Between the Great Door and the Lesser Door, tables, trestles and trenchers; benches, chairs and stools were all lying scattered hither and yon. Chairs lay ready to seat the guests and, in the centre, a huge gilded throne, backed with the arms of Outremer, sat ready to elevate the Baron Cotehel. Boards and costumes, props and playbooks were generally disposed. Chamber staff, kitchen staff, actors and onlookers bustled and gestured, rushed and dawdled and lolled. Somewhere a lutanist was practising an ancient air by Thomas Tallis. Somewhere a consort of viols was preparing the latest fashionable air by Peter Phillips, a musician popular amongst those who had spent time in the Low Countries, his 'Dolorosa Pavane' and 'Galliard'. It was mid-afternoon and the feasting was due to start at six.

After two hours of eating and drinking, accompanied by music and general entertainments, there would be dancing to music livelier than Phillips's 'Pavane', after which the Rose Company would give *Romeo*. Then Maestro Domenico Salgado would execute Master Thomas Musgrave for the amusement of the new Lord Outremer and in elegant completion of his designs for usurpation and revenge, and the company would go to bed at midnight.

Or that, thought Tom grimly, was the plan. He leaped easily up on to the low stage that stood to one side of the Lesser Door at the west end of the chamber, ready to be pushed into place beneath the gallery there when the feasting was done and the coming-and-going at an end. He needed to learn these boards, for it was likely that his duel with Salgado would be fought across them. But he needed to talk to Will Shakespeare more.

The playwright was pacing through Mercutio's death with the relevant actors. Luckily, the Rose's stage was small enough to be perfectly reproduced here – or Tom would likely have been distracted in earnest, called in to restage Romeo's mock duels with Tybalt and the County Paris before undertaking the deadly reality of his own. 'Will,' called Tom. 'Have you seen Kate Shelton?'

'No. But I've seen both Salgado and Baines. And I hear Constanza's here somewhere too.'

'Are you all staying after *Romeo* for the rest of the entertainment?'

'For your duel? Of course. I have laid ten angels that you best him within the first five passes.'

'Can I call on you? Can I count on you?'

'Is Ugo not standing with you?'

'Yes. But if I need to, can I count on you?'

Will looked straight into Tom's eyes. He said nothing. In spite of his light banter about betting, Will knew there was something more serious at hazard here. But would he stand with Tom if the dreadful need arose?

Tom thought of the summer Will had spent in Southampton House and moving through the Earl's country residences with the Earl, the Earl of Essex and their courtly circle. He was asking the playwright to walk away from undreamed riches, all but limitless influence. From the love of a powerful patron, bosom friend to Her Majesty's current favourite. 'I must spend the remainder of the day avoiding Salgado's poisons and Baines's bullies simply to stand on level ground tonight,' he persisted. 'Cotehel is the kind of man that hunts women through his parks with his hounds for his pleasure and holds Kate somewhere in this palace he has slaughtered a family to get, and he wants me dead and you know well enough why. I'm surprised he's let you live as long as this yourself, for you were there with me at the start.'

'Now why should I fear the fox,' asked Will quietly, 'when I have slept with the lion?' On that he turned back to his business and Tom went away about his, wondering why Will should leave it until this moment to confirm at last that he had read the long-banned, deadly dangerous works of Niccolo Machiavelli.

There were only two places Kate could be, thought Tom grimly. In a private chamber or a dungeon. If Morton's fears for her had any basis, then a dungeon seemed most likely, unless she, like Will and Constanza, was sleeping with the enemy already – or, like him, was destined to be exhibited tonight so their fates could be sealed in public. These thoughts were chilling enough, but the alternative was worse – especially to his ears that remembered the sounds Kit Callot had made on Topcliffe's rack when he had thought the tortured screams were hers.

Using the bustle that ranged throughout the castle, therefore – the fact that there were so many guests and servants stranger here, and most of them lost for much of the time – he spent the next two hours in fruitless search. It was only when a heavy hand fell on his shoulder and a flustered, familiar servant, discovering him in Lord Outremer's own quarters, backed this time by a dangerous-looking guard, insisted on guiding him back to his chamber, that he was forced to give up.

Ugo and Margaret were both waiting for Tom in his chamber and while one filled his ears the other filled his eyes. 'I've discovered a clear path for our retreat and escape if needed,' said Ugo. 'It was no easy task for I've been dogged every inch of my way. Whether you noticed or not, you have been yourself, Tom. It seems to me that every enemy we've crossed swords with during the last few days is here. I keep expecting to find Nick o' Darkmans lurking, or Topcliffe in the cellarage. Are you listening?'

'Aye,' said Tom. Constanza had put Margaret in one of her old dresses but the green-gold brocade suited her colouring well. The servant-girl had washed her breast, face and arms at least, and Constanza had lent shoes, so that she sat demurely, a high bodice pinned in place across a snowy cleavage and tiny golden toe-tips peeping from under her hem. They had not washed her hair but they had combed and brushed it until it sprang out into a riot of curls that swept over her shoulders and halfway down her back. A little white arsenic to pale her cheeks and a little rouge to redden her lips. There had been no need for belladonna to deepen the fathomless sparkle of her eyes.

'Even so,' persisted Ugo grimly, 'we'll be hard put to walk away from this, even had we just ourselves to care for. Your duel is to the death.'

'To the death,' nodded Tom. Slowly at first, then with gathering decision and energy as they talked, Tom began to wash and change.

'Then when you kill Salgado this Baron Cotehel's likely to call his people down on us, and even apart from Baines, there's a good number of well-armed guards about. Even if I didn't already have good reason to be nervous, I'd be extremely nervous stuck in this place tonight. There's evil afoot. Evil at the least of it. Have you sounded out Will and the others?'

'Will?' said Tom, pulling off his doublet and laying it, wrapped around the will, beside her on the bed.

'Can we count on him? What did he say?'

'He quoted Machiavel at me. *Il Principe*.' He stripped off his shirt and crossed to the ewer of scented water Constanza had left behind.

'God's death, the spy's bible. What did he mean by that?'

'He meant to tell me he was the Earl of Southampton's man, and that his life depended upon it.' He dashed a handful of water, violets and lavender flowers into his face. Rinsed his mouth and spat. He straightened, frowning, and crossed to

220

Villalar's box of potions. He lifted out the last vial, the sovereign remedy, and put a drop on his finger, tasted it and spat again. The vial, tightly stoppered, went into the purse at his belt. Then he spoke, slowly, thinking through the implications of Will's words. 'He meant that, like me, he's so deep in the toils of this thing that his life's worth nothing any more. And that only Southampton stands between him and the fate I can expect to meet before the stroke of midnight.' He caught up his doublet again and pulled out the will. 'Therefore I want you to take this through your escape route and bring it to Robert Poley at the Wainscott Inn with all the speed you may. Guard it with your life, and remember, even if Cotehel's plans for me run true, this will shall bring him down at my hand after all; though I be as dead as Will's Mercutio in the play, or poor Kit Marlowe down in Deptford.'

Tom took Lady Margaret down with him when he went to the Great Hall on the next stage of his march towards death. All he had to do was touch her and she seemed to become his puppet. She swept under Lord Outremer's coat of arms and into the glittering bustle like a queen, however, and for a moment her presence stilled every tongue and captured every eye. A lesser man might have hoped the sudden silence was a tribute to his black velvet doublet picked with silver and slashed with rose silk almost as dark as the rubies in his ears. Or the way his twin swords swaggered astride his black galligaskins above his Spanish kid boots. But Tom knew when he was bested – and he wryly hoped that this was the only time that he would be bested tonight.

He sat her at his side on the high table where, with Cotehel and his circle, he sat above the salt. But, having been placed – at the expense of some shuffling to allow the extra guest, right at the end of the table – neither Tom nor Margaret could be tempted by the feast.

The servants labouring in from the kitchens through the Lesser Door laden with course after course for the main tables and the long removes beneath the galleries could not catch their attention. The servants standing solicitously behind each one of them offering to pile their trenchers with food they could not reach, to fill their glasses with drink of every sort, got no reply to their enquiries and soon stood silently themselves. They joined politely in with the applause accorded to the Master Cook when he came in with his masterpieces, but nothing he had prepared passed down their throats.

Not the peacocks, swans and cock-pheasants brought in from Elfinstone Park, stuffed, roasted and served in their full plumage on plates of beaten gold could tempt either of them. Not the pike, eel and dolphin culled from the river below and swimming in lakes of herb sauce and butter on massive silver chafing dishes heated from below. Not the woodcocks and partridges baked in pies. Not the great sallets of parsley, sage, shallotts, leeks, borage, mint, purslain, fennel, cress and rosemary. Not the huge green sturgeon, boiled and sliced steaming at the table. Not the crane served with every feather in place and standing on one leg with a trout in its beak, nor the broiled baby herons served with it. Not the haunches of venison, hart and hind, roasted, boiled and baked. No jellies, potages, dates in compost. No lech of sugar, wine and spices, no damask sweet of sugared rose leaves, no suttletie, tart or fritter of strawberries or almonds could make them open their mouths. No salmon served in gold foil, no roast boar filligreed in silver and stuffed with piglets and rabbits, no dragon made of marchpane, no conger, lamprey or red herring passed their lips.

No wine of Egypt, Greece, Cyprus, Madeira, Italy, France, Portugal or Spain, chilled, mulled, syruped, sweetened, savoured or salted with dissolving pearls, could tempt their palettes. No mead or ale or beer or even water. If they talked to each other or the company, then none heard. If they laughed at the antics of the jester, the jugglers, the clowns, stilt walkers, acrobats, bears or apes, then none saw it. If they listened above the bustling hubbub to the pavanes of Peter Phillips, or the airs of Thomas Tallis or the boy who sang 'Greensleeves', then no one knew it. They did not eat, they did not drink, they did not talk, they did not laugh, they did not dance. Even under the questioning eyes of the laughing Constanza measuring a galliard, then leaping into a volte with Salgado as the music of Phillips was replaced by that of Dowland.

Tom sat moodily watching the great lords upon their elevated seats eating, drinking and laughing, then stepping down to dance – ever and anon glancing back down at him seeming to share some secret, sinister jest. Lady Margaret sat staring silently but fixedly at the beautiful little blue-eyed, golden boy who served the Earl of Essex as his page; but the boy was assiduous to his task and did not see the lady watching him. They did not move until it was time for *Romeo*.

For *Romeo* the room was rearranged. The tables that had made a great horse-shoe around three walls were carried away through the Great Door to be cleared elsewhere. The seats were arranged before the newly positioned stage. The lords and earls remained upon their raised dais. Their servants and the page boy remained standing at their shoulders. The rest of the company was put into long rows across the hall. The candles, lit long ago to illuminate the dancing, were darkened at the east end so that Lord Outremer's gilded arms burned dimly in the shadows and the stage stood under the light.

It was strange, thought Tom grimly, how the contrast between the light and darkness seemed to change the atmosphere. The Great Hall became a place of sinister whispering and shadowed scurrying even before Ned Alleyn heaved himself up on to the creaking boards and intoned the prologue to the play. Tom found himself torn. His eyes were keen to be exploring what was going on here, the increasingly worrying comings and goings; the thronging of the shadows with men who carried things that, like Lord Outremer's arms, occasionally gleamed amid the dullness. On the other hand, in spite of all the rehearsals he had attended and all the action he had staged, he had never seen the play. Even on a night such as this – in danger such as he stood in, with friends lost and enemies gathering and his death ticking nearer with every moment passing – he found he could become gripped by the simple power of the drama unfolding in Will Shakespeare's Verona.

At last he sat enraptured, lost to everything except the

terrible dilemma of Juliet and her vial of poison as she prepared to drink it and fall into apparent death – fearing all the while that she might awake in her tomb and run mad before Romeo could rescue her.

> 'Is it not likely that I,
> So early waking, what with loathsome smells
> And shrieks like mandrakes torn out of the earth,
> That living mortals hearing them run mad –
> Oh if I wake, shall I not be distraught,
> And madly play with my forefathers' joints
> And pluck the mangled Tybalt from his shroud . . .'

And even as the words were spoken, at the very instant Juliet uttered them on stage, a flash of light caught the corner of Tom's eye. No one else seemed to see it for he was positioned right at the end of the front row with no one beyond him except those sinister, shuffling shadows. With the poor girl's desperate words ringing in his ears, he looked across at the light. And there, just for a second, there and gone as a door into another, brighter, room swung open and closed upon her, there was Kate.

Kate was dressed in the very same costume as the boy playing Juliet – though she filled it more naturally. And she wore a gag of cloth across her mouth, above which her eyes rolled with a desperation close to madness indeed. For like Juliet in her nightmare vision, Kate was chained to a dead man. She crouched and he lay, green and mouldering like Juliet's slaughtered cousin might do in his tomb. Into Tom's mind flashed the vision of the open tomb he had passed in the grounds. The tomb he could see from his chamber window. The tomb in all probability he was destined to share with these two, if Cotehel's plans ran true.

For a moment Tom thought the corpse was Ugo Stell and all was lost indeed. But then he realised. It was the late Julius Morton. Morton taken up from the Plague Pit so that he was gone when Poley came to look for him. Morton brought to

Elfinstone as Cotehel's punishment for Kate, his contact. And punishment indeed, punishment beyond mere death, for Morton the intelligencer who had died trying to warn her with his dying breath. He tore himself half erect, but a hand crashed down upon his shoulder, pinning him relentlessly into his seat. There was a smell of oil and garlic lightened with a mouthful or two of sweet basil. Stunned and shaking, Tom looked back at the stage, thinking that the Lady Margaret sitting silently beside him, straining for a sight of the boy with the Earl of Essex, was probably the sanest person there.

As the applause died away, the stage was cleared and the actors joined the people thronging the shadows behind the rows of chairs and the raised dais at their centre. Between the dais and the stage stood an area of granite floor. It was perhaps ten feet wide and stretched the width of the room. Here, at the feet of Baron Cotehel and the Earls of Essex and Southampton, their assembled friends, acolytes and hangers-on, Tom at last stood face to face with Domenico Salgado. The silence in the room was massive, a thing of weight, as though the air had been transformed to stone. A black shape stepped out of the shadows to second the Spaniard and Tom recognised the knowing, brutal leer of the murderous Baines. The Englishman helped the Spaniard shrug off his doublet and prepare for the bout as one of Cotehel's courtiers stepped forward to referee the match.

Tom turned, alone, and tore off his doublet, pretending not to notice the stir as everyone realised he was without a second. Carelessly he wadded up the expensive velvet and threw it away to his left, up on to the stage. Then, after a moment, he followed it with the white lawn of his shirt. Naked to the waist, he unbuckled his sword belt and laid that on the warm pile of his clothes, then he eased the second belt that held his galligaskins and secured his money-pouch and dagger, tightening the black gloves that matched his kid boots so well. Pulling all his concentration in within himself, he eased his arms and shoulders, stretched his back, then tested the long muscles of his legs, ensuring his clothing did not hinder his movements and the grip of his boots on the granite floor was sure.

When Tom pulled out his rapiers the whole room seemed to sigh and he turned to face Salgado, realising that chance had made the Spaniard unsheath his weapons at exactly the same moment. They faced each other in silence until the Spaniard turned abruptly to salute Cotehel and Essex. Tom turned with a grim smile and saluted Constanza who sat beside Salgado's empty chair on the dais, behind a table laden with piles of fruit and sweetmeats; bottles, bowls and glasses of wine. Her eyes were wide and almost as dark as Lady Margaret's, to whom Tom addressed his second and final salute.

When Tom turned back, Salgado was awaiting him, already *en garde*. Baines was standing clear, behind him, and the referee was tapping impatiently with the staff he would use to control the bout. Salgado had chosen the Falcon, his right shoulder leading, rapier high, left rearing upward like a scorpion's tail. Tom, the slightly taller of the two, fell into the same pose, also leading with his right. The cane tapped the ground and vanished. Tom threw himself into the attack. Along the straight line of his progress he hurled his right blade. Down it swooped into the upper area of Salgado's breast, hissing in towards his collarbone. But the Spaniard riposted, securing the tip of Tom's sword with the solid base of his own and spitting it aside as his own deadly tip flashed in towards Tom's eye. Tom's right rapier was committed beyond recall and so he brought the left down, knocking Salgado's aside dangerously with the more flexible tip, knowing that Salgado too had another blade as yet uncommitted. And here it came, stabbing straight for his throat. Twisting his right rapier across his face, Tom caught the counter-stroke on his guard and stopped it short. There was an instant of stasis.

In that minim beat before he stepped back, Tom broke one of Capo Ferro's rules and looked away from his opponent's wrist. He glanced down at the point held inches from the pit of his throat and saw the sheen of the Solingen steel was discoloured. There was something dark and oily coating the last few inches of the point. Salgado was using poisoned swords.

'No score,' called the referee.

Tom disengaged, stepped back, assumed the Iron Door, and waited. Salgado again assumed the Falcon guard. This time, however, the Spaniard reversed his position and led with the left-hand sword. Tom's unguarded back was now under threat and only the greatest confidence, governing the swiftest blade, was likely to turn the trick. Tom looked up and laughed. Then, with the mocking echo of it still ringing on the air, he attacked fast and hard. He crossed his enemy's newly positioned body with lightning speed and committed his right point to an upward attack on Salgado's chest, reversing the point to swing back in and testing the power of the Spaniard's wrist as the attack was riposted.

He disdained to use his second sword when the slightly uncertain counter-attack came, using the strength of his own wrist and solidity of his footwork to step back out of range as the rapier sliced past his chest. He beat the half-hearted after-thought of Salgado's right-hand rapier aside like a herdsman directing a cow. An apt enough idea, for the Spaniard, un-balanced, staggered towards him like a bull to a matador. The casual mastery of it wrung a peal of laughter and some applause from his audience. The referee's cane whipped in between them and Salgado recovered, clearly resolving to risk the left-hand attack only in the final extremity. And in the meantime, to rely on the poisoned blades, thought Tom grimly.

For his third guard, Tom assumed the Crown, sloping his leading sword up towards Salgado's head. But he had reversed his stance now, and this time his leading sword was his left. Salgado now felt his own back and neck at risk – while Tom's own lead sword was guarding his breast. The Spaniard froze, clearly thinking with feverish speed. But the calculated humi-liation of that casual blow in the last bout stood well by Tom. Salgado was too proud to reverse his own stance now. Repeat-ing the pattern of the last two bouts, Tom threw himself into the attack the instant the cane vanished. Unsettled by Tom's reversal, Salgado reacted too quickly. Tom's attack was a feint. He froze for a beat of hesitation. In that fleeting moment, Salgado became the over-committed attacker. Tom accepted his thrust and enveloped it in his own riposte. He gathered Salgado's point against his own blade's base, trapping it and twisting with all his strength. Tom's own lead sword leaned far out of line, its point sliding harmlessly through the air above Salgado's head – but Tom's objective was not to run his opponent through. Salgado's sword tore out of the Spaniard's grip and soared tumbling up towards the stage to fall with a rattling clatter beside Tom's clothes.

But the bout was only half done. The Spaniard's second blade whipped viciously in towards Tom's face. His own lead sword uselessly extended, Tom slammed the hilts of his right hand sword across, only to feel the point of the Spaniard's blade slit through the wrist-guard of his glove and cut the skin on the back of his hand before it ground to a halt, trapped against the quillions above his basket guard. He disengaged and stepped back at once, leaving Salgado to recover under the protection of the referee again. He leaped up on to the stage and gathered Salgado's sword. Then he stepped down and reached into his purse to pull the little vial out. If anyone there understood why he wet his lips with the thick dark liquid it contained, no one said a thing. But the action was completed so quickly that few would have noticed in any case. Salgado was still straightening as he turned. Carelessly, Tom threw him one of the three swords he now held. Only when he picked it up and began to fit it to his hand did Salgado realise. The new sword was not his.

Face white, eyes and mouth wide and dark, Salgado looked at Cotehel and then at the courtier referee. 'He has my sword,' he said.

'And you have mine,' mocked Tom. 'Solingen and of the finest. Not good enough for you, *señor*?' As he spoke, he assumed the most dangerous of all positions, the *Posta Longa,* almost fully extended, with only attack an option, defence out of the question, even with the left hand sword sitting immediately above his head like a steel halo. As he moved, he felt the deadly lethargy creeping through his limbs. The distracting urge to void themselves clamping at his belly and bowels.

'Sir!' protested the outraged referee.

Behind him, Salgado assumed the more defensive Crown position, leading, like Tom, with a poisoned blade.

'Out, whoreson . . .' spat Tom at the referee and launched past him. With a scream that revealed all too much, the referee sprang clear, blundering into the dais and coming near to upsetting the drinks upon the table.

Poisoned blade sang along poisoned blade. As Tom had known he would, Salgado jerked back, fearing for his face. The Spaniard's own blade missed Tom's nose by a hair's breadth. The blade in Tom's fist wavered helplessly out of line. The two clean blades clashed above their heads, ringing like blacksmiths at work. The pair of them staggered over towards the dais and the referee, still squealing like a piglet, squirmed to escape the clashing blades. This time it was Salgado who disengaged, and Tom who staggered as they parted. But he remained erect, and he kept firm hold on Salgado's poisoned sword.

'Here!' Cotehel was calling abruptly to the referee. 'The men are parched, sir. Give them to drink.' He raised a broad green goblet of the thick Venetian glass and pushed it at the courtier still hopping along the front of the low wooden platform upon which he, Essex, Southampton and their guests were seated. The referee gave a kind of squawk and hesitated on one leg, like one of the courses at the recent dinner. Constanza swept forward. 'My lord,' she called, 'allow me!'

She took the goblet out of Cotehel's hand and stepped down off the dais. Between the men she paused and hesitated. 'God's my life,' she swore roundly. 'I do not know which one of you to feed first. Here's to both of you then, my lovers old and new!' And she toasted the combatants herself.

Tom, careful of the poisoned blade, caught her round the waist, hurling her sideways on to the stage. Thick red wine sprayed all over the floor, some of it from the goblet and some from Constanza's mouth. The Venetian vessel itself span away to bounce off the wooden boards and shatter across the grey flags behind Salgado, causing Baines to skip back with a cry. Constanza hit the edge of the stage and folded into a sitting

229

position like a broken doll. Her stomach heaved again. She looked up at Tom, her eyes huge. 'It was poisoned, *caro*,' she informed him, her voice blank with shock and surprise. Her words carried to every corner of the silent, shadowed hall.

Tom ripped Villalar's vial out of his purse. 'Drink this,' he told her. 'Every drop of it.'

Then he turned back to face Salgado.

For the last time he assumed his position. This time, again, it was the *Posta Longa*, but he led with the poisoned sword in the left hand. Shocked and shaken, but still caught in his bravado posturing, Salgado fell into the Crown position with the poisoned blade in his right hand, pointing at Tom's face. But the infinitesimal wavering of the point told Tom all he needed to know of the Spaniard's fear that Tom would cut his back, shoulder or neck before he could bring his envenomed point round.

Tom feinted. It was a large move, clearly false. Salgado treated it with the contempt it deserved, but he shuffled sideways, unconsciously moving the line of attack and defence to the very front edge of the dais. His toe-tips almost touched it, but he did not see the danger because he was looking back over his shoulder at the left-hand long attack.

Which came at once. His body numbing rapidly and the light in his eyes beginning to dim, Tom threw himself forward, tearing his arms into two immediate attacks. The poisoned blade struck straight and true, wavering not an iota from its line. The poisoned point went low – lower than Salgado had expected or could ever hope to counter – straight through the Spaniard's buttocks. Tom let go the hilts and pulled his hand free at once. His right sword, coming down over his head, collected Salgado's poisoned blade and threw it aside. Tom's left hand caught the reeling Spaniard by the shoulder and hurled him across the low dais, sword first. Essex and Southampton leaped wildly backwards, scattering fruit, bottles, tableware, tables. Cotehel was not so quick. He was still seated in the great, solid gilt throne he had made for himself when Salgado's poisoned blade sliced up the inside of his thigh to skewer his groin to the seat.

Tom pushed himself erect and stepped back to pick up his clean Solingen swords. The whole room sat in stasis. Even the Earls of Essex and Southampton remained frozen, crouched in their attitudes of fearful retreat. Only Baron Cotehel, no longer destined to be Lord Outremer on the morrow after all, twitched and whimpered, his voice shrill and tearingly high, like that of an Italian castrato.

Constanza slumped on to her side. The empty vial of remedy rolled out of her grasp and shattered on the floor. There, suddenly, astride her, standing at last as Tom's second, stood Will Shakespeare. Tom threw him up a sword and turned to pull the poisoned blade from the dying Spaniard's backside. 'Hugh Outram, Baron Cotehel,' bellowed Tom hoarsely as he moved along the front of the dais to pass the deadly blade up to Will, 'I charge you in the name of Her Majesty's Council, and of Lord Hunsdon, whose writ I carry, with the rape of Lady Margaret Outremer at Nijmagen in the summer before Armada year. I charge you and your creature Domenico Salgado with the poisoning of the family, heirs and servants of Lord Outremer in the second year of the great visitation. With the murder of Julius Morton, intelligencer to Robert Poley and servant to the Council. With the torture and murder of Seyton, chamberlain to the house of Wormwood in Jewry. With the murder of Mistress Hagar Kinch, the Searcher of Jewry. With the murder of sundry guards and Spanish prisoners in the Palace of Bridewell all within the last few days.' He took a deep breath.

Reality was coming and going in front of his eyes now as though the whole of God's creation could flicker like a candle flame. But he had to send Hugh Outram down to Hell with a full list of his sins around his neck. Domenico Salgado the same. And the time to make the list was drawing perilously short for all three of them. 'With the poisoning of the Bishop's Bailiff of the liberty of the Clink. For the attempted murder of Ugo Stell in Blackfriars.' Tom pulled the sword out of the dark, growing puddle between Cotehel's legs and fixed the helpless intelligence in those eyes that could no longer even blink as he continued relentlessly. 'With the ravishing into kidnap of Lady Margaret Outremer of Wormwood, Mistress Kate Shelton of Hunsdon House. For the murder of Mistress Constanza d'Agostino by poison this very minute.'

He swung round to look over Delgado's twitching body at Baines backing into the shadows, like a rat caught in the light. 'I charge you and your creature Baines with the murder of Master Poley's man Gil Brown in Hanging Sword Court, and with the incitement of Nick o' Darkmans and two friends to cripple me.'

Baines turned to run but the gathering darkness seemed to hold him back. Tom realised that the darkness was real. All the silent, sinister men from around the shadowed walls were closing in upon him. He felt the lightest of nudges against his back and realised that Will was standing back to back with him, one good sword in one hand and one dipped in poison in the other, holding them off to the last. For Tom was not yet done.

'My Lord of Essex . . .' he began.

'Kill them!' screamed Robert Devereux. 'Kill them both. A thousand pounds to any man . . .'

Baines hurled back again, seeming to swim through the thickening air towards Tom, swinging a great ornamental broad-sword as he came. Even a club would overcome him now, thought Tom, in the dreamy grip of the drugs at war within his body. And the huge old swords by the suits of armour looked well tended, well honed and cuttingly keen.

But even as Baines took his second step, swinging the great sword over his left shoulder like the headsman summoned from France to execute Queen Anne Boleyn, so there came a sharp report. Baines was blasted sideways and went sprawling over the stage, like an actor at the end of *Romeo*.

Robert Poley stepped into the light, his wheel-lock dag still smoking in his hand and Ugo Stell at his shoulder with the snaphaunce revolver primed. 'You were saying, Master Musgrave?' said the intelligencer quietly. But his voice filled the great hall, as did Tom's.

'My Lord of Essex, we must have the boy.'

'No!' cried Essex, white and shaking.

'We must, your grace. He can be nothing to you after all.'

'He is my . . . He is my . . .'

'Yes, your grace?' asked Tom, his quiet voice like doom.

'He is my page. *My page—*' Essex's voice broke. It was the cry of a defeated man.

'No, your grace,' said Tom with the last of his courtesy and strength. 'He is Lord Outremer. I have Lady Margaret his mother, and Master Poley has his grandfather's will.'

But Poley for once was pushed aside as well. A slight, stooped figure, pale of face and black of dress, stepped into the light like a spider come into the heart of its web at last. 'No, Master Musgrave,' said Sir Robert Cecil, Master Secretary, son to Lord Burghley, successor to Sir Francis Walsingham and head of the intelligence service. 'I have Lord Outremer's will and I hold it for the Council, the Court of Star Chamber and the Queen. I will have the boy, my Lord of Essex, unless you wish to publish any prior claim upon him. And, as I see you have nothing more to say, I must warn you that you and My Lord of Southampton are no longer welcome in his castle of Elfinstone.'

The golden boy came forward then, wide-eyed to be the centre of so much violent attention. But even as he did so he saw the golden woman standing in the shadows, framed in the great doorway beneath his golden coat of arms. 'Mamma!' cried Lord Outremer as he ran towards his silent mother. 'O Mamma!'

CHAPTER TWENTY-FOUR

Silence

The room was dark, as befitted the thoughts within it, and silent. A single candle burned in the centre of a small table illuminating the circle of faces around it but leaving the walls beyond – at whatever distance they stood – lost in velvet blackness. Away at some unplumbed distance a shape made of lighter darkness showed they were in a room with a window wide. The wind that breathed in through it was also silent and hardly strong enough to make the candle flame dance.

Elfinstone was noiseless; dead still after so much sound and fury. The young Lord Outremer and Lady Margaret his mother were finally safe at rest, watched over by the chamberlain, his wife and daughters. The earls and all their hangers-on were long gone. The actors, staff and servants were bedded down at last. Constanza lay at death's door in Tom's chamber aloft and Diego Villalar was holding watch beside her, keeping her last spark of life alight. Julius Morton lay in the cellar just below, awaiting his final placement among the lordly dead in the magnificent tomb outside – without the living Kate chained to his side. Without Tom Musgrave to keep him company.

Both of them sat, stunned into stillness, at the table in the silent room, with Will, Ugo, Poley and Sir Robert Cecil. The iron bell of the castle clock chimed midnight and the Master of Logic looked up. A combination of pallor, poison and shadow made his eyes seem huge and supernatural, able to see more than a normal man might. His voice when he spoke was weary, as though his knowledge came from far beyond the bounds of earth; as though he were the soul of the blind prophet Tiresias summoned back from the dead by Ulysses to guide him on his odyssey.

'Essex is caught in his own trap now. I see no way forward for him in the plans he has been following,' said Tom. 'He already has a son and heir, some two years old. He cannot acknowledge the boy upstairs as anything more than his page. We have seen that. You made us doubly sure of it, Sir Robert. He might father bastards the length of the land, but the ravishing of Lady Margaret Outremer would do him too much damage with the Queen. He stands high. All the world, except we few, knows he did well in Holland. He has done well since, boy and man. But like all of the moths that fly close to Her Majesty, he pays for his position with mounting debts. He owes her a fortune already and she pays but a pittance to her Master of Horse, as she did to her Lord Chamberlain. How many thousands did my Lord of Leicester owe her at the end?'

Cecil shrugged. 'More than he could ever have paid. He owed her all.' He was thin-lipped. They all knew he was doing the work of the late Sir Francis Walsingham with none of his pay at all.

'As does Essex, with a long life still to live and a place at Court to hold while parting with more and more of his money to finance his adventures overseas – which he must continue to undertake if he wishes to remain high in her esteem. Unless he beggars himself and his heirs in perpetuity, he stands no chance of holding the power that he really seeks. And if he does not establish himself at the Queen's side, on the Council and in such courts as the Star Chamber within the next few years he will be too late. It will all be gone. With Her Majesty.'

'Is that the heart of it?' asked Kate quietly. 'Money and power?'

'Yes,' said Tom. 'And a little revenge.'

He stirred himself. His voice gained strength; rose above a whisper. 'Consider. We begin at Nijmagen seven years ago.

Robert Devereux and Hugh Outram, Essex and Cotehel, become friends. They are little more than boys, though they carry
responsibilities because of their positions. In those days Cotehel
will rise to some little wealth – but nothing compared to that
enjoyed by his cousins Lady Margaret and Lord Henry. Margaret, wilfully and unthinkingly, puts herself in harm's way and
Outram tempts Devereux into an attack on her because she has
the riches and beauty Outram will never possess, and so he
wishes to despoil them. He is that sort of man. They are caught.
Outram, unsatisfied, is scarred and humiliated. Then both are
whipped. In person by the Earl of Leicester, Devereux's guardian.

'While they recover and plot further revenges, comes news
that Lord Henry is dead, slain while heroically bringing the
vital message from the Captain of Engineers to the Earl of
Leicester himself. While the nation mourns Sir Phillip Sidney
and Lord Henry together, suddenly Hugh Outram finds that he
is a large step closer to the inheritance of Outremer. Fabled
riches of such magnitude even the Earl of Essex is overawed. He
sees a way to augment his own great wealth and avoid the
grinding debts he knows await his guardian. Cotehel is well
worth cultivating, therefore. His plans are well worth nurtur-
ing, no matter how murderous they become.

'For five years the friendship persists. Essex rises slowly at
Court and Outram stays in his circle while Margaret runs mad
and is locked away. Only two younger children remain to Lord
Outremer for no one knows of the birth of Margaret's boy. But
Essex is impatient. He has great plans and still he stands in the
shadow of Leicester, his guardian. He reaches his majority but
his power and riches do not measure up to his plans. At last he
is free to take action. Leicester is old and ill. He is dying slowly,
but too slowly for Robert Devereux. And there is the matter of
a whipping to be revenged – the Earl of Essex does not like to be
chastised.

'Señor Perez is to hand, apparently at Essex House as an
advisor on conditions in Spain, of vital importance to all in
Armada year. He makes a potion to Essex's specification.

Baines the messenger substitutes it for the Queen's medicine. Leicester dies. Essex at once is revenged and made to advance most spectacularly. But being Master of the Horse is only the start. He does not sit on the Council as he wishes. He holds no position at the Star Chamber.

'But His Grace of Essex is a cunning man. He understands that if he wants to hold real and lasting power but cannot get it by sitting on these councils, then he must hold information on the men that wield it. Like many scholars, spies or not, he has read his Machiavelli and knows that knowledge can in itself be power. He and Perez go to work upon the only man who holds the sort of information that he needs. Mister Secretary Walsingham. But the Queen is never likely to send Sir Francis Walsingham a potion. So who is? His adopted son Tom, of course. But wait; Tom Walsingham would never use a man like Baines and this messenger must meet Sir Francis face to face. So who?'

'It was Kit Marlowe,' admitted Will quietly at last. 'My Lord Henry told me one night at Southampton House, full of Essex's cleverness in the matter.'

Cecil leaned forward, frowning. 'So the Earl of Southampton knew about it. Had he been a part of it?'

'No,' said Will. 'He told me later, in high summer, after Kit was dead. He was drunk and we were sporting. I think he forgot he ever spoke the words.'

'But it had to be Marlowe,' persisted Tom. 'He was the perfect messenger. And only that act, that one act of passing the poison to Sir Francis, would have called together Sir Francis's man, Tom Walsingham's man and the Earl of Essex's own man to settle things in Deptford last spring. To wit, Robert Poley, Ingram Frizer and Nicholas Skeres. Do you know why Marlowe did it?' Tom's eyes rested on Poley now.

'Money. He was desperate – and remained desperate. He was arrested for counterfeiting soon after. But I think he did not realise what was in the package. I think he did not know it was poison – until he had collected his thirty pieces of silver and Sir Francis was dead and it was too late to do anything but write *Faustus* about bargains with the Devil and to die.'

'But he told someone,' said Tom, looking back at Will. 'He told someone at the Rose what he had done, while they were rehearsing *Faustus* there, before they took it out of town to open it in the country, with the theatres here all closed. Before too many devils turned up on stage and poor Ned Alleyn got so frightened. Was it you, Will?'

'It was Morton,' said Will. 'Marlowe and Morton were lovers for a while. Morton told me, for the weight of the knowledge was great. We thought of taking it all to Master Poley here, but while we hesitated Kit was killed and Poley was there with the blood on his hands. So we wrote to Lord Strange.'

'And Strange died within the week. How did word leak out?'

'I could never find that out,' said Will.

'Nor could I,' said Poley. 'And I tried with all my might, for I was employed by the Council and the Court of Star Chamber to investigate.'

'There was a situation must have challenged your invention, Will,' said Tom, deadpan. 'The very man you trusted least was thrust into the heart of the matter when both Council and Star Chamber called on him to investigate Lord Strange's death. Suddenly Master Poley was demanding that you and Morton help with the investigation for you had all worked together in the past. He introduced elements into the equation that you could not control or trust. Suddenly Gil Brown was hanging around; and My Lady Determination here.' He looked across at Kate. 'But still you fought to control the game – and Morton fought to stay alive.

'And then Salgado arrived. He warned you to stay clear with the word "Mercutio" and the thrust to your ribs. I did not turn the point – I just got in the way of the thrust. But the message was delivered, was it not? Only someone sent from the Earl of Southampton would know the name Mercutio – for you had written the play at his house and discussed with him how the one new character you added to the drama was a portrait of your dead friend. Well warned, therefore, you stood as far back as you could. Even after Morton's murder demanded that you help us more, and Master Henslowe's voice was added to Master Poley's. And it all came back to money again.

'And money and power stayed at the heart of it. Like Southampton, Baron Cotehel heard what had been done by Marlowe – but he did not let the matter rest there. He added the dreadful knowledge to his own dark plans. As plague gripped the city and Salgado and Perez came and went to Essex House, Baron Cotehel hatched his own plan and took it to Essex, his friend and the Spaniards' master. Salgado went to Bridewell to consult with Villalar. What poison might destroy a household as easily as the tinctures that had snuffed out Leicester and Walsingham? What poison could capture for Cotehel – and his friends – the untold wealth of Outremer? Salgado got his answer and the household of Wormwood met its end. Or most of it did. For when he came to sniff around his new possessions before the Court of Chancery could award them to the nearest surviving heir, Cotehel heard of a chamberlain keeping the household open. And a little careful digging uncovered the continued existence of his cousin Margaret, the lady he had failed to rape in Nijmagen before. In went Salgado to find the lady and any documents referring to her. Instead, he found word of Margaret's son. And neither Cotehel nor Essex had to strain their mathematics to the limit to calculate who the father of the boy must be.

'And so my lord of Essex found himself trapped within his own toils. After all the death and the deception, neither he nor his acolyte Cotehel could lay their hands upon the wealth of Outremer, for it belongs to the son he dare not acknowledge in public. The bastard issue of an ignoble rape on the daughter of a noble house.'

'They had the boy,' said Kate. 'Why not kill him?'

'The Earl's own son? No. You do not yet understand the way they think. Why not keep the pretty boy – and his pretty mother to sport with for a while – and kill everyone else who knew? Everyone they could no longer trust? Me; you, Kate; Poley if they could; Villalar, Hagar Kinch the Searcher. You, Will.'

'Me? Even before I stood with you tonight I was marked for

death was I?' Will's voice was dry, his tone cynical and unsurprised.

'For death, tonight. For you were associated with Poley now, in their minds at least, and they began to wonder, were you Poley's spy last summer listening to guilty whispers in Southampton House? And you sent us into Wormwood, did you not? You, and only you did that.'

'I merely explained the secrets behind Morton's words as he died on the Rose's stage. Worm's meat . . .'

'A fine code, and well expounded. And there are mice, rats and cats on Outremer's coat of arms. But so much weight – to hang two great houses on a pair of unconsidered words.' Tom paused, watching Will.

After a moment's silent thought he decided to push the matter of Will's personal involvement no further. 'But perhaps you were right. Perhaps he thought swiftly enough, with his life ebbing, to marry Wormwood and Highmeet both within one curse. Or perhaps the houses he cursed are those of Southampton and Essex after all. Or those of Poley and Phellippes.' Tom turned to Poley once again, then glanced past him at the long pale face of Robert Cecil. 'For a deal of the blood-letting and strife here has come from Sir Francis Walsingham's legacy has it not? You have here civil matters of rape and murder, be they never so horribly and cunningly contrived. You have here great names and high ambitions, certainly; but base and lowly crimes. And you deal with these things using the two opposing halves of the old secret service as spies and counter-spies, secret agents and intelligencers. You fight deception not with honest plain dealing but with more deception of your own. You do this until everyone that stands between you is swept into the gutter, alive or dead. It is as though the whole world were Hanging Sword Court where Morton lived. On one side stand Phellippes and Baines and all the rest at Essex's beck. At the other stand Poley, Kate, Will and all the others, alive and dead, puppets worked by you, Sir Robert, through the Council, the Star Chamber and Lord Hunsdon. Behaving, all of you, as if there was no way forward but down the kennel with the filth, on to the great putrid rubbish pile where Gil Brown ended up.

'Now were I Morton with Salgado's Solingen steel slipped through my breast, those would be the houses on which I would call down a plague!'

'So,' said Sir Robert Cecil quietly, 'they decided to keep the boy – and the woman for a while – and kill the rest.'

'As part of the celebrations tonight. But again, you do not think like them. For just to kill us would never be enough. *Revenge* was all their cry. I had injured, disfigured and humiliated Cotehel. I was to be injured, humiliated and destroyed in turn. I was to be crippled first, then cut to pieces slowly, in public. But later, when Baines had let them down, Salgado had his blades envenomed; and to make assurance double sure, they poisoned one of the drinks. Will, you were to be slaughtered at the very point of knowing your play was preferred at Court and your future all secure. But, as Morton knew, who understood their mind the best, it was the women who were most at risk. You know what revenge was set for Kate, to be buried alive with Morton and me for ghastly company – they had even opened the tomb to be ready. You have heard how they proposed to serve the Lady Margaret, hunting her with horse and hound, then passing her from man to man. Constanza exercised their plans for her a little early, but she was marked for death as well – the speed and comfort of it dependant on Salgado's whim. But in saving me – by accident or by design – she has saved herself, if Villalar's remedy is as effective in her case as it has been in mine.'

Tom leaned back and stretched until the chair he sat on creaked. 'That is all of the past,' he said. 'But what of the future? This Robert Devereux, this Earl of Essex, owes us all a reckoning. There has been a deal of discomfort for each one here, leave aside the affronts he has committed against the laws of God and man. Shall we pull him down? He is ripe enough for shaking and never likely to rest until he has brought us all to silence.'

Robert Cecil leaned forward. 'Not with this,' he said. 'There is little enough of this that can be proved, and nothing such as we can use to hurt Essex or Southampton. Our word may carry weight with Council and Star Chamber but not with the Queen; not out in the light where Master Musgrave would have us stand. On whom would we call to venture out in full day and cry down the law on the Earl of Essex's head? Southampton's lover? The sister of Tom Walsingham's lover? The man who murdered Marlowe? An Italian bawd? A slave of the Armada? The mad woman? The boy?' The Queen's secret Secretary rose slowly, looming across the light. 'It is enough that we know,' he said. 'It is enough he knows we know so that he may hold his hand in the future.'

'And what of the future?' he continued softly. 'The man is compound of ambition and lust for power. There is nothing he will not do for power. So we will watch. We will remain in the shadows and we will say nothing, but we will watch and we will wait.'

He swept across the room as silently as the breeze, but turned in the door, the palest of faces hanging like a shrouded moon in the black of the doorway above the black of his clothing. 'In silence,' he said again, and was gone without even a footfall.

They sat in silence, digesting his words until the thunder of his horse hooves – and those of his bodyguard – died away into the stillness of the night.

Then Robert Poley put his hand slowly down over the spark of the candle flame. 'We have done well to have come through this with enough breath left in our bodies still to breathe, let alone to talk,' he said. The black shadows of his fingers loomed down from the ceiling like the legs of some unimaginable spider come to gather them all into his web, until his palm snuffed out the last tiny spark.

'But the rest must be silence,' whispered Tom wearily into the darkness. Then he gave a dry chuckle, reached unerringly across and took Kate's hot hand in his. 'For a little while, at least,' he said.

Author's Note

My records show forty-seven printed works consulted, not counting the works of Marlowe, Shakespeare and their contemporaries; twenty-seven Internet sites opened and several hundred pages of information downloaded; eighteen hours of assorted video research, including films, TV programmes and historical reconstructions of Renaissance fencing-bouts. I consulted experts from five major museums including the Guildhall, the Clink, the Rose, the Museum of London and the Manx Heritage Trust – especially at Castle Rushen. But I believe the reader interested in pursuing this subject would be better served by an indication of those works that suited my purpose most efficiently, rather than by a list of authorities. As my purpose was to use this particular part of the Elizabethan era (June 1594) as the setting for a murder-mystery adventure of the most authentic sort possible, the 'best' works tended to be the most specialised.

I could not even have begun without *The Reckoning* by Charles Nicholl – a work of immense academic insight and intense excitement and interest – ably supported by Judith Hook's *The Slicing Edge of Death* and, of course, Antony Burgess's *A Dead Man in Deptford*. All of these deal with the death of Christopher Marlowe and the Elizabethan Secret Service of which he was such an active and expendable part. My printed authority on fencing was *The Art and History of*

Personal Combat by Arthur Wise – which I have long used as a 'way in' to *Romeo and Juliet*. The most important video research was by Mike Loades – particularly his fascinating *Blow by Blow Guide to Sword Fighting in the Renaissance*. I was alerted to Mike Loades's work by my friend Dale Clarke, to whom I owe a special debt of thanks. Dale also lent me some of the consultancy work he has done for the Clink Prison Museum and took me round it in person – while taking time off from completing his MA thesis to 'walk the ground' with me. This allowed him to share his expert archaeological knowledge on the exact locations that I was describing. We went everywhere, from the footings of old London Bridge to St Mary Overie (now Southwark Cathedral), past the ruins of Winchester House to the Clink, the Globe, the Rose, the Borough Counter and the Museum of London which still holds at least one of his own discoveries in its exhibits. Dale also found me Tom's rapier (1590s Ferrara hilts but Victorian blade – unlike the one in the Museum of London which has the original Solingen blade, running wolf mark and all). As is often the case, I cannot thank Dale enough for the help, support and friendship he has shown throughout the whole project.

General historical works consulted included Alison Plowden's wonderful *Life in the Age of Elizabeth* as well as a range of 'Lives' of the queen and her father. Akrigg's fascinating parallel biographies of Shakespeare and the Earl of Southampton, as well as Katherine Duncan Jones's *Ungentle Shakespeare*, hot off the press, published as part of the Arden Shakespeare series, whose definitive editions of *Romeo and Juliet* and *Hamlet* I also used. Thanks as always must go to the librarians at the Wildernesse School, Sevenoaks Library, Tunbridge Wells Library (for the Tyndale Bible if nothing else), and the George Hardman Library, Port Erin.

I cannot end this list without recommending some more specialised work to the enthusiast. The HACA website is particularly good on period weaponry. The Internet also supplied George Silver's *Some Paradoxes of Defence* (almost exactly as it was published in 1590) and a truly awesome range of

Shakespearean information. There is even a website listing every actor and major figure associated with any Shakespeare play performed within his lifetime (www.clark.net/pub/tross/ws/bd/kathman.htm). This information is rivalled only by E. K. Chambers's seminal *The Elizabethan Stage* published over seventy years ago and the backbone of both my minor dissertation and my Master's Thesis a little more recently. E. J. Burford's *Bawds and Lodgings* details the disreputable history of Bankside while Martha Carlin supplied a less sensational but no less fascinating *History of Southwark*. Further north, Tom himself springs almost unreconstituted from George MacDonald Fraser's *The Steel Bonnets*, a work of academic research to rival that of Charles Nicholl and Martha Carlin, Alison Plowden and Katherine Duncan Jones. Finally, I was so simply overwhelmed by Gamini Salgado's *The Elizabethan Underworld* that I took the liberty of giving his name to one of its most sinister (fictional) denizens. I hope he does not mind.

The early part of this book was written as part of a series of lessons with Linda James and her writing school at the Trinity Arts Centre in Tunbridge Wells. I must thank Linda and the men and women of the Writing Group who gave so unstintingly of their advice and assistance – especially in the relationships between character, description, exposition and simple narrative. As always, it was the latter that won out with me. Much of the artistry and vividness came out of those wonderful Monday night sessions – thanks to you all.

My placing of events in and around London is based upon my map. This was supplied in book form (*The A-Z of Elizabethan London* by Adrian Prockter and Robert Taylor) by the Guildhall Museum Library to whom much thanks. I photocopied it, added Rose Alley and Maid Lane and the rest myself and it is now the size of a large double bed. Elfinstone (like Wormwood, Highmeet and everything else to do with the Outrams) is fictional, but it is squarely based on Castle Rushen in Castletown, Isle of Man. Here I was helped in my researches into Elizabethan foodstuffs, poisons and life in general by Lester Townsend and John Kerr of the Manx Trust and

Museum. Their unstinting help and advice went far beyond our original remit – to look at the life and (particularly) the death of Ferdinando Stanley, Lord Strange, Earl of Derby, Lord (if not King) of Man – patron of Shakespeare and his company and eater of poisoned strawberries.

And Lord Ferdinando brings us back to the heart of the book. Part of the fun of such an entertainment is to try and work out which of the personalities and events are rooted in history, and which are purely fictional. I have tried to remain as faithful as possible to the historical record. The Battle of Nijmagen has been moved a little in time. The incident of the walls was filched from Essex's Cadiz venture where the walls did in fact fall on top of the English Army, traditionally giving rise to Hamlet's wry observation about engineers being hoist by their own petards. Leicester and Walsingham died as I say (though traditionally of stomach cancer and a stroke) and Lord Ferdinando ate the strawberries. Tom, Talbot, Ugo and Constanza are fictional; Kate is only half so, being based on her 'big sister' Audrey who really was wife to Tom Walsingham, mistress to Robert Cecil and part-time amateur spy. Robert Poley is not fictional at all. He was spy and spymaster under Walsingham and Cecil in turn – and he was involved both in Mary of Scots' downfall and Kit Marlowe's murder. Will Shakespeare is real, too, of course, though maybe not as I have painted him. Julius Morton is not. The rest of the company are as according to Chambers and Kathman. According to Chambers again (and most modern authorities) the two greatest companies – later the Lord Chamberlain's and the Lord Admiral's men – worked together only once, from 5–15 June 1594. They actually seem to have been housed at Henslowe's southernmost theatre at Newington Butts, but for the purposes of this story I have moved them one mile north to the Rose, for which we have much more accurate records. There is nothing in Henslowe's diary to give details of what they played but *Romeo* was first put on about then and it is a play about poisons, young lust and family responsibilities – and swordfighting, in the deadly new style Mercutio mocks to his tragic cost.

The last major character in the book is the city of London itself. Except for Wormwood and Highmeet Houses, London is absolutely accurate. Everything is precisely located and what I say went on there did so. This is particularly true of Bankside; and Shakespeare himself recommended the Elephant. Alsatia was real. Bridewell Palace, a gift from Edward IV, contained both whores and Armada men below them. The one regularly liberated by the young bloods of the city and the other desultorily contacted by Senor Perez, poisoner, spy, writer, friend alike to Philip, King of Spain and Robert, Earl of Essex. Topcliffe really was the Queen's Rackmaster. Baines (perhaps our Baines) was hanged at Tyburn a year or two after these events. Tom's fencing school really was in Blackfriars – though he was not.

Whitehall and Westminster were almost a town outside London Town. The Star Chamber was as I describe it and it did give Kit Marlowe licence to wander, uniquely and suspiciously, less than a month before Ingram Frizer stabbed him in the eye with his twelve-shilling dagger while Nick Skeres and Robert Poley sat by (at the least) in a parlour of Eleanor Bull's house in Deptford, soon after six in the evening of Wednesday, 30 April 1593 – which is where, as I said, *The Point of Death* began.